DARK HORIZON

NEW DAWN

THE CHILDREN OF THE GODS
BOOK EIGHTY

I. T. LUCAS

Published by Evening Star Press

EveningStarPress.com

ISBN: 978-1-962067-29-4

MARGO

S unset in Cabo San Lucas was magnificent, and Margo had made sure to watch it every day since her arrival at the resort. The bright azure sky transitioned into an array of rich colors, with deep oranges, fiery reds, pinks, and purples reflecting over the pool's surface in a spectacular mirror-like effect. But as the sun dipped lower, so did the temperature, and the day's heat was replaced by the cool evening air.

Shivering, Margo draped a large pool towel over her bikini-clad body and cast a sidelong look at Lynda, who was collecting her things.

"Leaving already?"

"It's getting cold." Lynda wrapped a towel around herself and tucked the corner to secure it. "Are you coming inside?"

"I'm going to stay a little longer." Margo took off her glasses and put them on the side table. "I'm almost done with this book, and I have to know how the story ends."

Well, it was a romance, so happily ever after was guaranteed, but how the couple overcame the obstacles to get there was what made it interesting. So yeah, real life didn't come with guaranteed happy endings, but if Margo wanted real life, she could watch the news.

Not that all those who reported the news could be trusted to deliver objective truths either, and the view of the world that most of them broadcast was projected through the prism of their own agenda, but it definitely didn't promise happy endings. On the contrary, according to most of the media, the world was full of hate and strife and was about to end soon for one reason or another.

Perhaps they were right, but in either case, Margo preferred to spend her free time reading stories that ended in 'happily ever after.'

Lynda pursed her lips, which was a sure sign that she was going to deliver a lecture on all the ways Margo was disappointing her. "All you did during my bachelorette party was read, read, and read some more." She waved her hand for emphasis. "I've been sitting out here long after my friends left, hoping to have a nice chat with my future sister-in-law, but I should have known that you'd have your nose glued to your phone, reading."

Lynda scoffed at eBooks. She rarely read anything other than fashion magazines—the paper versions.

"I thought you were napping." Margo was well aware that Lynda hadn't been dozing off. She'd been watching the buffed-up lifeguard from behind the safety of her dark eyeglasses.

There was nothing wrong with that, but after what she witnessed during the bachelorette party, Margo wasn't sure that Lynda was faithful to Rob. Not that she was going to say anything to her brother. He would only accuse her of hating Lynda and trying to come between them.

The truth was that she wasn't fond of Lynda, but she didn't hate her either. The woman did have some redeeming qualities. Besides, Margo wasn't the one marrying her, and if Rob was happy with her, she was happy for both of them.

"I wasn't napping," Lynda huffed. "I was resting to conserve my energy for partying later tonight. Unlike you, I'm here to have fun and enjoy my bachelorette party." She pouted.

That pouty expression was what made Rob jump to fulfill Lynda's every demand, and it was also what Margo hated the most about her.

She assumed what she hoped was a pleasant expression. "I've had lots of fun with you and your friends. We drank, we sang karaoke, and we went dancing. It's been an awesome vacation." She smiled. "I'm so glad that you invited me."

That was a lie.

Margo would have been much happier if she hadn't been invited. Lynda hadn't paid for anything, and attending her week-long bachelorette party had eradicated Margo's meager savings. Also, calling the experience fun was an exaggeration. While Lynda and her friends had gotten drunk and flirted with the waiters and the lifeguards, Margo had mainly lounged by the pool, drinking virgin cocktails and catching up on her reading.

"Well, you are Rob's sister, so of course I had to invite you." Lynda sighed while collecting her bag from the back of the lounger. "It's our last night here, so I suggest that you take a break from your reading and join us on an outing." She slipped the strap of her oversized Louis Vuitton over her shoulder. "We are going to the Mandala, which is the most famous club in Cabo." Her eyes sparkled with excitement. "It's a must-see destination, and you can't skip it. You have to come."

"You girls enjoy." Margo cast her a fake apologetic smile. "As you know, I have a problem with loud music. My ears keep ringing for days, but I can join you for drinks later if you are still up for it when you return."

Lynda shook her head. "At this rate, you are going to stay single forever. You don't like any of the men that Rob and I introduce you to, you don't like nightclubs, and you work in an office with a bunch of other women. How are you going to meet any guys?"

"Online dating services." Margo put her glasses back on. "That's what everyone does these days." Except for her, but she wasn't going to admit that to Lynda.

"Oh well." Lynda tossed her artfully frosted tresses over her shoulder and put her feet into her Gucci three-inch-heeled slides. "Call me if you change your mind." She sauntered away.

Closing her eyes, Margo let out a relieved breath.

Everyone kept trying to set her up with someone as if being single was a terminal disease.

Margo went out on occasional dates, and sometimes she pretended she was out while staying home and turning her phone off just so people would leave her be. She even lied to her besties about her so-called dating life, complaining about the imaginary men she was supposedly seeing, who were all turning out to be disappointing.

The truth was that she hated dating. Her mother suspected that she was asexual or preferred members of her own gender, but Margo had proved her mother wrong by showing her the collection of her book boyfriends.

Margo just preferred fantasy over reality, and the heroes of her novels were all magnificent supernaturals. Suspending disbelief that they were as fabulous as the authors described them was easier when she didn't have to compare them to her underwhelming experiences in the real world.

Perhaps maturing too quickly and looking like a woman when she was still a child had something to do with it. At age thirteen, she had found that older men openly lusted after her and had made crude remarks which at the time had frightened and repulsed her, and she had never really gotten over that.

It wasn't rational, and she knew logically that there were plenty of nice men out there who weren't perverts, but it was a struggle not to think about what was going through men's minds when they looked at her and what they were planning to do to her.

Her mother had pressured her to get therapy, but Margo didn't like sharing her inner demons with strangers. She'd read self-help books and enough romance novels to fill up a library, and if that hadn't helped, she reasoned that nothing would.

She wasn't like other young women her age, who were obsessed with finding suitable partners, but she had learned to hide it. Going to bars with Mia and Frankie, Margo had flirted with guys like a pro, but she had never given any of them her phone number or taken any home. The only ones she'd actually gone out with had been friends or acquaintances of friends who had been vetted beforehand.

"Hey, pretty lady."

Margo tensed and opened her eyes, but the guy wasn't talking to her. He was talking to a leggy brunette with a huge hat on her head that hid her entire face from view.

The sun was almost all the way down, so the hat was no longer necessary, but it was an elegant accessory, and the woman looked like someone who paid attention to her accessories even more so than Lynda, and that was saying something.

Her sister-in-law was obsessed with designer labels.

Margo let out a breath and turned her phone on, going back to the eBook she'd been reading before the interruption. Still, she couldn't help but overhear the conversation going on two loungers down from her.

The woman was trying to make the guy leave her alone, but he was obnoxiously persistent.

"I can't join you at the bar," the woman said. "Please, leave. I asked you twice already."

"Just tell me your name, and I'll leave," the guy said.

Yeah, right. If she told him her name, he would ask another question, and when she answered that, another, and so on.

Some men didn't know when to quit.

"You are making me uncomfortable," the woman said. "My boyfriend is the jealous type, and if he sees you talking to me, he will get mad. Please go."

She was probably making up the story about the boyfriend, just like Margo had done countless times before, but the guy was either drunk or obtuse and refused to get the hint.

"Your boyfriend doesn't scare me." He thumped his hairy chest. "If you want a real man, dump the asshole and come with me. I'll show you a real good time, and I won't leave a precious jewel like you alone by the pool."

Margo turned on her side and gave the dude a bright smile. "You should do as she says. Marcello is a beast, and he's crazy. He will beat you up just for looking at Kitty."

"Oh?" The guy turned his attention to her. "What about you, missy? Do you also have a jealous boyfriend?"

"I'm happily married." She discreetly turned her ring around and lifted her hand to show him her fake wedding ring. "Patrick and I are expecting our second child." She rubbed a hand over her flat belly. "I hope it's a boy this time. What do you think about the name Solomon? I want my son to be smart, and King Solomon was supposedly the smartest man ever born."

Mindless chatter about children was a sure way to chase off even the most persistent flirts, but the guy was either smarter than he looked or good at detecting lies because he lifted a brow. "And where is this husband of yours?"

"Home with our daughter. I'm here with my sister-in-law, celebrating her last days as a single woman."

A convincing lie always had an element of truth in it.

The dude shook his head and pushed to his feet. "Slim pickings today." He walked away without saying goodbye.

"Thank you for the save," the woman under the large hat said. "Can I show my gratitude by buying you a drink?"

"Sure." Margo put her phone away and took off her reading glasses. "I'm Margo."

The woman chuckled. "I'm not Kitty. I'm Jasmine, or Jaz for short." She removed her enormous floppy hat, revealing a face that took Margo's breath away.

Jasmine was stunning.

"Is that your real name?" she blurted out. "Because you look too much like the princess from the Aladdin movie for the name to be a coincidence."

Black glossy hair tumbled in thick waves down Jasmine's shoulders, and her warm, olive-toned skin was so perfectly smooth that it seemed to be made of glass. Her almond-shaped eyes were deep brown with amber flakes floating around the pupils, their shade so striking that Margo suspected they were colored contact lenses. The high cheekbones, the straight nose that was slightly hooked at the end, and the full lips that were covered in berry-colored lipstick made Jasmine perfect for the role of an Arabian princess.

Her new friend laughed. "Believe it or not, but that's my real name. After the midwife placed me in my mother's arms, she took one look at my face and named me Jasmine."

Margo lifted a brow. "You looked like this as a newborn?"

"I can show you a picture." Reaching into a large tote bag, Jasmine pulled out her phone and frowned. "I'm so sorry, but you'll have to excuse me. I need to make a phone call first. I'll show you the picture after I'm done."

"The jealous boyfriend?"

Jasmine didn't smile. "Yeah. His name is not Marcello, but you must have some psychic powers because the rest of your description fits." She rose to her feet. "Can you watch my stuff while I take care of this?"

"Sure."

As Margo watched Jasmine walk away, the discomfort in her gut was a sure sign that there was a story there, and it wasn't a good one.

2

NEGAL

After scrubbing all the dirt and gore from his body, Negal stepped out of the shower and checked his nails to make sure they were clean. It was a bitch to get all the dirt and blood from under them, and he'd had to use a brush. He'd worked on them until they bled, but that wasn't a big deal for a god.

The skin healed immediately.

The clothes he had worn on the mission, though, were beyond salvageable, and he'd put them in a trash bag, but he wasn't sure what to do with the bag. The ship didn't have regular cabin service, and if he wanted clean towels and other supplies, he had to get them himself, which he might do after going down to the clinic and checking whether Dagor needed anything.

Dressed in a fresh pair of jeans and a black T-shirt, his hair washed and combed back, Negal finally felt like he was presentable enough to show up at the clinic.

Dagor, on the other hand, hadn't bothered to get properly cleaned up in his rush to see Frankie. He had jumped out of the lifeboat and had swum the last few feet to the ship. By the time the rest of them had gotten on board, he had used a hose to shower while fully clothed and had run to see the woman he loved.

It was very romantic and very unlike the crusty Dagor, but then love changed people, and in Dagor's case, it was for the better.

Hopefully, Frankie was okay. During their journey back to the ship, Dagor had called her every fifteen minutes, and she'd answered every time, so apparently, she wasn't slipping in and out of consciousness like Gabi had.

As Negal opened the door to the front room, the nurse smiled at him. "Can I help you?" Her smile was flirty, and he was about to put on the charm, but then the inner door opened, and Dagor stepped out.

Negal turned to him. "How is Frankie doing?"

"She's doing great." Dagor grinned. "Do you want to come in and see for yourself?"

Negal's eyes widened. Aru hadn't allowed them to see Gabi during her transition, so this was a very unexpected invitation.

"Are you sure she will be okay with me coming in?"

"Yeah. Toven and Mia were here not too long ago, and Frankie was very happy to see both."

"Okay then." Negal waved a hand. "After you."

When they passed through the front office, the nurse gave him an appreciative once-over, and he returned the favor with a smile and a wink.

He had to admit that being the most coveted male around was undeniably enjoyable.

Back on Anumati, Negal was a nobody. Just another guy from a family of modest means who hadn't had overly lofty aspirations. Serving in the interstellar fleet, he was content to slowly advance in the ranks, and the height of his ambition was to one day become a team commander. All positions above that required higher education that was nearly inaccessible for someone of his lowly status.

"Negal," Frankie beamed at him from the patient bed. "It's so nice of you to come visit me."

She looked so good that he had to wonder why the clan doctor was keeping her in the clinic.

"Hi, Frankie. I'm so glad to find you awake. How are you feeling?"

She shrugged. "Except for some fever and occasional nausea, I feel great. I was expecting to suffer much worse during my transition." She waved a hand at the lone chair in the room. "Please, take a seat. I want to hear what you've been up to."

Negal froze.

Did she know about his contribution to Karen's transition into immortality?

It was supposed to be a secret. Karen and Gilbert had asked him to supply his venom to aid in her transition, which was an uncommon thing for a bonded couple to even consider, let alone request. The venom bite was a very intimate act with strong sexual connotations, and Gilbert, who was a newly transitioned immortal, was even more possessive of his mate than he had been before that. But desperate times called for desperate measures, and Negal's godly abilities had been greatly beneficial to the successful completion of the procedure. Still, it wasn't something the couple wished to become fodder for clan gossip.

How had Frankie found out about it?

"What's the matter?" She tilted her head. "You look like you forgot something."

He shook his head. "I didn't. I just don't want to take Dagor's seat."

"It's fine." His friend clapped him on the back. "Sit down and chat with Frankie while I get us coffee. Gertrude doesn't mind as long as I bring her a cup as well."

So that was the nurse's name. Perhaps on his way out, Negal could flirt with her and make arrangements for tonight. The cruise was half over, and after that, there would be no more lovely immortal females vying for his attention.

His team was heading to Tibet to search for the missing Kra-ell pods, and it might be a long time before he found a suitable female to spend a few hours of pleasure with.

Negal wasn't looking forward to it, but he had a duty to perform.

He sat down on the chair and steepled his fingers over his knees for the simple reason that he didn't know what to do with them.

Frankie regarded him with a knowing smile. "You still haven't told me what you've been up to lately, and I don't mean the mission you've just come back from." She grimaced. "As glad as I am that those bad guys were dealt with, I don't want to hear the gruesome details. I'm much more interested in your love life."

He frowned. "What did you hear?"

She chuckled. "That you're very popular with the clan ladies."

Negal let out a breath. Maybe she didn't know about Karen after all and was just fishing.

"Indeed. I'm the only available bachelor on this cruise, so of course I'm popular. I could have warts all over my face and still get more attention than I could ever hope for."

"But you don't have warts. You are a god, and you are absolutely perfect." Frankie pulled out her phone. "Do you mind if I take a picture of you?"

"Why do you want to?"

"I want to show it to my friend Margo." She turned on her side and leaned closer to him. "I'm not supposed to take pictures of anyone on the ship, but we are inside a clinic that has no windows and looks like any other medical facility out there. No one will be able to recognize it, so I hope that whoever is monitoring outgoing calls, texts, and emails will let this one slide."

He really didn't want Frankie to show his picture to her friend and get her hopes up for nothing because he wasn't interested.

Wincing, Negal shifted on the uncomfortable chair. "Are you trying to play matchmaker?"

She rolled her eyes. "Obviously. Mia, Margo, and I are best friends, and two of us are mated to gods. It's only fair that Margo mates a god as well, and you are the only one left."

Negal groaned. "I don't want a mate. I'm perfectly happy being a bachelor and enjoying the attention of the single clan ladies." He leaned closer to Frankie, so they were almost touching noses. "Who are immortal and have the stamina to match. With all due respect to your friend, I don't want to waste the last days of the cruise on a human."

Frankie recoiled as if he had insulted her mother. "You are such a bigot, Negal. I was human until this morning, and yet Dagor chose me. Margo is beautiful, smart, and has the heart of a tiger." She leaned away from him and started scrolling on her phone. "Here. Take a look." She shoved the phone in his face.

Not wanting to antagonize her further, Negal took the phone and looked at the photo of a pretty blond human. She might be beautiful by human standards, but she was quite ordinary when compared to goddesses or even immortal females. That being said, there was a fierceness in her eyes that spoke to him. "I see what you mean by her having the heart of a tiger." He handed Frankie the phone back. "She looks formidable."

Frankie frowned. "That's it? That's all you have to say about her?"

"What did you expect me to say? That I fell in love with her at first sight?"

"Well, yeah." Frankie pouted. "I heard one of the immortals talking about falling in love with the picture of his mate before ever meeting her." She sighed. "Well, that was disappointing. Perhaps I should show Margo's picture to Max." She looked at him with a slight smirk, lifting one corner of her lips. "Perhaps he will react like I hoped you would."

"Max is an excellent choice for your friend." Negal pushed to his feet and dipped his head. "I wish you an easy and successful transition." He turned to leave.

"Wait. What about that picture?"

Taking a deep breath, he turned back to her. "What for? I'm not interested in dating your friend. You should take a picture of Max and send it to her."

"Ugh, Negal. You are such a party pooper."

"I'm sorry." He dipped his head again and walked out.

Outside her room, he found Dagor delivering a cup of coffee to the nurse.

"Leaving so soon?" his friend asked.

"Yeah. Frankie wanted to take a picture of me and send it to her friend. Can you please talk to her and ask her not to try to set me up with anyone?"

Dagor grimaced. "Why won't you give it a try? You might find Margo attractive."

Behind Dagor, the nurse cleared her throat. "Do you really want to have this conversation in front of me?"

Damn. Negal had plans for that nurse. Turning his best smile on her, he lifted his hands in mock surrender. "I'm sorry. I didn't come here expecting matchmaking." He lowered his hands. "I much prefer to court ladies of my own choosing."

3

PETER

Peter sat on the Lido deck and watched the sunset with an Old Fashioned in his hand, swirling the dark liquid around the large ice cube in the middle. It was getting cooler, which was a welcome respite from the day's heat.

He was a little miffed about not having been chosen to join the Guardian force that had dealt with the Doomer and cartel infestation. It would have been a nice break from thinking about Kagra and what had gone wrong in their relationship.

Things had been great between them during the joint Guardian and Kra-ell mission to China, the sex was phenomenal, and for a while Peter had thought that they had something special, but she had made it clear in so many words that he had been merely a passing curiosity. Kagra had wanted to experience what it was like to be with an immortal, and Peter had been conveniently available and willing.

Had she found him lacking compared to the males of her own race? Was that the reason she'd dumped him?

The Kra-ell males were faster, stronger, and could properly challenge her in the cruel Kra-ell mating rituals.

It was ironic that despite his proclivity for dominant bedroom games, he couldn't give her what she needed. Compared to the males of her species, he was too gentle, but he'd naively hoped that she would find his style of lovemaking revelatory.

Oh, well. When it wasn't meant to be, it wasn't meant to be, right?

It was her loss. He was wittier, funnier, and much better mate material than her fellow Kra-ell.

Still, despite the self-pep talk, the sting of rejection lingered.

Whatever. He was tired of mulling over the mysteries of love and the unpredictable nature of relationships.

Evidently, he was more clueless than he'd believed.

"Can I please have a mojito?" An unfamiliar female voice caught his attention.

It was heavily accented and a little nasal, which meant that it belonged to a human, and he had never seen one of the human servers on the Lido deck. It wasn't that they weren't allowed, but they preferred not to mingle with the immortals any more than they had to while serving in the kitchen and the dining hall and keeping the ship tidy.

Given their experience with the Kra-ell, that was perfectly understandable.

These humans were used to having been exploited by the powerful aliens, being treated as serfs at best and slaves at worst. The females had been given very little choice regarding accepting invitations from the male Kra-ell. Once they had produced a hybrid offspring or gotten beyond a certain age, they had been released from that obligation, but it must have been a miserable existence. Logically, they might acknowledge that their rescuers were different than their former masters and that no one would take advantage of them, but he could understand why they were wary of yet another kind of alien overlord.

Turning to look at the female, Peter recognized her as one of the servers from the dining room. Her blue hair and the piercing in her left eyebrow were her calling cards. He didn't like either, but he liked the rest. She was pretty, even beautiful, for a human, with smiling eyes and a mouth made for kissing. Her tiny T-shirt left her midriff exposed, and her waist was so small that he could encircle it with his hands. Low-hung jeans hugged her rounded hips and delectable bottom.

For a brief moment he considered flirting with her, a playful smile forming on his lips, but then he remembered where she had come from and changed his mind. During her time in the Kra-ell compound, she must have been subjected to the whims and desires of the powerful Kra-ell, and she might feel trapped.

The last thing he wanted was for the woman to assume that she had to suffer his advances the same way she had been forced to submit in the Kra-ell compound. He didn't want her to feel obligated to please him or to be caught in a situation where she felt powerless.

He had never asked Kagra about her own experience under Igor's rule. She had also been a victim and had suffered worse than the human females, so when she hadn't volunteered information about that time, he'd respected her choice to put the past behind her. It was better not to draw out pain that was best forgotten.

With a sigh, Peter shifted his eyes away from the woman and continued gazing at the horizon while sipping on his Old Fashioned.

"Is this seat taken?" the blue-haired server asked, standing with her mojito next to his table.

There was an abundance of empty chairs scattered across the outdoor bar, so it was clear that her interest was in him and not the other vacant chair next to his table.

"Not at all, please, have a seat." He waved a hand at the chair. "I'm Peter."

She flashed him a friendly smile. "I'm Marina." She put her drink down on the table and offered him her hand.

Leaning over, he took her slender fingers in the tips of his and resisted the urge to lift her hand to his lips. Instead, he gave it a gentle shake and let go.

"It's such a beautiful day, don't you think?" Marina gracefully settled into the chair across from him.

"It is. That's why I'm sitting up here and enjoying the view." He deliberately shifted his gaze to the ocean so she wouldn't think it was a come-on line.

"That's what I thought as well." She affected a sigh. "And I also thought that it was a shame to drink alone on such a lovely day."

Was she flirting with him?

She sounded a little nervous, so maybe she was, and if so, she was doing it in surprisingly good English. Most of the humans from the former Kra-ell compound spoke Russian and Finnish, and very few spoke English at all, let alone so well.

"You're absolutely right." He smiled to put her at ease. "Your English is excellent, by the way."

"Thank you." She grinned. "I've been studying for several hours every day." She crossed her legs. "My shifts at Safe Haven left plenty of free time, so that's what I dedicated most of it to. When the offer to work on the ship came, I saw it as a great opportunity to practice my new skills." She leaned a little closer, her perfume tickling his nostrils. "The community members in Safe Haven are a little standoffish. We basically keep to ourselves, and they keep to themselves. Still, I'm very grateful to them for inviting us to join them. It's a very nice place to live." She chuckled. "The problem is that we don't get to meet new people, so it gets a little boring."

Peter was pretty sure that she was flirting with him, but he wasn't going to assume anything. If Marina was interested, she would have to do more than hint.

He leaned in a bit just to indicate that he wasn't averse to the idea. "Your people keep to themselves here as well. You are the first human I've seen on this deck."

She shrugged. "It's mostly a language barrier thing. They are all taking classes, but the older ones don't learn as quickly."

"That's a relief." He leaned back. "I was concerned that your people were afraid of us."

"Some are," she admitted. "But I think it's stupid. Your people liberated us. You gave us choices, and you are kind and polite to us. You are nothing like the Kra-ell. It's like night and day."

He was relieved.

"I'm glad that you feel that way. Are you enjoying the cruise so far?"

Marina's expression shifted slightly, and she let out a small sigh. "Honestly, it's mostly work, and as you know, we've been on this ship before, so it's not a novelty either, but the pay is good so I can't complain." She shrugged, her blue hair shimmering in the waning sunlight. "The weather is also much nicer this time around. Sailing through the Arctic wasn't much fun."

"Can I ask you something?"

She smiled. "Of course."

"Why the blue hair?"

4

MARINA

arina leaned back in her chair, her gaze fixed on Peter. "It's my banner of freedom, my autonomy, my right to do with my body as I please and to paint my life any color I choose."

She'd been observing Peter since the voyage began, not only because he was handsome in a way that stirred something inside of her, but also because he looked lonely and sad. Even when sitting among friends and sharing laughs with them, his eyes had remained clouded and his expression defeated.

He was ripe for the taking, the perfect candidate to help her escape the drudgery of Safe Haven and her mind-numbingly boring job as a maid.

She had spent a lot of time observing the immortals in order to choose the right one, and approaching Peter had been a daring and calculated move.

Hopefully, focusing her attention on him wouldn't be a mistake like choosing to settle at Safe Haven had been. This time, she wasn't letting her emotions make the decisions for her.

She'd voted with the others to move there instead of to the immortals' village out of fear. Like the others, she hadn't wanted to exchange one type of tyranny for another, and just like them, she'd been convinced that humans could never be more than slaves to these powerful immortals.

The Kra-ell had been cruel masters, but she had learned what to expect from them, how to stay out of trouble, and how to minimize her exposure to the meanest amongst them. At the time of the vote, she hadn't known much about the immortals. All she had known about her rescuers was that they had defeated the formidable Kra-ell, which meant that they were even more powerful and scary than her former masters.

Over time, though, she had begun to change her mind about them. Every one of the Guardians posted at Safe Haven had been polite and kind. She'd thought they had been instructed to act that way, but she experienced the same on the ship. Everyone she'd interacted with had treated her like a person, with smiles and kind words. No one had looked down their noses at her, been impatient with her, or snapped at her.

The fortress of fear that had started eroding at Safe Haven had crumbled entirely during the cruise.

"I get it," Peter said. "I can't imagine how difficult it must have been." He took another sip of his drink before putting the empty glass down. "Were you born in the compound, or were you abducted?"

"I was born there." She lifted her hand to tuck a stray strand of hair behind her ear. "And before you ask, both of my parents are human. I'm not part Kra-ell, for which I'm thankful."

He winced. "Not all of them are bad. Igor was terrible, but even the males in his close circle weren't all horrible people. They were his victims, compelled to obey him just like everyone else."

Oops. She must have stepped on a toe. Or whatever the phrase was when someone said something they shouldn't have.

Evidently, Peter was a Kra-ell sympathizer.

"I know that. We watched the televised trial. Lusha did a great job defending them. She made us proud even though she has Kra-ell blood in her."

Lusha's quarter Kra-ell part was dormant, but it had been enough for her to get privileges that pure humans hadn't gotten in the compound. She'd been allowed to attend university and had become an attorney. Marina and others like her had been home-schooled, and their job prospects were limited.

"Lusha did an amazing job," Peter agreed. "Do you know that Jade is now mated to one of us?"

"I heard that. But so what? You are powerful immortals, and you defeated the Kra-ell who enslaved her and killed the males of her tribe. Mating one of you was a step up for her."

"She and Phinas fell in love."

Peter looked like he really believed that, but she doubted a female who had never spared her own daughter a kind look was capable of love.

Perhaps these immortals were a little naive when it came to the Kra-ell, thinking that they were like them.

"I heard that you entrusted the Kra-ell with safeguarding your village in your absence. Do you really trust them to do that?"

Peter nodded. "Jade saved Kian's life, and she's proved herself loyal many times over. Kagra, too."

His voice had hitched a little when he said Kagra's name. Were the two involved? Was being separated from her the reason he looked so lonely and sad?

If so, Marina had bet on the wrong guy.

Affecting a smile, she looked at him from under lowered lashes. "Is there something going on between you and Kagra?"

"Not anymore." He lifted his empty glass to signal to the robotic bartender. "Do you want another drink?"

So that was why he had looked so sad. He was getting over a breakup, which made him even more ripe for the taking. Now, she definitely wanted one more drink so she could keep talking to him.

"Yes, please." Marina emptied the rest of the mojito down her throat. "More of the same. The mint is very refreshing."

After Bob brought them their drinks, Marina leaned back with hers in hand. "So, what happened between you and Kagra?"

"Nothing worth mentioning." His eyes flashed as he sipped on his drink. "It was just a fling, and we both moved on."

Marina had a feeling that there was more to it, but if that was a touchy subject for him, she was perfectly fine with leaving it alone. "Very well. I won't ask about her. Tell me a little about yourself."

Peter regarded her with his intense dark eyes as if trying to read her mind. "What do you want to know?"

"You are a Guardian, right? I've seen you sharing a table with several males whom I recognized from the liberation of the compound and later the sea voyage."

"Yes, I am."

"Do you enjoy what you do?"

"Most days, I do. I've tried a few things throughout my life, but nothing has brought me as much satisfaction as being on the force and saving innocents from bad people, so I came back."

He was perfect. The guy was a protector, and that was precisely the type of male she needed. Someone who would want to take care of her.

"Can you tell me a little about what you do as a Guardian, or is it a secret?"

"It is a secret, but you are going to get your memories wiped after the cruise is over, so it doesn't matter."

That wasn't good. Her plan was to make the immortal fall in love with her, or at least care deeply for her, and invite her to live with him in the village.

"Why would they want to erase our memories? There is no need for that. We are under compulsion to keep the existence of Kra-ell and immortals a secret."

He shrugged. "I'm not the boss, and it's not my decision, so perhaps I'm wrong about that. It's just what they usually do to humans they employ after the job is done."

She let out a breath. "I hope you are wrong because I don't want to forget you."

It was almost jarring to see the change that her words evoked in him. Suddenly, there was desire in his eyes that hadn't been there a moment ago.

Leaning over the table, Peter reached for her hand. "Are you flirting with me, Marina?"

She gave him a coquettish smile. "What if I am?"

5

MARGO

While waiting for her new friend to return, Margo watched the clouds over the horizon. They were outlined in brilliant gold, looking majestic against the backdrop of the darkening sky. It was as if the world was putting on a show to celebrate the final moments of the day.

It would have been a tranquil and relaxing time if not for the unease churning in her stomach and the raucous sounds coming from the pool bar.

Margo had no doubt that the guy who had pestered Jasmine before was part of that bachelor party's rowdy and obnoxious crowd. The snippets of their conversations reaching her were a mix of brash jokes and boisterous toasts that were intermingled with bursts of loud laughter.

Ironically, the laughter was what sounded the most threatening to her. It was tinged with aggression, and she imagined that in that drunken and exuberant state, the men could be easily incited to do harm. She tried to rationalize that they were just having fun and that they might be decent men when they weren't drunk and away from the women in their lives, but right now, the members of that group were sad representatives of the male gender and further validation of why she was still single.

It was better to be alone than settle for a buffoon who spouted chauvinistic crap when in the company of other buffoons who laughed at his crude comments.

"Another round!" one of the men shouted, his voice booming over the others. "To Chuck's last night of freedom! It's drudgery and misery from now on!"

Margo's options to escape the unpleasant sounds were to put in her earbuds and blast music to tune the men out, or to leave.

The pool deck was mostly deserted, and if not for the waiters still circling the area, she might have felt uncomfortable there with all those drunks only fifty or so feet away. If she hadn't had to wait for Jasmine, Margo would have gone to her room.

Not that she would have had any peace and quiet there. Sharing it with Beatrice meant listening to the woman constantly talking loudly on the phone with her kids, with her husband, and mostly with her girlfriends back home.

How could one woman have so many friends?

Margo had only two, but they were the best.

Right now, Frankie and Mia were enjoying an all-expenses-paid vacation and mingling with Perfect Match employees, and she could have been there with them if not for Lynda's bachelorette party that she had been forced to attend.

The Perfect Match Virtual Studios company was supposed to be her next grand adventure. Becoming a beta tester for their revolutionary software was a dream that had kept her awake at night, imagining the possibilities. The beta testing would only be the first stage, an entry-level job that would hopefully give her a chance to present her ideas to whomever was running their marketing department.

Yeah, as if that had worked so well in her current job. She'd accepted an assistant position in an advertising agency in hopes of getting promoted to something more lucrative, but after nearly three years, she was still doing the same job she'd been hired to do initially.

She looked in the direction Jasmine had disappeared to, but there was no sign of her. Her things were still there, including her bag, so she had to return for them, and until she did, Margo was stuck watching them.

Tightening the towel around her, she thought about the ship's delays and the inconsistencies in Frankie and Mia's stories explaining them.

She was sure that the delay was more than just a logistical hiccup, and her conspiracy theory brain was working overtime but coming up empty. Mostly, it hovered around clandestine meetings the enigmatic owners of Perfect Match might have been conducting with other reclusive billionaires. Perhaps the ship had been intercepted by a luxury yacht, and they were negotiating while in international waters because it provided some kind of an advantage.

"Sorry about that." Jasmine plopped down on the lounger next to Margo, startling her out of her reveries. "Alberto checks on me constantly." She let out a breath and smiled apologetically. "What's with men and irrational jealousy?"

Was she being apologetic for making the claim or for the irrational men?

"Women get jealous, too," Margo said. "They are just not as dangerous when their jealousy turns psychotic."

The wince on Jasmine's beautiful face was all the proof Margo needed to confirm her suspicion that the boyfriend was bad news.

"Yeah, tell me about it." Jasmine leaned closer. "I shouldn't have agreed to come here with him. He was so charming and attentive back in Los Angeles that I never suspected he could be—" Jasmine stopped and waved a dismissive hand. "Never mind. I don't want to be a downer. Let's get that drink. What's your poison?"

Margo wanted to find out what Jasmine had stopped herself from saying. She had a feeling that the missing word was abusive, but given that the woman was in a tiny bikini, signs of physical abuse would have been hard to hide.

Maybe she'd meant to say jealous? Possessive?

Those weren't good traits, and they could quickly turn abusive, but it didn't look like Jasmine was in any immediate danger.

"Passionfruit mule," she said. "Have you had one of those? They are delicious."

"Not yet." Jasmine lifted her empty glass to signal for the waiter to come. "I'm going to rectify that oversight now."

After Jasmine placed their orders, she carelessly plopped the huge hat back on her head even though the sun had set, and it was dark. Seeing Margo regarding her with a quizzical look, she took it off. "Sorry. It's a habit. It usually keeps guys from hitting on me."

Margo snorted. "I very much doubt that. The hat might hide your face but not your body, and you have a very good one."

"Thank you." Jasmine gave her a small smile. "So, where are you from?"

"Same place as you. Los Angeles. More precisely, I'm from Pasadena."

"Awesome. We should get together when we get home. When are you leaving?"

"In two days. But I'm not going home right away. I'm going on a cruise that will end at Long Beach."

The amber flakes in Jasmine's eyes seemed to swirl. "I'm curious. Do they check passports on cruise ships?"

"They do. I was told to bring mine, but I needed it to get here anyway. My friend, who boarded the ship in Long Beach, had to show hers before being allowed on board. Why do you ask?"

"Never mind." Jasmine smiled at the waiter who had returned with their drinks. "I was just curious. I've never been on a cruise before."

6

KIAN

"I've changed my mind." Kian gestured for Kalugal to follow him. "Cigars first, and the Doomer's interrogation later."

The leader of the Doomers' Acapulco team was in the ship's brig, the same one that Igor had occupied not so long ago, and although Kian had intended to question him first and relax with a cigar later, he'd decided to reverse the order.

He and Kalugal needed to coordinate their line of questioning. Kalugal would have to ask the questions because he was the compeller, and Kian needed to tell him what to ask.

He was well aware that this was just an excuse to postpone an unpleasant task, but even though it wasn't his usual MO, he was cutting himself some slack for a change.

The cruise should have been about spending time with family and celebrating ten weddings. Instead, he was being forced to deal with the worst filth ever to mar the face of the Earth—vermin who rejoiced in causing pain and suffering—and consequently, he was consumed by rage instead of enjoying a well-earned vacation.

Kalugal grinned. "I'm delighted, cousin. Your cabin, I assume?"

Kian nodded. "Syssi is with Callie and her friends, and my mother has Allegra, so we can have the place to ourselves." He opened the door and motioned for Kalugal to enter. "Brundar might not want a bachelor party, but Callie wants to celebrate like all the other brides."

"I know. Jacki was invited to her bachelorette party, which delighted her to no end." He cast Kian an accusing look. "She wasn't invited to your sisters' parties or Wonder's, and she was starting to feel like a pariah."

He was sure that Kalugal was exaggerating. Jacki was well loved and respected, and she knew that.

Then again, they had invited Carol, who was Jacki's de facto sister-in-law, so perhaps that was why she felt slighted.

"Your wife was a bridesmaid at my sisters' weddings." Kian poured two glasses of whiskey and handed one to his cousin before heading to the balcony.

Kalugal followed him out. "True, but she would have loved to be invited to their bachelorette parties too."

"You should have told me." Kian opened the cigar box and offered it to Kalugal. "I would have dropped a hint to Amanda." He sat on the lounger and cut the tip off his cigar.

He lit his cigar and waited until Kalugal had cut the tip off his before offering him the lighter.

"I'm sure it was just an oversight." Kalugal leaned back on the lounger. "It's not a big deal. Jacki will get over it."

"I'm sorry," Kian said. "I'm glad that Callie invited her. I didn't know that they were close."

"They are not." Kalugal closed his eyes briefly. "I wish all of our troubles were as trivial as this. I'm not looking forward to interrogating that scum. Now that it's over and I have already showered, I don't feel like getting dirty again." He lifted his hands. "Even if I only need to dirty these. Can't it wait until tomorrow?"

"I wish." Kian took a sip of his whiskey. "I wish we could kill him and be done with it, but we have to find out what he knows and, more importantly, what he reported back to the Brotherhood."

Kalugal nodded. "Perhaps you should get Toven to compel Bud."

Kian found it amusing that the Doomers' leader had chosen such a mundane name for himself. Surely, that wasn't what his poor mother had named him.

Not for the first time, Kian wondered about the Dormants who were used to breed Navuh's mercenary army. Did they support his efforts, or did they feel victimized?

The women didn't know that they could be turned immortal, and they were probably just as brainwashed as the sons they birthed. They were told to feel proud for being the means by which the Brotherhood grew, and most of them probably believed that.

"Toven is not the right person for the job." Kian took a sip of his whiskey. "Why would you suggest that?"

Kalugal lifted his hand. "I know what you're thinking, but this is not about me trying to wiggle out of something that I'm not looking forward to doing. Toven is just a stronger compeller."

Kian cast him an amused look. "You are strong enough for Bud, and you are familiar with how the Brotherhood operates. Toven would need much more coaching before he could question the Doomer."

"You are right." Kalugal released a breath. "My knowledge is rusty, though. Perhaps we should have Lokan listen in."

"That's a good idea. If Bud throws names around, Lokan will know who he is talking about."

"I'll text him and ask him to come over." Kalugal pulled out his phone.

Kian grimaced. "I promised your brother a pleasant vacation with the family. I hate that he risked coming here, and then I failed to deliver on my promise."

"I'm sure Lokan will be happy to help." Kalugal put the phone on the side table. "The one I'm worried about is Luis."

"The tour guide?"

Kalugal nodded. "I thralled the two guys we left alive to spread a rumor about him being related to the Colombian cartel boss, but now I think it was a mistake. What if someone decides to use him as a bargaining chip again? The guy and his family have been through enough because of us."

"It wasn't directly because of us." Kian took another puff of his cigar. "But you have a point. What do you want to do with him?"

"We've already left Acapulco, so I'm not sure what we can do at this point."

"We can do plenty." Kian pulled out his phone. "I can arrange plane tickets to Los Angeles for him and his family, and once they are there, we can get them new identities."

Kalugal nodded. "Thank you. That will ease my mind. Luis and his family need trauma counseling after what they have been through. Do you think Vanessa could take them on?"

Kian snorted. "Poor Vanessa has enough on her plate. But I'll ask her. Maybe the volunteers in the sanctuary can help."

"That would be nice. Could Luis work in the sanctuary in some capacity? He will need a new job."

"I doubt it," Kian said. "But I'm sure I can find him something to do."

Kalugal lifted his glass, took a sip, and put it back on the side table. "I've noticed that the ship is going faster again. What's up with that? Now that we are not in a rush, I thought we would be going at a slower pace."

"That was the plan, but I decided to speed up our arrival in Cabo so we could have at least one more stop on the way home. As it is, this trip is a far cry from the vacation everyone expected. I want to salvage what I can."

Kalugal emptied his glass and put it back on the side table. "Higher speed requires exponentially more fuel, which makes it much more expensive, and the increased motion makes sailing uncomfortable. I don't think your guests care about visiting another port city as much as they care about enjoying themselves on the ship."

"I don't feel any difference in the comfort level." Kian took a long puff of his cigar. "And I'd prefer to put as much distance as I can between us and Acapulco as fast as possible."

Kalugal nodded. "That's a good point."

7

MARGO

Margo had a feeling that Jasmine's question about needing to show a passport to get on a cruise ship had to do with her boyfriend. She was an American, and she couldn't have boarded the plane at LAX without a passport. She had either lost it or it had been taken away from her, and Margo was betting on option number two.

The problem was approaching the subject in a way that wouldn't offend or scare Jaz away.

She was very pleasant to be around, and Margo wanted to befriend her. They had been chatting for more than an hour, and she found Jasmine knowledgeable about many subjects but not opinionated, and although she was stunningly beautiful, she didn't act like those women who thought that everyone needed to worship them because of their looks.

What was even more attractive about Jasmine was her ability to enjoy quiet camaraderie without having to fill every moment with sound. She was content to just lounge by the pool next to Margo and say absolutely nothing. It was so refreshing after spending nearly a week with Lynda and her friends, who felt like every moment needed to be filled with words, and every second of silence made them feel awkward.

"The bachelor party left the pool bar," Jasmine said after a while. "Do you want to get another drink before the night crowd arrives?"

They were the only two still lounging by the pool. The other hotel guests had left a long time ago, but some were enjoying drinks at the pool bar, which was just gearing up for nighttime activities.

The band was setting up their instruments on the podium while staff members were collecting the loungers and replacing them with tables and chairs.

"That's not a bad idea." Margo removed the towel that had been keeping her warm and pulled her cover-up from her satchel. It wouldn't shield her from the evening chill, but it was more suitable for the bar. "But this time, I'm buying."

"Don't be silly." Jaz waved a dismissive hand. "I'm putting it on Alberto's tab." She smiled with an evil glint in her eyes. "He said to charge anything I want to the room." She pushed to her feet and pulled a beautiful cover-up dress from her bag. "I bought this today in the hotel boutique."

"It's gorgeous." Margo slid her feet into her flip-flops. "It looks expensive."

"Oh, it was." Jasmine lifted her high-heeled slides and put them in her satchel. "But Alberto won't mind. He loves spending money on me." She winced. "He thinks that it makes everything else okay."

That was an opening Margo could pounce on. "What do you mean by everything else? Is he abusive?"

Jaz shook her head, but it was a very unconvincing gesture. "He's very controlling, so I guess that could be called abusive. But so far, he hasn't done anything physical." She padded toward the bar.

Margo fell into step with her. "I don't like how you said 'so far,' as if you are expecting that to happen soon."

"I didn't mean it that way." Jasmine's smile looked so fake that it would have been comical if not for the seriousness of the subject. "It's not going to happen because I won't let it."

"Good for you." Margo patted Jes's shoulder. "The moment you suspect that things are about to get ugly, walk away. No guy is worth it, not even one who lavishes presents on you."

"I know." Jaz sat on one of the barstools facing the bar and put her satchel on the floor next to her feet. "But it's not that easy."

"Why not?" Margo sat on the one to her right. "Is it a financial thing? If it is, you can move back with your parents for a while until you get back on your feet."

"It's not financial." Jasmine plastered a bright smile on her face for the barman. "Hi, can we have a couple of Cadillac Margaritas?"

"What's that?" Margo asked after the guy turned to fill their order.

"It's a supercharged margarita with a shot of Grand Marnier in it."

"Oh, my." Margo fanned herself. "I don't think I can handle such a potent drink."

"It's really tasty. But if you want something else, I'll order it for you." Jaz chuckled. "I've just pulled an Alberto, deciding for you what you wanted to drink. I'm sorry."

"It's okay. If I feel like it's going to my head, I'll just stop drinking. Speaking of Alberto, we are not done talking about him and why you are still hanging around despite the warning signs."

"Here you go, ladies." The barman put two large margaritas in front of them.

"Thank you." Jaz lifted hers and took several sips before turning back to Margo. "We haven't been dating for long, and we are not living together." She rolled her eyes. "Thank goodness for that." She leaned closer and whispered, "I'm mad at myself for agreeing to go on vacation to Mexico with him, but on the other hand, I might not have discovered what was hiding under the charm and affluence if I hadn't come here with him." She took another sip from her margarita. "I'll be fine. All I need to do is pretend that I'm having a great time until we get back to Los Angeles, and then I can dump his ass."

Margo wasn't convinced that was true, especially in light of Jasmine's passport question. Given that Jaz was reluctant to speak about her boyfriend within anyone's earshot, Margo leaned closer and whispered in her ear, "You asked me about boarding a cruise ship without a passport. Is Alberto holding yours?"

Jes's eyes widened for a moment, and then she nodded. "He says that it's unsafe because of pickpockets and that hotel safes are not really secure because every employee knows how to open them. He also took all my credit cards and left me with just forty bucks in my wallet, telling me I could have whatever I wanted and to just charge it to the room. I don't doubt that he will return my things, but his excuse about my so-called safety is bogus. That's just how he ensures that I can't leave the hotel. If he's so concerned, why isn't he here?"

"Good question. Where is he?"

"God knows." Jasmine sighed and cast a furtive look at the barman. "Perhaps we can continue our talk in your room?"

Margo's hackles rose.

What if this was an elaborate setup to rob her? Usually, guys fell for pretty girls with sad stories who needed rescuing, but it seemed that women could also be manipulated that way.

On the other hand, what if Jasmine's story was genuine and she needed help for real?

Margo cast a glance at the woman's large satchel. She could be hiding a machine gun in that thing, and as soon as they were alone in Margo's room, she could rob her at gunpoint.

"I share my room with a friend. Maybe we can go to yours?"

Beatrice was on her way to the Mandala club, but Jasmine didn't have to know that.

Or did she?

Margo hadn't noticed Jasmine until that obnoxious guy had started pestering her, but she could have been there when Lynda had told Margo about her plans for tonight.

Jasmine grimaced. "We could, but I have a feeling that we won't have privacy there either." She pursed her lips. "But maybe we can sit on the balcony." She leaned closer to Margo again. "I suspect that Alberto bugged our suite. I've searched for cameras or hidden bugs as best I could, but I didn't want to be too obvious about it. The balcony might be safe, though. Even if he planted anything there as well, we can sit near the waterfall, where it's really noisy."

The hotel had a huge waterfall running down its front, starting from just below the penthouse and spilling into the artificial lake below, so Jasmine might be right about the balcony being safe. Still, it surprised Margo that the woman suspected her boyfriend of bugging the place.

Someone who had been naive enough to fall for charm and lavish gifts couldn't be an overly suspicious type.

Margo was precisely that type, though, and it tickled her that Jasmine and she might have that in common.

"Why do you suspect that he bugged your hotel suite?"

"Because he never calls to check on me when I'm there. Only when I'm away. He doesn't even try to hide that he knows I'm not in the room. He asks me where I am and what I'm doing."

"That's suspicious."

Jasmine waved a hand. "Right?"

"Totally."

8

BRUNDAR

I t had been a good day for Brundar, and he felt a rare sense of contentment.

He'd killed some vermin and made the world a tiny bit better for a little bit of time and for a small enclave of people. It was not even a blip on the tapestry of existence, but it gave him some small measure of satisfaction.

Everyone assumed that finding one's fated mate was a cure-all and that happily ever after was guaranteed, but it wasn't. Brundar loved Callie with all the good that had managed to survive the devastation of his trauma, but most of him still needed to stay deadened most of the time, or he would become overwhelmed by rage.

He still had hordes of demons to deal with.

Most people tried to run away from their tormented pasts, but Brundar had discovered a long time ago that there was nowhere to run. The demons were with him wherever he went. They were there when he woke up, and they were still there when he got to bed at night, keeping him awake until his eyes burned with fatigue and he could no longer hold his eyelids up.

Thankfully, when he finally drifted into sleep, he enjoyed a few hours of peace. Since Callie had entered his life, he no longer suffered from nightmares, so the few hours of shuteye he managed were a reprieve.

Love might not cure all, but for him, it cured some.

Stepping out of the shower, he dried off with practiced, efficient moves, combed out the knots from his ass-long hair, and padded to the closet.

There was still plenty of time until the wedding, so there was no point in getting into his tux, but he pulled out the garment bag and unzipped it, nonetheless.

Perhaps he needed reassurance that it was actually happening.

Callie was his miracle, and his gratitude to the universe for sending her to him was the only good thing he had to say to it, or the Fates, or whatever other sadistic power was in charge.

Sometimes, he mused that perhaps this world was nothing more than a computer game played by an alien sociopathic child.

There was too much suffering and misery in the world for him to believe that the powers that be up there were any more interested in the well-being of people than the politicians down on earth.

When the doorbell rang, he rehung the garment bag, pulled on a pair of workout pants, and padded to the living room to open the door without bothering to take a look at the screen to see who it was.

Only his big brother would come to bother him on the evening of his wedding.

"Come in." He threw the door open.

Anandur arched a brow. "That's a surprise. I expected you to slam the door in my face like you usually do."

"I don't do that anymore."

Anandur chuckled. "That's because Callie is around, and you know it will upset her."

"Usually, you also show up with Wonder, and I don't want to be rude to her." He walked over to the bar and poured himself a shot of whiskey. "What do you want?"

Anandur rubbed the back of his neck. "I came to convince you to attend a little get-together. We will not call it a bachelor party, and I promise not to goof around or even tell jokes. All we will do is smoke good cigars, drink premium whiskey, and share battle stories. You will like that, right?"

For a moment, Brundar was tempted, but he knew he wouldn't be able to handle so much social interaction in one day.

"Sorry, but I can't." He took in a deep breath. "I need this time alone before the wedding."

Anandur shook his head. "What are you going to do here by yourself until then?"

"Watch television."

"Right. You never do that."

That was true. The movies and sitcoms were either too saccharine and made a mockery of real life, or too violent, which was more reflective of how things really were, but he hated the glorifying of killing. There was nothing glorious about it, although he had to concede that heroism was real, and some people went above and beyond the call of duty to save their friends or protect the innocent. He liked to watch those kinds of movies, but there weren't many of them.

"Perhaps I'll take a nap." Brundar walked over to the door and opened it. "When and where am I meeting my groomsmen?"

"We will come here to get you. Be ready by eight-thirty. We need to be in formation precisely at nine."

"I'll be ready."

9

CALLIE

arol released Callie's hair from the loose, wet bun on the top of her head and spread it over her shoulders. "I love your hair. It's such a pleasure to play around with it."

"How would you know? You've never played with it before."

They had been friends while working together in the café, but they hadn't hung out outside of it. Callie had been busy finishing her degree and serving drinks in Brundar's club at night. That hadn't left time for anything else.

Then Carol had left with Lokan, and they barely talked because it was too dangerous for Carol, or maybe just because she was too busy building a fashion empire in China.

Callie was also busier now than she had been before, even though she'd finished her studies and wasn't working in the café or in Brundar's club. Her restaurant was a full-time job even though it was only open for dinner.

"I imagined doing it so many times." Carol reached for the curler. "I always wanted a little sister."

Sitting on the bed behind them, Wonder sighed. "I miss Tula. For me, it wasn't that long ago since the last time I saw her, but she lived for thousands of years while I was in stasis, and she probably barely remembers me."

"She remembers you," Carol said. "She's never forgotten you or Annani or Esag or Khiann."

Callie tried to see Wonder's expression in the mirror, but Carol was blocking her. The rest of her guests were in the cabin's living room, and given the laughter coming through the open door, they were having fun.

Amanda had brought Onidu with her, and he was mixing drinks for everyone and getting them in a good mood for the wedding.

The successful end of the mission had something to do with the mood as well. Everyone had been worried about the tour guide and his family and what those monsters might be doing to them. Now, the guy and his family were safely home.

Brundar had returned from the mission in a good mood, too, which Callie was thankful for. The wedding was stressing him so having an outlet for the stress had been good.

She didn't want to think about what he had done to release that stress. Sometimes, it was better not to let imagination run free.

"You haven't shown me your wedding dress yet," Carol said. "Is it another one of Amanda's designers?"

"No." Callie smiled. "I went to a wedding shop and bought a ready-made dress. I'm not a designer clothing kind of girl."

Carol paused with the curler. "Are you telling me that Amanda agreed to wear a bridesmaid dress that wasn't custom-made for her?"

"I didn't leave her much choice." Callie chuckled. "Not only that, the tulle inserts are made from nylon. I hope she doesn't have an allergic reaction to the material."

"You'd better not tell her about that." Carol wound another lock of hair around the curler. "She might refuse to wear it, or worse, refuse to be your bridesmaid."

Callie doubted that was true, and Carol was probably exaggerating to poke fun at Amanda.

"That's why I brought the dresses with me and didn't let any of you try them on. I just hope everything fits."

Callie had collected everyone's measurements and delivered them to the bridal shop, so they should be okay, but it made her anxious to think that her bridesmaids might not approve of her choices.

"I'm sure they will fit perfectly," Carol said without much conviction in her voice.

"Now that I think of it, I shouldn't have done that," Callie murmured. "I should have let all of you choose your own dresses, go to the fittings, and have everything done perfectly instead of trying to save time and money. I keep forgetting that I don't have to do that anymore. Brundar makes a very good living as a Guardian, the club is finally making a profit, and my restaurant is doing extremely well. I could have hired Amanda's designer to do all the dresses, including mine."

"Are you unhappy with your choice?" Wonder asked.

"I love the dress." Callie smiled at the mirror. "Wearing it, I feel like Cinderella going to the ball. All I'm missing is a pumpkin-made chariot and mice-made horses. Oh, and glass slippers."

"If you're happy with the dress, that's all that matters." Carol released the curl and wound another section around the device. "I'm glad you didn't hire the designer. I couldn't have made the fitting appointment, and I bet the others would have hated running all around town to try on bridesmaids' dresses for ten weddings."

"That's what I was thinking, but now I'm having second thoughts. What if everyone hates what I've chosen for them?"

Carol shrugged. "I'm sure I'm going to love mine, and even if I don't, it's not a big deal. It's just a dress, and most bridesmaids' dresses are horrible. It's your night, and you are the only one who matters."

"Brundar matters too, and I'm worried about him as well. Anandur is so disappointed that he didn't even agree to a small get-together with the guys. It is difficult for Brundar to be around people. If he spent time with the guys, he would have been emotionally exhausted by the time he needed to show up at the altar. It was one or the other."

Wonder pushed to her feet and loomed over Carol as she looked at Callie through the mirror. "He spends long days with Kian in meetings. How does he handle that?"

"By pretending to be a statue." Callie looked up at her friend. "Everyone thinks that he does that to look intimidating. The truth is that he needs to retreat into himself for self-preservation."

"Ha." Wonder pursed her lips. "It's so obvious now that you say it. I remember him pulling the statue routine when Tim had me describe that woman Anandur had been with. What was her name? Was it Rosie?"

"How should I know?" Carol waved the curler in the mirror. "Does it matter what her name was for the sake of your story?"

"Not really," Wonder admitted. "Anyway, he looked so damn scary. I wish I had known it was an act."

"Well," Callie scrunched her nose. "It's not entirely an act. Brundar can be scary sometimes. He's not the soft and fuzzy type."

"Not even when the two of you are alone?" Carol asked.

"Not even then. If I get a smile out of him, I feel like it's a great accomplishment."

"And yet, you are marrying him." Wonder put a hand on her shoulder. "It must be love."

"It is." Callie smiled. "Brundar is a work in progress, and the road to recovery is still long, but I wouldn't trade him for anyone else. I love him so much."

10

MARGO

"Wow." Margo turned in a circle, taking in the luxurious suite. "I've never been in a presidential suite before. This is amazing."

The opulence was intimidating.

The entrance led to a sprawling living area with floor-to-ceiling windows. Two plush purple sofas faced each other with a massive black marble coffee table between them. The artwork on the walls looked original, probably done by local artists.

"Do you want a tour?" Jasmine asked.

"Of course. Can I take pictures? I want to send them to my besties on the cruise ship."

A brief shadow passed over Jasmine's eyes, but it was gone almost as soon as it appeared. "Of course." She smiled. "Take as many as you want."

As they moved through the suite, Margo was struck by the sheer size of it. There were two master bedrooms, each with a king-sized bed, and the linens and pillows were of much better quality than what she had in her room.

Running her fingers over the fabric of the duvet cover, she marveled at its softness. "I wish all the rooms in this hotel came with this kind of luxury bedding."

Jasmine arched a brow. "They don't? I was sure that hotels used the same linens for all their rooms."

"I thought so too, but I was obviously wrong."

Each of the bathrooms was like a private spa, equipped with rain showers and Jacuzzi tubs that gleamed under the soft lighting. Designer toiletries were lined up neatly on the vanities, and the towels looked so fluffy that she had to run her fingers over one of those, too.

She cast an apologetic look at Jes. "I hope you don't mind that I'm touching your stuff."

"Not at all. Everything in here is clean. The housekeeping comes twice a day to replace all the towels and the toiletries."

"Impressive," Margo murmured under her breath. "I bet this suite costs thousands of dollars a night."

"I have no clue." Jasmine leaned against the vanity and crossed her arms over her chest. "Alberto doesn't share details like that with me. He tells me not to worry my pretty little head over stuff like that."

"Ugh." Margo grimaced. "I like him less and less with each new thing you tell me about him. Does he have any redeeming qualities?"

"He's a generous tipper, and he's friendly and polite toward the staff." Jasmine closed her eyes and sighed. "He's also awesome in bed. In fact, he's one of the best I've ever had, but that's probably because I like dominant assholes. It's a terrible character flaw."

"Which is the character flaw?" Margo put down one of the little soaps that was shaped like a mermaid. "Alberto being a dominant asshole or your attraction to the type?"

"The second one." Jasmine pushed away from the counter. "I should find myself a nice accountant or engineer who will worship the ground I walk on and answer every question with 'yes, honey,' 'of course, honey,' 'as you wish, honey.'"

Margo laughed. "You've just described my dream man. We should go hunting together. Maybe we can snag a couple of Google engineers. Computer geeks are my favorite type."

"You're on, sister." Jaz high-fived her.

When they returned to the living room, Margo looked around for the bugs Jasmine had hinted at, but the truth was that she wouldn't know one if it stared her in the face and maybe not even if it landed on her nose. What she knew about spyware came from books and not the illustrated type.

Given that she called herself a conspiracy theorist, that was a gap in her education that she needed to rectify. How could she talk about conspiracies if she didn't know the first thing about espionage?

Nevertheless, Margo could tell that cutting-edge technology was seamlessly integrated into every corner of the suite, with a smart system controlling everything from the lighting to the curtains covering the huge floor-to-ceiling windows. The bar in the corner of the living room was stocked with an array of premium bottles, and there was even a kitchen tucked behind a discreet door where the staff could prepare private meals for the guests of the suite.

"It's too large for just the two of us." Jasmine opened the sliding doors to the terrace. "We have the entire floor to ourselves, and this balcony wraps around the suite. We have the ocean on one side and the city on the other."

"So, this is how the rich live." Margo felt as if she had stepped through the looking glass into another world.

"I'm not rich." Jasmine dragged one of the patio chairs all the way to the railing, where the nearby waterfall was indeed loud enough to drown out their conversation.

Margo hefted the other chair and brought it next to the one Jasmine was sitting on. "I wonder where he could have planted bugs out here."

"You've just said it. The planters," Jaz said without hesitation. "I checked under the chairs and tables, so I know those are clean, but I didn't want to get my hands dirty by sifting through the soil."

It seemed like Jasmine had given this a lot of thought, which once again raised Margo's hackles.

"Were you expecting to invite someone up here?"

"No." Jaz crossed her legs. "I was just curious to what lengths Alberto's possessiveness and jealousy would go. I was afraid to search the interior because I didn't want him to realize that I was suspicious, but out here, it was easier. I pretended to be concerned with real bugs, the type that crawled. If he was watching, I gave him a very convincing show of fearfully checking under the chair and jumping with a scream when I saw a suspicious speck."

Imagining what Jaz had described made Margo laugh. "I hope you added a few juicy curses to make it seem even more convincing."

"I did." Jasmine tossed a lock of hair behind her shoulder. "I acted in school and college productions, so I'm a semi-professional actress."

"Is that what you do for a living?"

Margo hadn't seen Jasmine in any movies, but she couldn't claim that she had seen them all.

"When I get lucky, I play in commercials," Jaz said. "The rest of the time, I work in customer service. I'm the one people call when they don't understand their electrical bill."

"That sounds even more boring than what I do."

"Which is?"

Margo sighed. "I work at an advertising agency, but that sounds much more glamorous than it is. I'm an assistant, which is another term for a paid servant. Whatever my boss says, I do. Thankfully, she is not a total bitch, but she's a workaholic and thinks that everyone around her needs to put in just as much effort even though we are paid a fraction of what she gets."

"Life is not fair." Jasmine pushed to her feet. "Can I get you a drink?"

"Water or Coke would be great. I'm still a little tipsy from that Cadillac Margarita."

"Yeah, me too." Jasmine walked into the living room, leaving Margo alone on the terrace to admire the view.

"It's good to be a queen," she murmured. "Except, neither of us is royal."

11

NEGAL

egal walked through the sliding doors onto the Lido deck with Gertrude's phone number in his contacts, a promise of a dance at the wedding, and a much better mood.

He wanted to check up on Karen and see whether she was showing any early symptoms of the transition, but he didn't want to call Gilbert because it felt too intrusive. Perhaps the couple or one of their many relatives were enjoying a drink by the pool so he could casually inquire about her.

On second thought, he should limit the inquiry to the people who knew for sure what went down last night, and that was a much smaller group. One of them was Max, and he spotted the Guardian sitting at the bar and talking with one of his friends. Negal walked over and sat down on Max's other side.

"Good evening, gentlemen," he greeted them. "Mind if I join you?"

"Not at all." Max turned to him, which meant that he had his back to the other Guardian. "How did it go last night?" he asked.

The question was general enough not to hint at what Max wanted to know.

"Very well. The mission was accomplished."

"Excellent." Max grinned. "Any plans for tonight?"

"Of course. But with a different lady." Negal tacked on that last sentence to insinuate that they had been talking about his nightly exploits with the single clan ladies. "How about you?" He lifted his hand to get Bob's attention.

Max snorted. "The only single ladies I'm not related to on this cruise are underage or recovering from trauma, so it's another lonely night for me."

"Not for long." Negal turned to Bob, who was waiting expectantly for his order. "I will have a whiskey sour, please."

"Coming up, master."

Max frowned. "What do you mean by not for long?"

"Don't you know? Frankie's friend is coming on board in Cabo, and Frankie plans to introduce you to her. She has her matchmaker hat on."

A grin spread over the Guardian's face. "I was sure she would try to get you for her friend. You know, three best friends all mated to gods and all that."

"I'm not interested." Negal lifted the drink Bob had put in front of him and took a sip. "I like my freedom, and I'm not looking for a mate."

"I hope she's pretty," Max said.

"She is. Frankie showed me a picture." Those fierce blue eyes were what Negal remembered best about her.

They were the eyes of a warrior.

"And..." Max waved his hand. "What does she look like?"

"Blond, blue eyes, the same age as Frankie and Mia, looks fierce."

Max's brow furrowed. "Do you mean angry? Because I don't dig angry women."

"No, not angry, just fierce. Not afraid, not mellow, and not accommodating. It's hard to explain. If you visit Frankie, I'm sure she will show you her friend's picture. Be ready for her to take your photo too and send it to her. She wanted to take mine, but I said that I wasn't interested."

"Oh, so she offered the match to you first. I knew it."

Negal didn't know what to say to that. It was true, and Max seemed offended to be the second choice.

The Guardian sitting on Max's other side snorted. "I'll leave you two to gossip. See you later."

"We are not gossiping," Max said. "We are talking."

"Whatever." The guy waved and walked away.

"Asshole," Max muttered under his breath.

"Are you talking about my brother?" Anandur commandeered the vacated seat.

"No, I was talking about James."

"Aha." Anandur turned to Bob. "Your finest whiskey, please."

"Right away, master."

Anandur glanced at Negal's drink. "What's that?"

"Whiskey sour."

Anandur looked down his nose at the glass. "That's a waste of good whiskey."

"That's how I like it." Negal took another sip. "Did you have an argument with your brother and that's why you are calling him names?"

"I didn't. Max did." Anandur leaned over the bar. "Brundar refused to have a bachelor party, and I'm bummed about it. Not only is it a tradition, but he's my brother, and he's only getting married once. I tried to convince him to at least smoke a cigar with a few of our closest friends, but he's so antisocial that he didn't want to do even that. I have no idea how he runs a club."

"Maybe he likes the people in his club more than he likes us?" Max suggested.

"Not likely." Anandur lifted the whiskey glass to his lips. "He doesn't like anyone other than his bride."

"I'm sure he likes you," Negal said.

"Sometimes, I'm not sure he does. He tolerates me, but he doesn't like me." Anandur took a sip from his drink. "Wonder is with Callie and the other ladies, and I'm all by my lonesome."

"Why aren't you with Kian?" Max asked. "Wasn't he planning on interrogating the prisoner?"

"Kian decided to do that later." Anandur pulled out his phone. "He said he would call me when he was ready to go down there, and I hope he didn't go without me. The Clan Mother would be displeased."

The mention of the princess got Negal's attention. Anandur was close to Kian and, therefore should have more insight into the heir than most.

"Why is she so careful with her son and not her daughters?" Negal asked. "From what I've heard, she doesn't require the daughters to take bodyguards everywhere they go."

Anandur chuckled. "The answer to that is simpler than most people assume, but it's a well-guarded secret, so you can't tell anyone."

Max made a sign over his lips that meant he would keep them shut, and Negal mimicked it.

Anandur leaned closer to Max. "The daughters would have never agreed to that, and the Clan Mother knows which battles are worth waging. She got them to agree to take their Odus with them, but Amanda refused to do even that. She almost never takes Onidu with her to the university."

Max looked doubtful. "That doesn't sound right. Kian is more stubborn than all of his sisters combined, and yet he agreed to the bodyguard rule."

"They made a bargain," Anandur said in a conspiratorial tone. "The Clan Mother agreed to follow a safety protocol that Kian insisted on, provided that he followed hers. The truth is that hers is as minimal as her daughters', but even that was a hard-won concession. The Clan Mother believes that she's invincible, and she might be right, but Kian still worries about her."

"That makes more sense." Max lifted his empty glass to signal to Bob that he wanted it refilled. "Although I'm sure it's not the entire story."

"It never is," Anandur said with a wink.

12

KIAN

"He's ready for you, boss," Anandur said as he walked out of the brig, leaving the door open.

"Thank you." Kian followed the Guardian inside, with Kalugal a step behind him.

The fear in the Doomer's eyes as he and Kalugal entered the antechamber sang to Kian's soul. It was satisfying to see the maggot, who had anointed himself a deliverer of death and suffering, cower before a superior force.

The cell had two sections, with a small area at the front separated from the actual cell in the back with reinforced bars. It had been strong enough to hold Igor, so it was definitely strong enough to hold the Doomer calling himself Bud.

His ankles and wrists were cuffed, even though there was no need for that. He had a feeling that Anandur had insisted on the cuffs as another way to intimidate the guy, but again, Kalugal didn't need the help. His compulsion was enough to make the Doomer sing whatever tune they wanted him to sing.

Roger, the Guardian whom Onegus had chosen to fill in for Brundar, stood with his hand on his sidearm, ready to intervene if needed. The guy was an experienced veteran of the force, and Kian had no doubt that he could step into Brundar's shoes for the next few days.

It hadn't been easy to convince Brundar to take time off after his wedding. Allowing the Guardian to join the mission earlier in the day had been a strategic decision on Kian's part. He'd used the concession as a bargaining chip to pressure Brundar to take a leave of absence.

"What do you want with me?" the Doomer asked in his heavily accented English.

"I want you dead, but first, I want some information." Kian turned to Kalugal. "The stage is yours. Go ahead."

Lokan had seen the guy through the camera feed and hadn't recognized him, which meant that he was a junior commander of no importance in the Brotherhood. Still, he wasn't a complete moron because he could speak English quite well, and that wasn't common in the Brotherhood, even though immortals learned languages easily.

Well, not all immortals, as evidenced by Syssi's difficulty with learning Spanish.

"With pleasure." Kalugal leaned his elbow on his knee and rested his chin on his fist. "What did you report to the Brotherhood about us?"

The Doomer looked at Kalugal with defiance in his eyes. "I don't know who you are, so how could I have reported anything about you?"

The guy knew that Kalugal was a compeller, and he was trying to be smart and work around the compulsion, but it wasn't Kian or Kalugal's first rodeo, and the tactic was not going to work on them.

"Nicely done, evasive answer," Kalugal said. "I'll make sure to be more precise with my questions. After you discovered the bodies and figured out that they were killed by immortals. What did you report to your superiors in the Brotherhood?"

The veins in the guy's neck bulged as he tried to fight the compulsion. "We didn't report anything until we conducted an investigation and found Luis."

Kalugal sighed and cast Kian a sidelong glance. "This is going to take longer than I expected." He shifted his gaze back to the Doomer. "What did you learn from Luis?"

"We pumped him for everything he knew, and then we reported what we suspected."

That was bad news. Kalugal had wiped Luis's memories of them and the incident. He shouldn't have remembered anything useful to the Doomers, but apparently, he had remembered something that had made the Doomers suspicious.

In any case, Kian was glad for Kalugal's insistence on getting Luis away from Acapulco. If Bud reported the tour guide to his superiors in the Brotherhood, whoever was sent to investigate what happened to the unit of missing Doomers would no doubt search for Luis because he was the only connection they would have.

"That still does not tell me what you learned from Luis," Kalugal said. "What did he tell you that you did not know before?"

The Doomer shook his head like a dog trying to dislodge a tick, but Kalugal's compulsion was a force only a few were immune to, and fortunately, Bud wasn't part of that exclusive club.

"He didn't remember much beyond picking up a bunch of tourists at the harbor and taking them to Tehuacalco," Bud said. "He said that he was injured when some bandits started shooting at them, but he and the tourists managed to escape. We figured that he'd been thralled and his memories had been tampered with."

Kian released a relieved breath. Luis didn't remember anything useful about them.

"What else did he tell you?" The element of compulsion in Kalugal's voice was so strong that it reverberated through the cell.

The Doomer looked like he was about to vomit, but instead of emptying the contents of his stomach, he vomited words. "Luis overheard someone talking about picking up a woman from the Grand Allure all-inclusive resort in Cabo San Lucas."

That was not good.

"Did he tell you the woman's name?" Kalugal asked.

"He didn't remember it."

"What else did Luis tell you?"

"Nothing. That was all Luis remembered." The Doomer looked Kalugal straight in the eyes, but Kian knew he was lying, which should be impossible under the power of Kalugal's compulsion.

Bud must have found a loophole.

Kian leaned sideways toward Kalugal. "He could have sifted through Luis's memories without having him talk. Ask him about that."

"Good point." Kalugal turned to the Doomer. "What else did you pick up straight from Luis's mind when you looked at his memories?"

"Names," the Doomer spat.

"Tell me all the names you or any of the others picked up from Luis's head."

The power of Kalugal's compulsion was so strong that Kian felt like reciting names, but thankfully, the question had been very specific and referred only to the names the Doomer or his friends had learned from Luis.

"Kevin, Gunter, Jacki, Edna, Rufus, Doug, and Frankie."

Kian was grateful for Kalugal's foresight in calling himself Kevin Gunter. His real name would have been a dead giveaway and endangered all of them more than the incident with the Doomers.

Navuh had never truly believed that his son had died in WW2, and he had been searching for Kalugal for decades. He would have sent half of the Brotherhood to look for him.

His cousin turned to him. "Those were all the passengers in Luis's vehicle. I must have forgotten to erase that from his memory."

"Did Rufsur call himself Rufus?" Kian asked.

Kalugal nodded. "We wanted all the names to sound American, and I had a little fun with playing my favorite alter ego, Professor Gunter. There isn't much they can learn from these names. They are all common."

"They know the name of the hotel in Cabo," Kian pointed out.

"Right." Kalugal turned to the prisoner. "What did your superiors tell you to do with the information?"

"Nothing."

"That doesn't sound right," Kalugal said. "Tell me precisely what your superiors told you to do?"

"They told me to lure the immortals into a trap, catch them, and interrogate them to find out where the rest of them were hiding. After I got that information out of them, I was supposed to hold them captive until my superiors verified the information and wait for further instructions."

"To kill us," Kian said.

The Doomer nodded. "They might have wanted to bring you to the island."

"What about the kidnapped women?" Kalugal asked.

"They were a secondary consideration. We could always get more from other villages. You were the big fish we were told to catch."

Kian's blood boiled in his veins when he imagined another slaughter of innocent villagers and the violation of women and children, but he forced himself not to react. The Doomer would die soon, but before that, they needed to get every morsel of information out of him.

"What are your superiors' plans regarding Cabo?" Kalugal asked.

"I don't know. They didn't tell me."

"Do you know or suspect that they will send a team to the hotel in Cabo?" Kalugal asked.

"When we don't report back, I suspect that they will. They will also send a team to Acapulco to investigate what happened to us."

13

MARGO

J asmine returned with two cans of Coke and handed one to Margo. "How come you are not partying with your friends tonight?"

Margo frowned. "Have you been watching me?"

"It was hard not to notice your group, and you stuck out like a sore thumb."

"What do you mean?" Margo popped the can open and took a grateful sip.

Jasmine sat down and popped hers. "While the others were chatting, getting drunk, and flirting with the waiters, you were reading. The only reason I know you were with them is because I overheard you talking with that lady with the Gucci slides."

"That was Lynda, my future sister-in-law. It's her bachelorette party."

"Makes sense." Jaz took a sip of her Coke.

"How come I didn't notice you?" Margo asked. "You're hard to overlook."

Jaz chuckled. "It's the hat. I turn invisible when I'm wearing it. Besides, I only got here two days ago, and yesterday, I didn't spend much time at the pool. Alberto took me to the city for lunch and then shopping. After that, he left me alone in our suite and didn't return until late at night. He said something about visiting a friend and playing poker, but it sounded like a brush-off. When I told him so, he got angry, accusing me of being irrational and ungrateful after the good times he showed me, and then he left. He didn't return until morning."

"What did he say?"

Jasmine shrugged. "He gave me a half-assed apology, excusing his behavior with stress at work. The thing is, he never told me what he did for a living except for saying that he was a trader."

Alarm bells went off in Margo's head. "Where is he now?"

"More business meetings, or so he says. I'm not jealous because it doesn't make sense for him to drag me out here and spend so much money on me only to screw around. I'm just suspicious about what he's involved in."

That was precisely what Margo was thinking, too. "What do you suspect?"

"Drugs," Jasmine whispered. "He says he's a trader, but he doesn't tell me what he trades in, and he throws money around like he has an endless supply of it. What else am I supposed to think?"

There were worse things to trade in than drugs, but Margo kept that thought to herself. The woman was distraught enough. Then again, a stunning beauty like Jasmine could be sold for top dollar, so maybe it would be better to warn her.

"Trafficking," Margo said quietly. "I'm worried about you. If that's what he is involved in, and he isn't too attached to you, he might try to sell you. You are like a rare jewel that some perverts would pay a lot of money to possess. Not only that, it's a known tactic of human traffickers to seduce their unsuspecting victims and get them to voluntarily travel to a foreign country, where it is easier to have them disappear. That's why it's called trafficking instead of a more appropriate name that sounds much more brutal."

Jasmine waved a dismissive hand. "I'm flattered by your compliments, but you are exaggerating. I'm not such a great catch." She smoothed a hand over her hip. "No matter how much I exercise and diet, I can't get rid of these thunder thighs."

Margo rolled her eyes. "Your body shape is perfect for your type of beauty, and you are exquisite. You don't need to get rid of anything."

"Thank you." Jasmine smiled. "That's very sweet of you to say, but I know what I see in the mirror."

"It's called body dysmorphia," Margo said. "Only you can see the imaginary imperfection."

"Not true. Alberto sees that, too. He said that I should have plastic surgery to remove these pockets of fat."

What an asshole. "Did he offer to pay for it too?"

"No." Jasmine leaned back in her chair. "That's over the limit of what he's willing to spend on me, and I don't expect him to. We haven't been dating that long, and we didn't make any commitments to each other, although he said that he loved me."

Lies.

The wheels in Margo's head started to spin again. "So, I assume that he never bought you expensive jewelry either."

Jasmine shook her head. "As I said, we've only been dating for a few weeks, so I don't think that's significant."

"He's a rich dude who likes to impress people with his money. If he wanted to keep you long term, he would have bought you an extravagant gift to make you feel obligated."

"He paid for this vacation." Jaz waved a hand over the view. "Which is quite extravagant. This suite probably costs thousands of dollars a night."

Margo shook her head. "And yet he left you here alone."

"True." Jasmine worried her lower lip. "And he took away my passport and my credit cards so I couldn't escape." She winced. "I was so stupid for agreeing to come here with him. I've known him for less than three weeks."

"That's still a lot of time to invest in a woman he intends to sell, but regrettably, the rest of his behavior points in that direction."

"You are right." Jasmine let her head fall back and closed her eyes. "What if those meetings are about me? He might be negotiating my sale as we speak. I can't leave, and if I go to the local authorities with this story, they will laugh in my face."

"Maybe you should go to the American Embassy? I don't think they will dismiss your story, and maybe they can help you get away."

Jasmine shook her head. "I can't believe that's what he's really up to. He's a controlling jerk, but he wouldn't have treated me to a stay in the presidential suite only to sell me. Also, my family knows where I am. I can ask my parents to buy me a plane ticket, but I don't have my passport or even my driver's license. I have no way to prove who I am."

It was a conundrum, and Margo wasn't sure how she could help.

"Perhaps I can get you on that cruise ship if I explain your predicament. It's a private cruise for the employees of Perfect Match, so maybe my friend can speak to the boss and convince him to let you hitch a ride with us. The problem is that even if he agrees, the ship will not get here until Thursday, and if we are right about Alberto's nefarious intentions, it might be too late."

Jasmine's head snapped up. "Did you say Perfect Match?"

"Yeah?

She gaped at Margo. "The same Perfect Match Virtual Adventure Studios that are running commercials on all the channels?"

"Yeah. I hope to get a job as a beta tester for their adventures. But this isn't the time to get excited over virtual reality. We need to figure out how to keep you safe first."

"What if I come to stay in your room? You could hide me."

"Not a good plan. First of all, my roommate won't be leaving until tomorrow, and secondly, a lot of people saw you and me talking and drinking together. My room would be the first place your boyfriend would search." Margo scratched her head. "I can get you a cheap Airbnb somewhere in town. Or even better, I can ask my friend to book it, so it won't be under my name. You can hide there until the ship arrives. But first, I need to call her to see if getting you on board is in the cards."

"Thank you." Jasmine leaned over and took Margo's hands. "I promise to repay you and your friend every penny once I get back home."

Margo needed to call Mia without Jasmine listening in, but was it wise to leave her in the suite and go make the phone call from her room?

On the one hand, it would be better if Margo wasn't there when the boyfriend returned, but on the other hand, she was afraid to leave Jaz alone. Then again, what could she do to help her if the guy decided to abduct both of them and sell them?

She wasn't some ninja fighter, and besides, if Alberto was a thug, he was probably armed.

"I'll call my friend from my room. In the meantime, I suggest that you go back to the bar where you will be surrounded by people. I'll find you when I'm done."

Jasmine nodded. "I need to shower and change first. But as soon as I'm done, I'll head to the pool bar."

Margo pushed to her feet. "Don't take too long."

"I won't."

14

KAREN

Karen sat in front of a mirror and regarded her freshly cleaned face. She looked her age, not younger and not older, which was an improvement over the tired and washed-out look she'd been sporting lately.

It was the venom's effect.

Lifting her hand, she feathered her fingers over the spot where Negal had bitten her. She didn't remember the bite because he had thralled her to ignore him when he had done it, and there was no sign left of it, but she could feel its phantom echo on her skin, a prickling that was most likely psychosomatic.

Since she had no memory of the bite, all she had to rely on was what she'd heard from others, and her imagination.

In the mirror, she saw Gilbert walking out of the shower with a towel wrapped around his hips, looking absolutely perfect. The few pounds he'd been carrying around his middle had disappeared, and he had gained muscles even though he rarely visited the gym.

He smiled at her through the mirror. "Anything?"

She knew what he was asking about and shook her head. "I feel exactly the same as I did before the bite."

Well, that wasn't true. She felt invigorated, which she'd been told was one of the residual effects of the venom.

When Gilbert's venom glands and fangs became functional, she would be able to enjoy these wonderful effects daily.

If she survived.

Heck, if she survived the transition, she would become immortal, and she wouldn't need the energy boost that a venom bite provided. The other benefits were more than enough to look forward to, though.

She vividly remembered the string of orgasms and euphoria that had followed and the psychedelic trip that had lasted for hours.

In her case, it wasn't a question of whether she would enter transition. She was a confirmed Dormant. The question was whether she would survive it.

Letting the towel drop, Gilbert gave her a great view of his ass as he walked toward the closet. "I know better than to offer a little hanky-panky when you are getting ready, but in case you are randy..." He looked at her over his shoulder with a hopeful expression on his face and shook his ass. "Cheryl has the kids in her bedroom, and you know how good the soundproofing is here."

"I do, but I also know our kids. Idina could burst in here at any moment. Besides, I do need to get ready."

He sighed dramatically. "We can lock the door..."

Karen closed her eyes. "I'm sorry, sweetheart. I really need to get ready."

"Yeah, yeah." He pulled on a pair of boxer briefs, walked over to the bed, and turned the television on. "You don't mind if I watch something while you do your makeup, right?" He lay down on the bed without waiting for her response.

"I don't. Enjoy your channel surfing."

Gilbert had always been a virile male with a healthy appetite for sex, but since his transition, he'd become insatiable, and his stamina was through the roof. She tried to keep up, but he was exhausting her, and as much as she hated disappointing him, she couldn't handle one more session.

She would never admit it to him, but she was starting to dread getting in bed.

It was temporary, she reminded herself. Soon, she would be immortal, too, and their energy levels would match.

With a sigh, Karen began her routine, first dabbing a light moisturizer onto her skin and patting it down until it dissolved into a silky smoothness. Next came the foundation, which she'd had formulated to match her exact skin tone.

She used to love the process, the transformation she could achieve with contouring and shading, but her skin no longer looked smooth, and the foundation was accentuating every little wrinkle and crease.

Perhaps it was better to go without?

Nah. No one would see the imperfection in the dim light of the transformed dining room, but the shading and contouring would transform her face.

Reaching for the eyeshadow palette, she opted for earthy tones that complemented her eyes, and blended the colors with gentle, circular motions, creating a soft, smoky effect that was neither too bold nor too understated. After cleaning up the corners, she drew a thin line of black eyeliner along her upper lash line, giving her eyes a defined look.

"You look beautiful," Gilbert said from the bed.

"Thank you." She slanted him a smile. "I'm not done yet."

"You look beautiful without any of the war paint."

She chuckled. "War paint? Is that what it looks like?"

"I'm just teasing. You look great. Which dress are you wearing tonight?"

"The silver one. Why are you asking?"

He shrugged, his shoulders looking so much more defined and muscular now, even though he hadn't increased his exercise routine after his transition. It was just happening, the same way his hair was regrowing, and his midsection had lost its padding of fat.

He turned on his side. "I was just imagining dancing with you, and I needed a dress to go with the fantasy."

"You're weird." She dabbed a hint of blush over her cheeks, bringing a warm, rosy hue to her face.

Gilbert propped his head on his hand. "It's not weird to imagine the good things in life even if they are readily available. It enhances the experience. You should try it. Close your eyes and imagine yourself with me on the dance floor, looking into my eyes and telling me that you love me and that I'm the hunkiest male there."

She narrowed her eyes at him. "Do you imagine yourself telling me that I'm the sexiest, most beautiful woman on the dance floor?"

"I do. That's why I needed to know what dress you are planning to wear."

Shaking her head, Karen picked up a lipstick that was a shade darker than her natural lip color, but then changed her mind and went for something bolder, a deep burgundy red.

As she pressed her lips together to blend the color, Karen admired the overall effect. "Not bad if I say so myself."

"Magnificent," Gilbert said.

She turned to him. "Do you ever imagine how I will look after the transition?"

"I don't have to imagine. I know what you will look like."

"And that's what?"

"The way you looked when I first met you. Although, to tell you the truth, in my eyes you haven't changed. When I look at you, I always see the woman I fell in love with."

15

MARGO

As Margo made her way to her room on the second floor of the hotel, her stomach churned with unease.

She didn't like leaving Jasmine alone and vulnerable in that fancy suite, but she had to concede that there wasn't much she could do for her other than make the call she had promised.

Hopefully, tonight's wedding hadn't started yet, or Mia wouldn't be able to help her with anything. To bother the boss in the middle of the festivities would result in a guaranteed refusal.

Margo wondered whether the weddings were of employees who had met their Perfect Match through the algorithm. If so, it could be a wonderful marketing opportunity. The question was whether anyone would let her pitch her idea.

She was supposed to start as a lowly beta tester, and chances were that no one would want to hear what other things she could bring to the table.

So far, she'd gotten the impression that the boss Mia had been referring to was even more intimidating than Mia's fiancé, which was hard to imagine, but since Tom didn't have the authority to approve Jasmine coming on board, the reclusive partners were the ones in charge. Mia hadn't mentioned which one of them was the boss, but since she referred to 'him,' it was a man, and given the tone of her voice when she talked about him, she had a lot of respect for the guy.

Closing the door behind her, Margo locked it as if that was going to keep her safe, dropped her bag on the floor, and sat down on the single armchair in the room.

The contrast to Jasmine's luxurious suite was stark. The room, which Margo had thought was so nice, suddenly looked cramped and basic. The two queen beds and one armchair took up most of the floor space, and the small table by the armchair couldn't even hold her bag.

The bathroom was basic as well, with a bathtub and shower combo, a shower curtain, a toilet, and a single sink.

Oh well, even that simple room, which she had split the cost of with a roommate, had made a big hole in her savings account. That and the plane ticket. The other things were incidentals that weren't too costly.

Pulling out her phone, Margo placed the call and waited for Mia to answer.

When the call went to voicemail, her heart sank. Mia was probably at the wedding already, and it was too noisy to hear the phone ringing.

Maybe she should call Frankie?

Frankie couldn't help her, though. She wasn't close to the boss, and besides, she was probably at the wedding too.

When her phone rang a few minutes later, Margo let out a relieved breath. "Hi, Mia. I thought you were at the wedding reception already."

"No, not yet. These weddings start really late. I didn't answer because I was in the shower when you called, and Tom was helping me. Did you talk with Frankie today by any chance?"

Margo tensed. "No, why? Is she okay?"

"She's fine. She came down with some sort of a bug, and they put her in the infirmary. But that's not why I asked. I didn't know whether she told you that we were going to get to Cabo tomorrow afternoon instead of the following morning. The boss decided to crank up the speed so we can make an excursion to one more port of call before heading home."

"Great." She would have been thrilled to hear that only this morning, but now she was worried about Jasmine. She needed more time to put her rescue plan in motion.

"You don't sound happy," Mia said. "What's up?"

"I met someone who might be in danger, and I need a favor." She proceeded to explain the situation and her suspicions about Jasmine's boyfriend.

When she was done, there was a long moment of silence. "Are you sure that you are not jumping to conclusions? No offense, but you tend to see a conspiracy around every corner."

"That jerk took her passport, her driver's license, and her credit cards. He left her with forty bucks in her wallet. Don't tell me you don't find that suspicious."

"So, the guy is a controlling asshole. It doesn't mean that he's a trafficker."

"What if he is? Do you want Jasmine's abduction and sale into sex slavery on your conscience?"

"Of course not." Mia sighed. "But I would hate to make a big brouhaha about nothing."

"It's not nothing, and even if it is, I'd rather be wrong than sorry. That's how people get killed, Mia. Those who should recognize the warning signs and do something don't want to believe that bad things are about to happen."

After every big terrorist attack, the news was full of warning signs that should have been heeded but had been ignored. Evidently, those in charge of security often suffered from the same idiotic optimism and false sense of safety as the clueless victims in horror movies.

"Yeah, you're right," Mia sighed. "Better safe than sorry, right? I'll tell Tom what you told me and have him ask the boss if he will allow your friend on board."

"Thank you. You are the best. I need one more favor, though."

"What is it now?"

"I want to rent an Airbnb in town so Jasmine will have a place to hide from her boyfriend, but if I book it, I'll have to use my credit card, and he might be able to trace the place. People saw Jasmine and me hanging out together, so he wouldn't have much trouble figuring out who was helping her. If you book the rental, though, he won't be able to find her."

"That's actually a smart idea. I'll book a place, and I suggest that you join her. If he's the bad apple you think he is, you don't want him coming after you when he searches for his girlfriend."

"Good point. I might even save a few dollars by canceling my extra night in the hotel. I'll pay you back, of course."

"*Pfft*. That's the last thing you need to worry about. I'll try to find a place that's walking distance from the hotel. You don't want to take a taxi because that could also lead him to you."

Margo chuckled. "Look at us. We are like a couple of sleuths. I'll leave my luggage in the hotel and go with just a large satchel. I'll tell Jasmine to do the same."

"I'll call you back once I make the reservation."

"Thanks, Mia. I really appreciate it."

"No problem. I'm happy to help. Getting the boss's approval for your friend to come on board might take a little longer, but at least she will be safe in the meantime."

"True that. If the boss says no, I'll try to get her to the embassy. Maybe they can help, although I doubt it. She can't even prove who she is without at least her driver's license."

"Let's keep our fingers crossed that the boss agrees."

When Mia ended the call, Margo slumped in the armchair, her energy level dropping like a rock now that she had done all she could.

But was it all?

She needed to think creatively. Perhaps one of Jasmine's parents could fly in and bring her birth certificate along with some pictures. That was another way to prove who she was. Or maybe she had an expired passport that they could get. That should be helpful as well. After all, it wasn't uncommon for people to get mugged while abroad and have all of their documents and money taken, and yet they somehow found a way to return home.

16

KIAN

"Do we have time for another cigar before the wedding?" Kalugal glanced at his watch. "Or do you need to get ready?"

Kian chuckled. "How long will it take me to put on a tux? Let's go to my suite."

His cousin grinned. "I was hoping you'd say that. Jacki is still with Callie, so I assume Syssi is too. They are getting dressed in Wonder's suite."

"Can I join?" Anandur asked from behind them. "I was told to stay away from the suite until they were done. My tux is in Brundar and Callie's place, and I'm not in the mood to hang out with my brother. Or I should rather say that he's not in the mood to hang out with me."

"Is he nervous about the ceremony?" Kalugal asked.

Anandur shrugged. "Probably. I can't imagine what his vows to Callie will be like. He does not know how to express his emotions, so this must be difficult for him. I just hope he wrote something because I'm sure Callie did. She doesn't suffer from the same limitations he does. She's a loving, caring sweetheart, and she knows how to express herself in words."

Kian nodded. "He'll be fine even if he doesn't have anything profound prepared. All he needs to say is that he will love her forever, which is a given, and it will be enough for her."

Anandur made a face that indicated he disagreed. "It might be true on the day-to-day, but I bet she is hoping for him to say something more profound in front of the entire clan."

"Your vows were great." Kalugal clapped Anandur on the back. "I laughed so hard, and I even teared up a little."

"Thank you." Anandur put a hand over his chest. "It means a lot to me to hear you say that. I worked on them for months."

"Really?" Kian arched a brow.

He was never sure whether Anandur was serious or joking.

"Really, and hearing that Kalugal was touched by what I wrote makes me so proud."

"Your vows were beautiful." Kalugal sighed dramatically.

Kian rolled his eyes as he opened the door to his suite. "I didn't know you were so emotional, cousin." He ushered his guests inside.

Kalugal batted his eyelashes. "I have many layers."

Snorting, Kian walked over to the bar and pulled out a bottle of whiskey. "As lovely as it is to share this touching moment with you two, I need to think about what we are going to do. I don't want to engage another group of Doomers while I have my entire clan on the ship, and especially my mother." He lined up three glasses on the counter and poured whiskey into them. "Any suggestions?"

As Kalugal and Anandur took their glasses, Kian walked over to the balcony doors and opened them.

The humid heat outside was not as bad this late in the evening, but it was still an adjustment after leaving the air-conditioned space behind.

"We can just keep on sailing." Kalugal followed him to the balcony, with Anandur a couple of steps behind him. "Mia and Frankie will be disappointed, and so will their friend, but that shouldn't influence your decision. Safety first, right?"

Kian opened the humidor he had left outside and presented it to Kalugal. "Maybe we can pick Margo up with a lifeboat. She can head to one of the nearby beaches, and we will collect her from there. I doubt the Doomers will be following her since they don't know who she is." He offered the box to Anandur.

Anandur pulled out a Cuban. "It doesn't feel right to run. We took out those directly responsible for the massacre, but that's not enough. We need to take out the entire leadership, and we can't, which frustrates me."

Kian and Kalugal both nodded.

"Perhaps eliminating the team they sent to Cabo will send a message," Kalugal said.

"What kind of a message?" Kian offered him the cutter. "That we are in charge of this area? We are not. They will send an even larger force, and by the time it gets here, we will be long gone. It's futile to engage them." He lit his cigar and took a grateful puff. "We need to stick to what we have always done, which is hiding the best we can. I don't like it, and I wish we could take on the entire Brotherhood and eliminate them, including Navuh, but we can't, not even by bombing the hell out of their island. There are civilians on that damn island, including your mother and Wonder's sister."

"We can get them out first." Anandur lit up his cigar. "The same way we got Carol out. Her rescue was proof that it could be done."

"My mother doesn't want to leave." Kalugal sat down on a lounger and put his feet up. "We would have to knock her out. But since she is the only one who we could coordinate the rescue plan with, that would be a problem. And even if we managed that, I wouldn't want to be on the receiving end of her wrath if we killed my father. She would be enraged and inconsolable."

Kian couldn't argue with that, and he didn't want to. It was a futile discussion at this point, and he had more urgent matters to think about.

"We are getting carried away." He sat on a lounger next to Kalugal. "We need to decide what to do about Cabo. Let's consider the timeline. By now, the superiors know that something is up because they lost communications with Bud's team. They will want to investigate what happened, and they will want revenge. Bud is right about them sending two teams. One to Acapulco and one to Cabo. But even if they are on the plane right now, it will take them at least eighteen hours to get here. Probably more. They need to fly to the Maldives first, and as far as I know, there are no direct flights from there to Acapulco or any of the other nearby airports. They will have to book a flight with a layover. Then, they will need to get weapons from a local supplier, which will probably take a few more hours. In short, I can't see them being ready to engage us sooner than forty-eight hours or so from now. At the speed we are going, we can dock in Cabo, get Margo, and be out of there before they even get there."

Kalugal puffed on his cigar for a few quiet moments before turning to Kian. "Even if you are right about that, which you might not be, they will ask their buddies in the cartel to intervene."

Anandur snorted. "What can a bunch of humans do to us?"

"Plenty," Kalugal said. "We have less than eighty Guardians, and even with my men, our entire force is just a little over a hundred. Humans can easily overwhelm us with the right weapons. My compulsion is a formidable weapon, but it has to be used strategically. They have to be able to hear my voice, so it won't help us at all if they fire a torpedo at the ship from a safe distance. We are lucky that they don't know for sure we are on a ship or which one. One well-aimed anti-ship cruise missile could sink us."

Kian frowned at his cousin. "What did you mean by if I'm right about the timeline?"

"You are assuming that they will send a force from the island, but that's probably not what they will do." Kalugal took a puff from his cigar. "They probably have teams stationed across Mexico and other South American countries that they can deploy on short notice. They could also send a force from California, where they have a large presence. In my opinion, we can assume that they are already waiting for us in Cabo with a large force stationed at the hotel."

17

MARGO

Margo showered and checked her phone. She got dressed and looked at her phone again. She packed a suitcase and her satchel and checked her phone once more, but there was still no response from Mia.

She thought about checking on Jasmine, but then it occurred to her that they hadn't exchanged phone numbers. Besides, even if she had Jasmine's number, it wouldn't be prudent to call her. Alberto might be monitoring her calls.

In fact, when Jasmine fled to the Airbnb, she should leave her phone behind in the suite so Alberto couldn't trace her.

With a sigh, Margo picked up her phone and headed out to the pool bar, where Jaz was supposed to wait for her.

She didn't know why it was taking Mia so long to book the Airbnb. Perhaps there was no availability?

If so, one of the nearby hotels would do. They were all clustered in the same area, and Margo was sure they had rooms available. Maybe she should call Mia to tell her that?

Nah. Mia was smart enough to figure that out on her own. Something else must have caused the delay.

As Margo exited the elevator at the ground level, she had a sudden flare of panic. What if the dastardly boyfriend had shown up while she had been gone and dragged Jasmine away from the bar to deliver her to a buyer?

Shaking her head, Margo chided herself for possibly getting carried away again.

Was she making a logical leap with this situation or was she creating a storm in a teacup by weaving yet another conspiracy theory?

Both scenarios seemed plausible.

She was the first one to admit that she had a penchant for defaulting to the worst possible outcome for any given situation. The thing was, being paranoid didn't mean that she was wrong. The world was decidedly a more nefarious and hostile place than most people believed, and safety was an illusion.

Margo was always prepared for the worst to happen. Well, prepared was an exaggeration. She was mentally ready, but she still didn't own a gun or even have a security alarm in her apartment. If she could, she would rent a place in a secure building with a guard in the lobby, so at least she would be somewhat protected, but she couldn't afford the rent in a place like that.

When she got back, the first thing she would do was contact one of those alarm companies, and the second thing was to apply for a gun permit.

The problem was that not all life's calamities could be blamed on murderers, rapists, terrorists, traffickers, and drug dealers. More people died prematurely from diseases, hereditary defects, and natural disasters than from wars and murders.

Perhaps it had been Mia's heart failure that had turned Margo into such a pessimist.

Mia's mother had died from the same heart defect that had almost killed her daughter years later, but everyone had seemed to think that it wouldn't happen to Mia, including Mia herself.

Then it had, and Mia had almost died, and her legs had been amputated.

It had been like a punch to the gut, a rude wake-up call, making it glaringly apparent to Margo that bad things happened to good people for no good reason. Since then, she had never taken anything for granted again. Not her health, not her safety, and not her happily ever after, which was the biggest lie of all.

Most people didn't get to live a happy life, so why would she be so lucky?

Well, miracles happened; Margo was willing to admit that, and that realization too, was because of Mia, or rather thanks to her. Her bestie had met Tom, a multi-billionaire who had taken her to Switzerland and gotten her the best medical help in the world. The details were a big secret because the procedure had not yet been approved, but Mia was regrowing her legs.

Still, stories like Mia's were so rare that it was safe to assume they didn't happen for the vast majority of people, including Margo.

"Ain't I the cheerful sort." Margo chuckled as she walked through the sliding doors out onto the pool area.

The bar was packed, the music was loud, and people were laughing. Life seemed good for this single moment in time.

Seeing Jasmine sitting at the bar with a drink in her hand, Margo let out a relieved breath. Two guys seemed to be vying for her attention, but given her easy smile, she was doing fine.

Heading toward her new friend, Margo took another glance at her phone, but there was still no message from Mia.

She was almost at the bar when her phone finally rang.

Taking a slight detour, she sat on one of the chairs and answered the call.

"I've got the Airbnb," Mia said. "It's fifteen minutes on foot from the hotel. A nice two-bedroom condo in a secure building. I'll text you the codes for the building's front door and the condo. If you want, you can go there right now. I rented it for five days, starting tonight. In case the boss says no, your friend will have a place to stay until she figures something out."

"Thanks. So, I guess you don't have an answer from the boss yet."

"Regretfully, no. Everyone is busy getting ready for the wedding, so I might not have an answer for you until tomorrow."

"Is there a chance you or Tom could talk to the boss during the wedding?"

"We might, but these parties usually end really late. It might be after three in the morning when Tom can catch a word with him."

"That's fine. Call me or text me the moment you have an answer."

"Will do. Are you going to move with your friend tonight?"

"If Jasmine wants to go, I'll escort her there and come back. Lynda and her friends are leaving tomorrow morning, and I'll never hear the end of it if I don't say goodbye to them."

"Yeah, I hear you. Things got better between you two during this week, right?"

"Yeah. I can tolerate her now, but it takes an effort, and I can only do it for a short period of time. The woman's middle name is entitled. I don't know how Rob can stand her, but I gave up on trying to understand their dynamic a long time ago."

"To each their own." Mia sighed. "Good luck to your friend."

"Thank you. For everything."

"If there's anything else you need, let me know. I can rent you a car, send you cash, just say the word."

"Cash would be nice. I'd rather not use my credit cards because charges can be traced, too. I'll pay you back. You know that."

"Don't be silly. Of course, I do."

18

KIAN

"Thank you for coming so quickly." Kian motioned for Lokan to follow him to the balcony. "We need your input."

"I'm glad you called. With Carol gone, I had nothing to do, and I was bored. Besides, I wouldn't mind a cigar and a glass of whiskey, and the company, of course."

Lokan was already dressed in his tuxedo, which was good since they were pressed for time. The wedding was in less than half an hour, which wasn't enough time to devise a strategy, but it was enough to get Lokan's perspective on the situation. He was still an active member of the Brotherhood and had more insight into its workings than Kalugal and Kian had.

Kian opened the lid of the cigar box. "Choose your poison."

"Since we don't have much time, I'll take the Short Story."

"Good choice." Kian handed him the cutter and poured whiskey into a glass from the bottle he had brought outside.

Lokan cut off the tip of his cigar. "I was hoping for another get-together for Brundar's bachelor party and some male bonding, but given that he participated in the mission earlier, I understand why there hasn't been one."

"It has nothing to do with the mission. He just didn't want to have one. He's not very social."

Lokan nodded. "I've noticed." He took the lighter from Kian. "So, what is this about?" He lit his cigar and took a puff.

Kian handed Lokan the glass. "Kalugal and I interrogated Bud earlier, and it turned out that Kalugal hadn't been as meticulous as he should have been erasing the tour guide's memories. The guy remembered a few things that he'd overheard, and Bud was able to coerce him into revealing them."

"It's not easy to thrall so surgically," Kalugal said. "I couldn't erase all of his memories because that would have been suspicious, so I had to sift through them and decide what needed to go and what could stay, and as you all know, looking into someone's head is not like reading a book."

"We know." Kian put a hand on Kalugal's shoulder. "I'm not accusing you of negligence."

"It sure sounded like you did." Kalugal tapped on his cigar, dislodging a big chunk of ash.

Ignoring his cousin's pout, Kian turned to Lokan. "Anyway, Luis overheard someone mentioning Cabo and the name of the hotel where Mia and Frankie's friend is staying. Kalugal says that the Brotherhood have probably moved locally stationed teams, either from here in Mexico or from California, to investigate what happened to their brethren in Acapulco and to wait for us at the hotel. What's your take on this?"

"Kalugal is right. If time was not a factor, they would have sent teams from the island, but the disappearance of an entire team is an urgent matter, especially since they reported their suspicions about who killed their cartel partners. They have several teams in Mexico and other Latin American countries to oversee their drug operations. Those are the teams they will most likely use."

Kalugal smirked. "That's precisely what I said."

Lokan tilted his head. "What is the plan, then? Are we still stopping at Cabo, or are we sailing past it to the next stop? My advice is to keep going. You don't want a confrontation with the Brotherhood."

"No, I don't." Kian took a puff of his cigar. "What I'm worried about is them figuring out which ship we are on and sending the Mexican navy after us. They don't have any compellers other than Navuh on hand, and no one will dare to ask him to get involved in such a marginal matter, but I bet that they have plenty of Mexican politicians, generals, and admirals who they can either bribe or extort to do their dirty work for them."

Lokan shook his head. "They wouldn't go that far. As much as they want revenge, they need to stay under the humans' radar as much as you do. Starting an international incident over twelve members of the Brotherhood is not reason enough to risk exposure, and neither is the prospect of capturing or killing a few clan members. No one in the Brotherhood's leadership would expect that the entire clan is on one ship. Nothing in the clan's behavior over the centuries would lead them to think that. They are used to you doing your best to hide. If I were the one evaluating the situation, I would assume that several clan members, most likely Guardians, were on vacation or on their way to doing some business in Mexico. They ran into the cartel thugs who were holding the women by chance, and being the goody two-shoes that they are, they appointed themselves the champions of the weak and killed the bad humans. When the Brotherhood's team demanded the victims' return and threatened to harm Luis and his family, the Guardians attacked and killed the team and their human cohorts."

Kian let out a breath. "That's the problem right there. They were prepared for us, and they marshaled a large military force. To overcome them, we had to have a superior force. They would no longer think that they are dealing with just a few members of the clan. They don't know about you or Kalugal or Toven, so they might assume that Annani disabled all those soldiers and made them easy to pick off."

A long moment of silence stretched over the balcony as the others considered what he had said.

"Again, not likely." Lokan pushed to his feet and walked over to where Kian had left the bottle of whiskey. "To assume that the Clan Mother was there in person is a leap of logic none of them would make. They might consider cooperation with the local army or police, though. Or maybe even an aerial attack since we are not that far from the clan's base, which they know is in Los Angeles."

"We left no evidence," Kalugal said. "All the bodies were burned, the vehicles and the weapons were delivered to Turner's arms supplier, and the two boys we left alive were thralled to remember that it was a Colombian cartel attack."

"They'll know that the boys were thralled." Lokan returned to his chair. "Since there will be no bodies for them to find and no vehicles, they might assume a coup. The cartel thugs could have overpowered their immortal overlords. It wouldn't be the first time something like that happened."

Kian snorted. "We should be so lucky." He took a puff from his cigar. "So, what's our next move, gentlemen?"

Kalugal pushed to his feet. "We don't stop in Cabo, and we keep sailing back to Long Beach without stopping anywhere. This ship can defend itself in case of an attack, but a hasty retreat is best."

"I disagree," Lokan said. "Ships get tracked, and it's easy to access that information. The mention of Cabo will lead them to believe that the clan members involved in the attack are traveling by ship, and they can follow all the ships that left Acapulco earlier today and are sailing north. We are already going faster than any cruise ship in the area, which will make us stand out, but if we continue all the way to Long Beach as if the hounds of hell are on our heels, they will figure out right away that the *Silver Swan* is their target and wait for us in Long Beach. We should stop in Cabo as planned and have a few groups go ashore and do all the touristy activities that people do there. If possible, they should disguise themselves to look like humans, meaning older and less attractive."

"Good idea." Kian put his glass down and pulled out his phone. "I need to talk to Eva about disguises. I hope she can do something with what's available."

"One more thing," Lokan said. "You should slow down to a normal cruising speed. First of all, it will appear less suspicious if you are going at the same speed as all the other cruise liners, and secondly, it will give us more time to prepare."

19

MARGO

Since Jasmine seemed to be enjoying herself at the bar, Margo continued chatting with Mia for a few minutes longer. After all, it would have been rude to get what she needed from her friend and not talk with her about the things they usually talked about.

"I have to go," Mia said. "I'm sitting here in my underwear while Tom is already dressed in his tux."

Margo laughed. "I'll let you go. Get dressed and have fun at the wedding."

"I intend to. Stay safe, and get Jasmine to the Airbnb." Mia ended the call.

Mia was the best. It helped that she had a very rich fiancé, who made sure that she didn't lack for a thing.

A tiny pang of envy coursed through Margo, but she quickly shoved it away. If anyone deserved a major happily ever after, it was Mia. She had gone through so much. Losing both her legs at such a young age was terrible, and she had been so brave, learning to walk on dual prostheses, which was a very hard thing to do that not many managed well.

Mia might look small and fragile, but she was a fighter.

At the bar, Jasmine said something to the guy sitting next to her, and he turned to look at Margo with a hostile look before getting up and motioning for her to take his seat.

"Someone isn't happy," she muttered under her breath.

Not that she could blame him. If she were a guy, she would also be mad if her flirting with a gorgeous woman was interrupted.

"See you later, Liam." Jasmine waved.

Margo took the seat Liam had vacated. "You probably won't. My friend got you an Airbnb that's walking distance from the hotel. It's under her name, and the door has a code lock, so you don't even need to meet the owner, and no one can trace you there."

The music was loud, so Margo felt okay talking with Jaz about it in the open. Unless someone had bat hearing, their conversation was private.

"I don't know." Jasmine grimaced. "I'm sorry to have put your friend through all that trouble, but I had some time to think, and I realized that we might have overreacted. If Alberto wanted to sell me, he would have shown me to prospective buyers, but he hasn't introduced me to anyone."

That was a good point. But he didn't need to show her in person. There could be hidden cameras in the hotel penthouse.

"What if he put tiny cameras in the bathroom so prospective buyers could see you naked when you are showering or taking a bath?"

Jasmine recoiled. "I didn't think about that angle. Let's check. It's much harder to hide a camera in the bathroom than in the other rooms. If he put one in the shower, we should be able to find it."

Margo slid off the stool and stood up. "Let's do it."

"One moment." Jasmine signaled for the bartender to come closer. "I need to sign for the drinks."

"Check, please," she said.

He nodded. "Give me a moment."

It took him a little longer than that to put a receipt in front of her with a pen on top of it. "Here you go, ma'am. Sorry for the wait. Have a good night."

Jasmine wrote down her room number, added the tip amount, and signed the check. "Let's go."

They rode the elevator in tense silence, and as it opened on the penthouse level, Jaz rushed out with the card key in hand. Once they were inside, they didn't waste any time and walked straight into the master bathroom.

"The shower is the most logical place," Margo said. "Either that or above the bathtub. Do you take baths?"

"Sometimes, I do." Jasmine walked into the shower and started patting the tiled surface. "But mostly, I take showers. How small can those cameras get? I don't know what I'm looking for."

"I read somewhere that they can be as small as a pinhead."

"Great." Jasmine grimaced. "With this pebbled tiling, he could have hidden it anywhere."

"Not really." Margo took off her shoes and climbed on top of the bathtub platform. "It's not like he had access to it while they were building the place, and a retrofit is never seamless." She pointed her phone's flashlight at the ceiling, methodically scanning the entire expanse.

Jaz stopped her tile patting and leaned against the wall. "What if the suite was built to serve as a viewing room? They could have embedded the cameras in the walls."

Margo chuckled. "And I thought that I was the queen of conspiracy theories."

"Jaz? Where are you?"

They both froze.

"It's Alberto," Jasmine whispered.

Margo winced.

"What are we going to do?"

"Follow my lead and act natural." Jasmine smoothed a hand over the flowing skirt of her halter dress and sauntered out of the bathroom.

"Alberto, you're back," she said with such cheer in her voice that Margo had to admire her acting skills.

"Here you are." A good-looking guy swept Jaz into his arms and planted a kiss on her lips. He stopped kissing her only when he noticed Margo behind his girlfriend. "Who are you?"

Jasmine untangled herself from his arms. "This is my new friend, Margo. We met at the pool and hit it off right away. I was just showing her around the suite."

"This place is amazing." Margo put a hand over her heart. "I've never seen a presidential suite before. I didn't even know rooms like this existed in hotels." She snorted. "This place is so big that it needs its own serving staff."

Alberto plastered a charming smile on his handsome face and offered her his hand. "I am very pleased to meet you, Margo." His handshake was firm but not too hard. "I'm so glad that my Jaz found a friend. Regrettably, the business deal I'm working on requires much more of my time than I expected, and I'm forced to neglect my beautiful Jasmine." He made a pouty face and wrapped his arm around Jaz's waist, pulling her toward him. "My precious jewel should not be left by her lonesome."

"I agree." Margo regarded him from under lowered lashes.

Usually, she was good at reading people, but Alberto was either very good at putting on a show, or he was innocent of the nefarious intentions she'd assigned to him.

"You must join us for drinks and a late supper." Alberto walked Jasmine out of the bedroom. "I'll order room service, and we will get to know each other."

"I would love to." Margo granted him a bright smile.

For a brief moment, she considered that Alberto might want to sell her too. Margo wasn't nearly as beautiful as Jasmine, but she was a natural blonde, had a decent figure, and had a pretty face.

She could fetch a good price.

Nah, she was just an average, nothing-special twenty-seven-year-old. Most of those in the market to buy flesh would regard her as too old. They wanted the young and innocent.

How old was Jasmine, though?

The woman appeared ageless. She could be twenty or thirty or any age in between, but she was far from innocent. She was also one of the most beautiful women Margo had ever seen, so maybe it didn't matter that she wasn't as young as the perverts preferred.

20

BRUNDAR

Brundar stood in front of the mirror and debated whether to gather his long hair at his nape like he usually did or leave it to fan out down his back.

The choice to keep it that long had been about making a statement. He could look as feminine as had been claimed by those who had attacked him as a kid and shattered his innocence forever, but no one would ever think that he was easy prey again. He was lethal, and even those who didn't know him could figure that out with just one look.

Still, he didn't need to make a statement onboard a ship that carried mostly his clan. He was an accepted and respected member of the community, and no one would mistake him for someone who needed protecting or rescuing.

He was the protector and rescuer now, and he was damn good at his job.

Pulling the leather tie from his pocket, he brushed his stick-straight hair back with his fingers, gathered it at the nape, and tied the string around the thick, blond column.

In the other pocket of his tux was the folded piece of paper containing his vows to Callie. He pulled it out, unfolded the page, and read through it once more. By now, he could probably recite them in his sleep.

Anandur had pestered him for weeks about writing his vows and memorizing them, warning him that things might get a little emotional during the wedding ceremony and that he might forget some of the words, but Brundar had enjoyed tormenting his brother by pretending that he didn't care about that and wasn't going to bother.

Had Anandur believed him?

He shouldn't have.

His brother was probably the only one other than Callie who knew that Brundar's stoic appearance was a mask, and that inside he was just as susceptible to the turmoil of emotions as the next person, maybe even more so. Except, as soon as he felt anything, he immediately shoved that feeling into the armored safe inside his mind so it wouldn't interfere with his work or training.

The only emotion that Brundar would allow himself to feel was his love for Callie. He didn't shove that into the safe. Even so, it required a conscious effort not to do so, and that was not because his feelings for her didn't run deep because they did. It was just that he'd gotten so used to suppressing his emotions that it happened on autopilot, and reprogramming himself was still a work in progress.

When the doorbell rang, Brundar took one last look at his reflection and walked into the living room to open the door for his brother.

"I don't have much time." Anandur rushed by him, dripping water from his freshly washed hair. "I have two minutes to get into my tux and tame my hair."

Brundar followed him to the bedroom. "Where did you shower?"

"Kian's place. I figured you needed your alone time before the wedding."

"Thank you. That was uncharacteristically considerate of you."

"You're welcome." Anandur pulled his T-shirt over his head and dropped it on the floor. "Don't get used to it. I'm only making an exception for your wedding. The rest of the time, you're fair game." He dropped his pants in the same unceremonious way.

Brundar shook his head at his brother's nudity. "Do you ever wear underwear?"

"Yeah, I do. But I didn't want to borrow Kian's, and I didn't have any fresh ones with me, now did I?" He unzipped the tux bag and pulled the tux out.

With a sigh, Brundar collected the discarded clothing and carried it to the laundry hamper in the bathroom. "I can give you a fresh pair. I have a pack of new ones."

"Thank you. That would be awesome." Anandur shrugged on a white dress shirt and started buttoning it. "I wanted to wear something fun for your wedding, but since you are not fun, I decided it would be a waste of effort."

"And there goes the one day of reprieve you just promised me." Brundar tossed the package at Anandur.

"Thank you. And that doesn't count because it's the truth. You wouldn't have appreciated my humor."

Brundar shrugged. "I thought that the Superman T-shirt was a nice touch."

"Really?" Anandur's brows hitched nearly to his hairline. "Why didn't you say so?" He tore the plastic bag and pulled out one of the boxer briefs.

"Your head is too big already." Brundar leaned against the dresser, waiting for his brother to be done.

"How do I look?" Anandur asked and turned in a circle.

"Just as good as you did at your own wedding." Brundar pushed away from the dresser. "Do you need cologne?"

"Yes, please."

Anandur's hair was still as messy as always, but they didn't have the time or the products for him to tame it, so Brundar didn't mention it.

"Do you have your vows ready?" Anandur asked after spraying himself with the cologne.

Brundar nodded.

"Did you come up with anything good?"

"I hope so, and if not, Callie will forgive me. She knows I'm a man of few words."

Anandur straightened to his full height and looked down at Brundar. "Yeah, everyone knows that. But you've been more talkative than usual just now. Is it because you are nervous?"

"Not about the wedding. It's just a formality. I'm nervous about having everyone looking at me and expecting the same stoic Brundar they are used to seeing every day."

Anandur frowned. "What are they going to see instead?"

Brundar smiled, and the shock on Anandur's face was just precious. "They are going to see the face I've only shown Callie. It's going to come out for one night in honor of my bride and go back into dormancy tomorrow."

21

CALLIE

Callie stood at the entrance to the beautifully adorned hall and smoothed her hand over the voluminous skirt of her gown. She'd chosen a traditional white dress even though it wasn't her first wedding, because the first time didn't count.

She'd married a monster who would have murdered her if Brundar hadn't shown up in her life and given her the courage to escape the trap of her disastrous marriage.

Her destined mate, the love of her life, had almost died while trying to defend her, and if not for Anandur, who had saved them both, they wouldn't be here today.

But she didn't want to think about that now. The past belonged in the past, and today, or rather tonight, it was about her and Brundar and the love they shared.

This was the only wedding that mattered, and this time she was marrying an angel. He certainly looked like an angel to her, and most of their guests, being family, would share her opinion of her mate, but they probably thought of him as their Guardian angel. There were only a few who knew that he was as beautiful on the inside as he was on the outside.

Brundar might look like a killer to some, and when circumstances called for it, he was, but he was also a savior, a protector. He was a guardian.

As tradition dictated, he hadn't seen her dress yet, and she hoped he would love it as much as she did. Callie had seen it in an online catalog and knew that it was the dress she was going to wear on her special day. A trip to the bridal shop had confirmed her choice. The dress fit her so perfectly that no alterations had been needed, not even the length, even though she was of average height and expected the skirt to be too long.

What made the gown truly stand out were the delicate tulle inserts interspersed within the skirt. The sheer fabric pieces played with the light, creating an ethereal, almost magical quality to the gown. As Callie moved, the tulle pieces swayed gently, making her feel like a fairytale princess.

"You look beautiful," Wonder whispered.

Callie smiled at her soon-to-be sister-in-law. "Thank you." She looked over Wonder's tall frame encased in a peach-colored bridesmaid's dress. "The color really suits you."

"I know, right?" Wonder looked at the other bridesmaids, who all wore the same style of dress, just in different colors.

Amanda had joked that they looked like assorted candy or ice cream cones, which was the kind of look Callie had been going for. The dresses were simple satin sheaths with spaghetti straps and of varying lengths, and all of her bridesmaids looked beautiful in them.

Amanda's was blue, Syssi's was orange, Carol's was pink, and Jacki's was yellow. Cassandra's was bright red, Mey's was purple, and Jin's was emerald.

It had been tough to choose her bridesmaids from her many female friends in the clan, but since Brundar's groomsmen were mostly his fellow Guardians, she'd decided to choose their mates in addition to Carol, Syssi, and Amanda.

"That's our cue," Amanda said as the wedding march started playing.

As the double doors to the dining hall were opened by two Guardians, Callie took a deep breath before taking the first step.

With her bridesmaids flanking her, four on each side, she entered the hall and followed the red carpet to the podium, where Brundar waited for her with his seven groomsmen and one groomsmaid by his side.

In addition to the head guardians, his groomsmen included Kian and Dalhu.

Callie smiled, her eyes trained on Brundar, who surprised her by returning her smile and nodding.

She was so stunned by that smile that her step faltered, and she had to steady herself to regain her footing. She'd been graced by his smiles on rare occasions, but never in public. Was this the start of a new Brundar? Or was he only lowering his shields for this one night?

When Brundar averted his gaze to look at the Clan Mother, Callie was finally able to tear her eyes away from him and shift her attention to the goddess who was presiding over their wedding.

Just as in the three preceding nights, Annani wore a gleaming white gown with long sheer sleeves that looked like angel wings when she raised her arms.

It was a different gown every night, but it was a variation on the same theme.

Shifting her eyes back to Brundar, Callie glided toward him on the wings of love. Or at least it felt like that because all she could feel was the smile stretching her face. It probably looked manic, but she couldn't help it because Brundar was once again smiling at her across the room.

As she and her bridesmaids reached the podium, she took her place by Brundar's side while her bridesmaids joined the groomsmen.

Brundar reached for her hand and clasped it gently, pouring strength into her.

The Clan Mother lifted her arms, and the last of the chatter stopped.

"My dear children. We are gathered here tonight to celebrate the union of Callie and Brundar. It is most fitting that this joyous occasion follows a great victory of good over evil, and on this eve, our hearts are filled with joy and hope for a better future."

Smiling, she lowered her arms and trained her glowing eyes on Brundar. "Brundar's journey has been one of courage and determination, of triumph over adversity and the relentless pursuit of excellence and growth. You have been a staunch defender of the clan. With bravery and skill, you have walked a path of honor, courage, and personal growth. In Callie, you have found a safe harbor of calm water, peace, and unconditional love."

The goddess shifted her warm gaze to Callie. "Callie's journey paralleled Brundar's. With courage and determination, you triumphed over hardship while retaining a spirit bright with optimism and hope, a guiding light of compassion, and a testament to the healing power of love. You are proof that the gentlest of touches can move mountains and that kindness can illuminate the darkest of paths. In each other, you have found love and a mirror reflecting back the best of yourselves, and together, you are stronger than the sum of your parts."

She turned her gaze to their gathered family and friends before returning it to the two of them. "May your joined journey be an odyssey of growth, filled with shared joys and enduring companionship. Your love is a sanctuary, a haven of peace and renewal, not just for yourselves but for all who are touched by it. May you walk hand in hand as partners, mates, and scions of hope and inspiration in the Fates' great tapestry of life."

The goddess smiled, and Callie's heart missed a beat. "In the presence of your family and friends, you may now recite your vows of love and commitment to each other."

22

BRUNDAR

Callie was always beautiful to Brundar, but today she looked like a fairytale princess in her white dress and her low-heeled white slippers that he had to examine to make sure they weren't made from glass.

He might be the last male anyone could mistake for a prince, but Callie was dancing only with him, and if anyone was to find her glass slipper, it would be him.

The silly thought brought a smile to his face, but it melted away when the Clan Mother spoke of love's transformative power. Brundar knew what she was referring to, but he hoped that the rest of the assembled clan did not.

In fact, Annani wasn't supposed to know either, and he wondered who had told her.

148

It couldn't have been Anandur, who had sworn to take the tale with him beyond the veil, but his mother could have said something to the goddess. She also didn't know the details of what had happened to him, but she'd seen him when Anandur had brought him home, and it hadn't been difficult to guess what had been done to him.

Anandur had protected him as he had always done and prohibited their mother from asking questions.

His secret should have never reached the goddess's ears.

"You may now recite your vows of love and commitment for each other." Annani's words pulled him out of his thoughts, and he turned to Callie, the love of his life and his savior in so many ways.

Her brilliant smile and the sheen in her eyes melted some of the ice that had formed around his heart, and he smiled back. "I'll go first if you don't mind." He took her hands and waited until she nodded.

"Callie, my light in the darkest of nights. From the moment our paths first crossed, I knew deep in my heart that we were destined to be together. You were married to a monster, but at the time, I didn't know the extent of his monstrosity, and I tried to stay away. But the Fates whispered in my ear to keep an eye on you, to guard you in case you needed my help, and that was my excuse for watching you like a stalker."

Callie smiled. "You were not a stalker. You were my guardian angel, and you saved me. I felt you watching me, and your presence was reassuring rather than threatening. The Fates must have whispered in my ears as well."

Brundar gave her hands a light squeeze. "We saved each other. You have been my guiding light. In your eyes, I found a world filled with hope and a future I didn't think was possible for the likes of me. You have shown me that love is more than a soft feeling. It's a force that can move mountains, heal the deepest wounds, and bring light into the darkest corners. In your love, I have found a sanctuary."

"Oh, Brundar." A single tear slid down Callie's cheek. "I love you so much."

"I love you more than words can express. I vow to honor the love you have given me, to cherish it, nurture it, and protect it against all. In the quiet moments and the chaotic ones, in the challenges and the triumphs, I promise to stand by your side as your partner, your best friend, your guardian, and your greatest ally. I promise to be the warmth in your winter, the breeze in your summer, the harvest of your autumn, and the bloom of your spring."

He'd read the last sentence somewhere, and it had stuck in his memory. Hopefully, Callie wouldn't mind that not all the words in his vows were original.

He had to let go of one of her hands to pull the ring out from his pocket. "We don't need symbols to represent our everlasting love, but it's tradition, so here goes. This ring has no beginning and no end, and symbolizes my eternal love, faith, and commitment." He slid the ring on her finger. "With this ring, I bind my life to yours."

He leaned down and kissed her lightly on the lips. "I know that I'm supposed to wait until the Clan Mother pronounces us joined, but I needed this."

"Me too." She wiped the lone tear that had slid down her cheek.

Taking a deep breath, Callie took his hands. "Brundar, my guardian, my strength. In the tapestry of my life, the threads of darkness were once overwhelming until you entered, bringing light, hope, and incredible courage. When shadows loomed large and the path ahead seemed insurmountable, you became my protector, my shield, my guardian angel. I will never forget that you were willing to sacrifice yourself to save me or the terrible injuries you sustained while rescuing me from a monster. You have shown me what true bravery is. In the solace of your strength, I found the courage to dream, to be unapologetically myself, and most importantly, to love as I will."

This was the only mention of their shared proclivities, and it was subtle enough for most of their guests to gloss over, but those who knew them well and were aware of the games they liked to play smiled and clapped.

Callie gave them a slight nod before continuing, "I vow to honor the sacrifices you've made and to cherish the love you've shown me every step of the way. With every beat of my heart, I promise to be your sanctuary and safe harbor as you have been for me."

She turned to Anandur, who stood first among the groomsmen. "Neither of us would be here if not for you. In our darkest moment, in the crucible of despair, you came to our rescue, and for that and all the other times you stood by your brother's side, you have my eternal gratitude."

For a change, Anandur didn't retort with a jest or a joke. Instead, he put his hand over his heart and dipped his head. "For as long as there is breath in my lungs, you will have my protection. As you know, I take my big-brother responsibilities very seriously, and once you became Brundar's mate, you also became my little sister."

"Thank you." She blew him a kiss before returning her gaze to Brundar. "In the human world, when you marry a man, you marry his whole family. I'm overjoyed to be part of yours." She waved a hand over the gathered crowd. "You are all the best people I've ever met, and I love you all."

As applause and cheers erupted, Callie smiled and waited patiently until they subsided. When the room fell quiet again, she turned back to face Brundar. "Today, as I stand with you, I see a future filled with promise. I vow to weather every storm with you, and to glide through every calm. I promise to support you in every struggle, and to celebrate your every triumph."

Callie extended her hand to Wonder, who placed a ring on her palm.

"This ring is a symbol of my eternal gratitude, my unending love, and my commitment to our joined journey." She slid the ring on his finger. "Brundar, my love, my angel, my knight in shining armor. You are my fated mate."

As the crowd erupted in a new wave of cheers and applause, Annani lifted her arms. "In the presence of all gathered here, I pronounce you bonded for eternity. May your love shine as a symbol of hope and transformation and the unyielding power of the heart." She waved a hand. "You may kiss the bride."

23

MARGO

"The food was delicious." Margo leaned back in her chair and rubbed her tummy. "It's good that I don't get to eat like that every day."

"Why not?" Alberto asked.

She smiled. "I don't want to gain weight."

He waved a dismissive hand. "Women think too much about their weight. Men might like to look at skinny models, but they don't want them in their beds." He threw a charming smile at Jasmine. "They don't want a bag of bones under them. They want their woman to be soft."

His words rubbed Margo the wrong way even though she couldn't totally dispute them. She wouldn't be attracted to a guy that was all bones either, but she wouldn't phrase it like that. She would never say that she didn't want a pile of bones in her bed.

Alberto talked about women as if they were sexual objects and not people with minds, feelings, and thoughts.

It wasn't unusual for men, and maybe even for some women, to think about possible partners exclusively in sexual terms, but it was small-minded and offensive.

"Are you calling me fat?" Jasmine asked teasingly.

"I'm calling you perfect." He took her hand and kissed the back of it. "One of a kind." He kissed it again. "A rare and coveted jewel." He kissed it for the third time.

Hadn't he told Jasmine that she should get plastic surgery to slim her thighs? Maybe Jasmine had made that up?

The guy acted as if he worshiped the ground she walked on, even if he was only infatuated with her body and gorgeous face and couldn't care less about her personality or her mind, both of which Margo found lovely. Jasmine was effortlessly friendly, she wasn't conceited, she didn't act entitled, and she was intelligent.

Jasmine smiled. "You are such a charmer."

That he was, and Margo had reconsidered her initial suspicions about him wanting to sell Jaz, but there was still something about him that bothered her.

Perhaps it was just his Latin machismo.

Not that she knew enough about Latin men to pass judgment. Growing up in Los Angeles, she'd been surrounded by Latinos, but she had never dated one. The truth was that she hadn't dated many men in general, so maybe she just didn't know much about them, regardless of their ethnicity.

Crap, she was committing the same offense she'd accused Alberto of. She wasn't thinking of men in terms of people but in terms of their gender, and that was as wrong as any other generalization.

Okay, so what did she know about Alberto as a person?

He spoke English like a native, which led her to believe that he had studied in the US, and his vocabulary was rich enough to indicate that he had at least some higher education or read a lot. Still, she could easily detect the traces of the Spanish accent he was trying to hide. He might have even been born and raised in the US, but his first language had been Spanish.

The guy was too young to have so much money to throw around, but that didn't necessarily mean that he was a drug dealer or a trafficker. Maybe he came from a wealthy family, and the business deal he was negotiating was on behalf of his family business and had nothing to do with drugs or trafficking.

Lifting her wine glass, Margo turned to Alberto. "You mentioned a deal you are working on. What is it about?"

A shadow passed over his eyes, but his lips lifted in a smile. "I'm afraid it's confidential."

Margo's hackles rose again. "How come?"

He sighed. "I'm trying to negotiate a deal between two large companies. If word got out about the possible merger, it would influence their stock prices, which is a big no-no. Anyone who bought or sold their stocks after hearing about it could be accused of insider trading. I'm therefore very careful about saying anything regarding the merger."

"I don't invest in stocks," Margo said. "I have a 401(k) retirement savings through the company I work for and a savings account. That's all."

Alberto let go of Jasmine's hand and reached for the wine bottle. "You might have friends and family who invest." He refilled her glass. "The bottom line is that I can't tell anyone who isn't directly involved in the talks." He refilled Jaz's glass, and lastly his own.

"Is that why they are conducting the negotiations in Cabo?" Jasmine asked.

He nodded. "It's easier to hide from the media. The executives of both companies are staying in different hotels, and I doubt anyone in the media will figure out the connection between the two companies organizing retreats for their executives at the same time and in the same city."

It all sounded perfectly logical, and Margo's earlier suspicions were diminishing by the minute.

"I thought that you were dealing with local businesspeople," Jasmine said.

"What made you think that?" Alberto asked a little sharply.

Jaz shrugged. "You said something about a long drive. All the hotels are clustered in the same area."

He reached for his wine glass. "They are thinking about building a new manufacturing plant in the area, and we are scouting possible building sites."

Again, it sounded legit, but something about it bothered Margo. Did it make sense for the two companies who were negotiating a possible merger to be already looking for a site for their future joint endeavor?

Shouldn't they conclude the first step before going to the next?

If all of that was an elaborate fiction, Alberto was a skilled liar who could spin tales on the spot, which he might very well be.

Still, Margo's usually suspicious mind was getting a little lazy tonight, and she was more and more convinced that she had overreacted. It didn't make sense for the guy to invest so much time and money in a woman whom he intended to sell. There was no reason for him to put her in the presidential suite or to try to charm her new friend into liking him.

On the other hand, Alberto had taken Jasmine's passport, her California driver's license, and her credit cards, and that was a big-ass red flag.

24

KIAN

"That was so beautiful." Syssi dabbed under her eyes with a cloth napkin. "I never suspected that Brundar could be so poetic."

Amanda snorted. "Don't judge the book by its cover, right? People are more than their appearance."

"That reminds me." Kian drummed his fingers on the table. "Eva will need your help tomorrow. We need to disguise a large number of people to look like humans, and Eva can't handle so many on her own."

"Why do you need to do that?" Dalhu asked.

"So, the Doomers don't suspect this ship is ours." He explained Lokan's arguments and why he agreed with them. "But if we hope to pull it off, we will have to do a really good job of appearing like any other cruise ship. A large percentage of passengers will need to disembark and do touristy things while looking like average cruisers, which means much older and less attractive."

"Eva doesn't have her chest of professional makeup and costumes with her," Amanda said. "How does she hope to create the illusion with what's available to her?"

Kian turned to look at Brundar and Callie walking hand in hand toward the dance floor. "Eva said that she could do it with regular makeup, padding, and coaching on how to act. I assume she means walking hunched over, maybe shuffling a little, but it shouldn't be overdone because it will look obvious."

"What about Margo?" Syssi asked. "They don't know who she is, only that we are supposed to pick up a woman from the hotel. We should tell her to take a taxi to the airport and collect her from there."

That was actually a pretty good idea, and it was much simpler than what he had in mind, which was picking up Margo at a mall or a coffee shop. That still didn't solve the problem of getting her on the ship with the Doomers watching. If he were in their shoes, he would have counted the number of passengers leaving the ship and compared it to the number of those who returned. If there was an excess of one, that would prompt them to further investigate the *Silver Swan*, including boarding it.

There was another problem that he hadn't considered before. If any of the Doomers were lurking nearby, they could sense the immortal males. Still, if only females went ashore, that would appear suspicious as well. Hopefully, they would be watching from some distance. The alarm only worked in close proximity.

"I should tell Mia to contact Margo and tell her what the plan is." He pushed to his feet. "The question is how to explain that to a human who doesn't know who we are."

"Let Mia worry about that," Amanda said. "She can invent some story about the cartels."

"Can't it wait?" Syssi took his hand. "I want to join Brundar and Callie on the dance floor."

"There is no rush." He tugged on her hand. "In fact, it can wait for tomorrow morning. We've slowed down, so we will only get to Cabo in the evening, and Mia will have plenty of time to tell Margo what to do."

Syssi rewarded him with a bright smile. "It would be nice to have at least one night to just enjoy ourselves."

"I couldn't agree more." He led his wife to where several other couples were dancing. "Did I tell you already how stunningly beautiful you look tonight?" He put one hand on her waist and took her hand in the other.

"Yes, you did." She followed his waltz steps. "Several times. You look very handsome tonight as well, my love."

"It's the same tux I wore to the other weddings."

"You've looked dashing every night, but you need to wear your other tux for the upcoming weddings."

He looked down at his pants. "Why? Did I get stains on this one?"

She laughed. "No, but it's no longer in immaculate condition. It's time for a fresh one."

"As you wish, my darling." He dipped his head and kissed her cheek, only because she was wearing lipstick, and he didn't want to mess it up.

Not yet, anyway. Once the wedding was over and they were back in their cabin, he planned to mess up a lot more than just her lipstick.

Syssi chuckled. "I love that lopsided smile of yours. Are you thinking the same thing I'm thinking?"

"That depends on what you were thinking."

"You go first."

He pulled her closer against his chest and whispered in her ear, "I was thinking about messing up your lipstick."

Syssi laughed. "That's all? I was expecting something much naughtier."

He lowered his hand and gave her ass a loving squeeze. "I didn't say how I was going to mess it up."

Predictably, her cheeks pinked. "And how is that?" She licked her lips.

"I think you've got the right idea."

25

PETER

As the vows were concluded and Brundar kissed Callie, Peter cheered and clapped with everyone else, but his eyes scanned the hall for Marina. None of the servers were out, though, and he remembered that they wouldn't be allowed into the event hall until Annani departed.

The Clan Mother never stayed long during the celebrations, usually retreating to her quarters after the ceremony was over, so it wouldn't be long before the servers would start delivering trays of food.

His fellow Guardians were particularly revelrous tonight, which was to be expected after a mission. There was nothing like killing scum who truly deserved it to put everyone in a good mood.

Peter was still clapping when the newlyweds took to the dance floor for their first dance as an officially married couple. Brundar and Callie had been mated for a while, and yet seeing them swaying in each other's arms, lost in their private universe, made him a little emotional.

Thankfully, he wasn't the only one. Anandur was wiping tears from his eyes, and for once, he wasn't pretending.

Who would have thought that the stoic Brundar could deliver such beautiful vows to his bride?

Callie and Brundar's vows had been touching, but then Peter had found all the previous couples' vows moving.

Love was truly a beautiful thing, and he hoped to one day find his own fated mate, but the waiting line was long, and there were many ahead of him.

No one knew for sure why the Fates rewarded some with the boon of a fated mate and not others, but the belief was that it had to do with the sacrifices one had made for other people or the terrible suffering that one had endured.

The only hardship Peter had ever suffered was when Emmett had abducted him, and he'd been afraid of being used as a stud bull for Kra-ell Dormants, but even though it had been a scary experience, he really hadn't been harmed, so it probably didn't count as enduring great suffering.

166

Bottom line, he wasn't expecting his truelove mate to appear anytime soon.

After Annani departed, Peter waited until the servers emerged with their trays and scanned the room. Looking for a glint of blue hair, he spotted Marina weaving between the tables while expertly balancing a tray laden with champagne flutes.

She'd promised him a dance at the wedding, and he intended to collect on that promise sooner than later. He also had plans for her later that night, and he had a feeling that she would be more than amenable to those plans.

Rising to his feet, Peter made his way through the crowd, zeroing in on Marina.

Seeing him heading her way, her eyes widened, and a smile ghosted her lips. She shook her head slightly, hinting that she wasn't ready for him to collect on her promise, but he was impatient, and he needed to hold her in his arms right away.

Hell, he'd been imagining that since the moment she'd promised him that dance, her lips curving in a seductive smile and the scent of her arousal nearly bringing him to his knees.

It had flared for only a moment, but it had been enough to imprint itself on his psyche for eternity.

Kagra's words suddenly sounded in his mind, chilling his fervor. *You are a romantic, Peter, and you fall too easily. You are enamored with the notion of love.*

So what? Love was the spice of life, and even though neither Kagra nor Marina could be his fated one, he wasn't looking for a forever love. For-now love was good enough, for the simple reason that it was the only kind available to him.

When he reached Marina, he plucked the tray from her hands, put it down on the nearest table, and took her hand. "Come dance with me."

"I can't. I'm working." She reached for the tray.

"You can take a break. If anyone has a problem with that, they can take it up with me."

She still hesitated.

"Just one dance. The world won't crumble if the champagne is served a minute later."

"Fine," she said in a resigned tone. "Just one dance, and if Mila comes to scream at me, I'll point her in your direction." She untied her apron and draped it over the back of a vacant chair.

"Attagirl." He took her hand. "This morning, you spoke of freedom and choices. I'd say choosing to take a break to dance embodies that sentiment."

Marina laughed. "That's a great argument. I wonder what Mila would think of it."

"I don't really care." He wrapped his arms around her, pulling her close against his body.

She laughed again, nervously this time. "This is not a slow dance."

"I don't really care," he repeated. "I've dreamt of doing this since you promised me a dance this morning."

Her eyes sparkled as she looked up at him. "Me too," she whispered.

As an electric charge of attraction pulsed between them, he wanted to kiss her so badly, but he was acutely aware of the eyes on them. Some were smiling, others seemed curious, and still others looked disapproving.

Was it because he was dancing with a human while everyone else on the dance floor was immortal?

Well, that was their problem, not his or Marina's.

Ignoring the looks, he let the melody envelop them and drew Marina even closer, their bodies touching and electrifying one another. He could sense her heartbeat quicken, her breath hitch, and that delicate aroma of her arousal flare.

She wanted him as much as he wanted her, and unlike Kagra, she didn't find him lacking in any way.

To Marina, he was a god.

MARINA

Originally, Marina had seen Peter as a mere steppingstone, a part of her calculated strategy to escape the mundane life in Safe Haven. He was supposed to be a means to an end, but it seemed like she was falling into her own trap.

Moving across the dance floor, she was acutely aware of every point of contact between their bodies, of the way Peter's arms felt around her, of how solid his chest was, and of the substantial erection pressing against her stomach.

It had been so long since she'd been with a man, and she missed it.

She was nearing her mid-thirties, so the Kra-ell had lost interest in her a long time ago, and out of the limited selection of human partners in the compound she had chosen Nicolai, who was many years younger than her and had Kra-ell blood in him, which hadn't worked in his favor as far as she was concerned, but the fact that he'd been chosen to attend a university had. It was what had attracted her to him the most.

The problem was that the university offered him many more choices than what was available in the compound, and eventually he had lost interest in her as well.

Marina had been heartbroken for a while, and then the liberation had happened, and then she had found herself in Safe Haven with community members who held on to strange beliefs that were closer to the Kra-ell way of life than what the humans in her former compound practiced. They were into free love, which just meant multiple partners and no individual commitment. It wasn't what Marina wanted out of life, so she had stayed away from them.

She couldn't even remember the last time she'd had sex. It had been during one of Nicolai's monthly mandatory visits from college, but she didn't recall which one.

It seemed like a lifetime ago.

Everything had changed so drastically that looking back to life in the compound seemed like ancient history, when in fact only a couple of months had passed since the liberation.

The problem was that hooking up with an immortal might help her get out of Safe Haven, but it wouldn't get her any closer to having a man to call her own.

Marina wanted children, and she wanted to make a home for her family, but the only way to achieve that was in the outside world, and she wouldn't be allowed to do that. She knew too much, and there was no way to make her forget that two alien species were hiding among humans.

Her plan had been to play coy, to weave a slow web around Peter and make him chase her. She had thought to draw this out, to savor the dance of seduction, but as their bodies moved in perfect harmony, with Peter's gaze so intently focused on her face, her strategy began to crumble. The desire she felt was too intense, too urgent to be stifled, sacrificed on the altar of strategic games.

He seemed to see beyond the calculated façade and stir something within her that she had long given up on.

Escaping the intensity of his gaze, she put her cheek on his chest and inhaled his scent. He had applied his cologne sparingly, for which she was grateful, and not just because she didn't like overpowering scents. It allowed her to smell his own unique scent, and it was much better than anything that could be bought in a store.

As the song reached its crescendo, Marina lifted her head and whispered, mindful of all the immortals around them with their super hearing, "I want you, and I know that you want me." She leaned away and forced her voice to remain steady as she looked into his eyes. "The only question remaining is your place or mine?"

In that instant, the world seemed to stand still. The dance floor, the watching crowd, the twinkling lights—all faded into a distant blur. There was only Peter and the way he looked at her, with eyes that promised a world of passion.

"Mine," he finally said. "I have my own bedroom, but I share the cabin with another Guardian. Are you okay with that?"

She nodded. "Can you sneak me in without him knowing?"

He frowned. "Are you embarrassed about being with me?"

"No, but you might be embarrassed about being seen with me." She chuckled nervously. "Slumming with the human."

His hold on her tightened, becoming almost bruising. "Never say that. I don't slum. Any female who invites me to her bed or invites herself to mine honors me."

Peter looked so offended and so sincere that she couldn't bring herself to doubt him. He'd really meant that, and it eased something in her chest, a memory of past humiliations that she had buried deep inside and pretended that they had never existed.

"What about your roommate? Does he think the same way you do?"

Peter must have realized that he was hurting her because his grip on her loosened a fraction. "The only thing that my roommate will feel is jealousy that a beautiful woman is spending the night with me."

Was that true, or was he just saying it to make her feel good?

She felt compelled to challenge his assertion. "What if I want to stay more than one night?"

He smiled. "Then he would be even more jealous, and I would be even happier and more honored."

"Okay, then. But you have to wait for me to be done for tonight, and it's going to be really late. I can't leave before the kitchen is clean."

"I'll wait for you, and when you come, I'll draw you a bath and massage your aching feet."

The groan that escaped her throat sounded more like a lust-filled moan. "If you keep saying such wonderful things to me, I might fall in love with you."

"Is that bad?"

"Of course, it is. You are immortal, and I'm mortal. There is no future for us."

He dipped his head and took her lips in a gentle kiss. "I'm not thinking about forever love. For-now love is good enough for me."

27

MARGO

"Margo." Alberto lifted his wine glass and leaned back with it in his hand. "We've been talking about me and Jasmine the entire evening, but you didn't tell us anything about yourself."

"What do you want to know?"

"Who are you with? I'm sure a beautiful woman like you isn't vacationing alone."

The guy probably told all the women he talked to that they were beautiful, but Margo couldn't help but feel pleased by it. "I'm attending my future sister-in-law's week-long bachelorette party."

He arched a brow. "So why aren't you celebrating with her tonight?"

Margo didn't want to tell him about Lynda and the others being away in the club. She no longer thought he wanted to sell Jasmine to the highest bidder, but there was a lot about the guy that still seemed shady, and she didn't trust him.

"After nearly a week, I needed a little break from Lynda and her girlfriends."

Alberto smiled knowingly. "Did you have a fight with your future sister-in-law?"

His mocking tone annoyed her. In fact, a lot about the guy grated on her, but she couldn't put her finger on what it was. He was unapologetically chauvinistic, so maybe that was it.

"I didn't have a fight with Lynda." There was really no harm in telling him that Lynda was away from the resort at the moment. It wasn't as if she was a factor in his decisions, even if they were shady. "She and her friends went to a club, and I decided to pass. I don't like the club scene, and I've been a good sport about partying with them so far."

"I can understand that." His tone turned compassionate, and his eyes conveyed commiseration. "How much longer is this bachelorette party going to last? You sound like you've had enough of it."

Now she was back to liking him. The guy was very attuned to her, which meant that he was an attentive listener who heard more than just what was said. He got the emotions behind the words, which was pretty rare for men.

Crap, I'm doing that again. I shouldn't generalize.

It was the wine's fault, and the Cadillac margarita before that, and that other drink she'd had before that one. She really needed to cut back on the alcohol, or she would start acting like Lynda and her girlfriends, flirting with waiters and making a fool of herself.

"It's almost over. Tomorrow is the last day."

The smile Alberto gave her looked predatory. "Are you happy to be going home?"

"I'm not happy about going back to work, but I miss sleeping in my own bed."

She didn't want to tell him about the cruise, and she cast a loaded glance at Jasmine, who nodded that she understood her meaning.

Evidently, she wasn't completely drunk and could still think semi-clearly. The ship might still be an option for Jasmine in case their suspicions proved correct after all, and telling Alberto about it would be stupid.

"What about the person sharing your bed?" Alberto asked. "Are you happy to go back to them?"

It was pretty progressive of him not to assume the gender of her bed partner, but then he might have suspected that her interest in Jasmine was sexual in nature.

"I have no partner at the moment." Margo took another sip of the wine.

"That's a shame. A beautiful woman like you shouldn't be alone. Perhaps I could introduce you to some of my friends? Do you have particular preferences I should know about?"

He was definitely fishing for information about her sexual orientation, and for a moment, Margo considered toying with him and answering vaguely, but perhaps it wasn't a good idea to make a possessive, jealous man think that she was interested in his girlfriend.

Smiling sweetly, she lifted the wine glass to her lips, took a dainty sip, and put it back down. "Tall, handsome, well-educated, and open-minded. The rest is negotiable."

"What about rich?" Alberto reached for the second wine bottle on the table and uncorked it.

"I don't care about money."

He refilled her glass and Jasmine's. "Most women want a man who can take care of them and their children. It might not be politically correct to say that, but that's reality. It's instinctual." He refilled his glass as well.

"Well, I want my dream guy to have a good job and make a decent living. I didn't say that I was willing to settle for a pauper. But I don't need a lot of money to be happy. Just enough to pay the bills and have some saved up for emergencies."

Jasmine laughed a little too loudly. She was definitely drunker than Margo. "With how much everything costs these days, you need to be wealthy just to afford rent and pay for groceries, and rich if you want to go out to restaurants and buy nice stuff from time to time."

Margo nodded. "I've been thinking about renting out the second bedroom in my apartment to make ends meet, but I might not need to do that after I start the new job I'm hoping to get." She took another sip of her wine and then put the glass down when she remembered that she needed to cut down.

The wine was so good, though. Tomorrow, she wasn't going to touch alcohol.

"What kind of a job?" Jasmine asked.

Margo frowned. Hadn't she told Jaz about it? She was sure that she had told her about the cruise being a private retreat for the Perfect Match company staff and that she hoped to get a job as a beta tester for their adventures. She even remembered Jasmine gushing over it.

"Didn't I tell you about it?" Her words came up a little slurred.

How much wine did they drink? They'd finished the first bottle and were on their second, and they had been drinking before that.

She was certainly overdoing it, and so was Jasmine.

"I don't remember." Jasmine lifted a hand to her temple. "I'm not feeling so great. I think I need to lie down for a few moments."

"What's the matter, love?" Alberto asked, rising to his feet.

"I'm dizzy," Margo said, even though his question had been directed at Jasmine. "Maybe I should call it a night and go to sleep." She snorted. "I'm sure to wake up with one hell of a hangover tomorrow."

28

KIAN

"I wish immortality made wearing high heels painless, but I guess that's asking for too much." Syssi plopped down on the chair and kicked off her shoes. "You can go talk to Mia now." She lifted her leg, crossed it over her knee, and started massaging her foot.

"I can also stay here and massage your feet." Kian sat down, took her foot, and put it over his thigh. "After all, it's my fault that your feet are hurting."

She frowned. "How is it your fault? I was the one who wanted to keep on dancing."

"If I wasn't as tall, you wouldn't have felt the need to wear high heels."

On the other side of the table, Amanda snorted. "Men. They think that the sun orbits around them. Syssi is not wearing high heels because you are tall. She's wearing them because they make her look good. Why do you think I always wear them even though I'm tall?"

"Because you are vain?"

She rolled her eyes. "Well, duh. I want to look my best at all times."

"You don't need heels for that." Dalhu draped his arm around her shoulders. "But what do I know? I'm just a simple-minded male."

Amanda chuckled. "Oh, stop it. We all have our hobbies, and one of mine is looking fabulous. Anyone have a problem with that?"

"Nope." Kian reached for Syssi's other foot and lifted it onto his lap. "No one dares."

As the whiz of Mia's motorized wheelchair alerted Kian to her approach, he turned to look at her over his shoulder. "Mia. You're just the person I need to talk to."

"Really? I came over to talk to you." She waited for Toven to move one of the chairs away so she could get closer to the table. "I spoke to Margo earlier, and she asked me to ask you for a favor."

Kian arched a brow. "She isn't supposed to know about me."

"She doesn't. We only refer to you as the boss or Tom's mysterious and eccentric partner, who should remain unnamed."

That got a smile out of him. "I like that. So, what's the favor?"

Mia took a deep breath. "Margo met a woman named Jasmine at the hotel, and they started chatting. Margo thinks that Jasmine's boyfriend is about to sell her. He took her passport, her driver's license, and her credit cards, claiming that he needed to keep them safe from thieves and pickpockets. The bottom line is that Jasmine can't escape him without her passport, and she needs to return to Los Angeles. Margo is asking if she can hitch a ride with us."

Kian grimaced. "It sounds fishy to me. Did that woman ask Margo if she can come aboard?"

"I don't think so, but maybe she did. Margo asked me to book an Airbnb for her so she could hide from her boyfriend until the ship arrived. If you don't allow her to come on board, having a place to hide will give her time to contact her family and have them try to help her. She said that people at the hotel had seen the two of them hanging out together, so if she booked the Airbnb under her name, the boyfriend could easily trace it through her. That's why she wanted me to book it under mine."

Syssi put her feet down and leaned over the table to look at Mia. "Did Jasmine ask her boyfriend for her passport, and he refused to give it back?"

"I don't know. I told Margo that she might be overreacting and making a big fuss over nothing, but her answer convinced me to help Jasmine anyway. She said that she might be wrong, and the boyfriend could be just a controlling jerk, but if she was right and did nothing, it would be forever on her conscience that she hadn't helped Jasmine."

"That's a convincing argument," Toven said. "I think we should allow the woman on board. We already have a group of rescued victims. What's one more?"

Kian sighed. "I might have been agreeable to letting Jasmine on the ship, but there are developments you are not aware of, which will make even getting just Margo here difficult."

"What's going on?" Toven asked.

"We interrogated Bud, the Doomers' leader, and it turns out that Kalugal left some memories in Luis's head that they were able to retrieve. One of them was that we were picking up a woman from the Grand Allure Resort in Cabo San Lucas. They don't know Margo's name, but we expect the Doomers to have a large presence at the hotel."

"That's not good," Toven said. "Are we still going to Cabo?"

"Yes, but we are putting on a charade, pretending to be a ship full of humans. That's why I wanted to talk to you. We slowed down so we wouldn't stand out among the other cruise ships that left Acapulco around the same time we did, and we will be arriving at Cabo late in the evening instead of early afternoon. Several groups will go to local clubs and restaurants, pretending to be tourists, and I plan on having the human staff intermingled with them to reinforce the perception. You need to tell Margo about our late arrival and also make up an excuse as to why we need her to take a taxi to the airport. We will collect her from there and find a way to smuggle her aboard, probably in a supply crate."

Mia chewed on her lower lip for a moment, and then she perked up. "I know what we can do. Jasmine can take a taxi to the airport from the Airbnb, and we can collect her from there together with Margo. If we can smuggle one in a supply crate, I don't see why we can't smuggle two."

Except for the law of unintended consequences, which was a major bitch, Kian couldn't find a fault in Mia's plan.

"They can both go to the Airbnb," Amanda said. "And we can pick them up from there. All the Doomers know is that we are picking a woman up from that hotel. They don't know who she is, so no one is going to watch Margo specifically."

The girl had probably told everyone in her group about being picked up by a cruise ship, and if she was the talkative type, she might have told many people about that. The Doomers could find out who she was very easily, which meant that she might be followed to the airport.

"Here is what I want you to tell Margo." Kian leaned back so he could see both Mia and Toven. "Tell her to go to the Airbnb and stay there until you call her. I will have Guardians watching the Airbnb to check that no one is following her and Jasmine to the airport. If they are compromised, we will have to change plans accordingly."

29

PETER

Peter didn't want to take any chances and risk Marina changing her mind. After everyone had left and the dining room was empty of guests, he started collecting plates with the other servers and putting them into the plastic bins.

"What are you doing?" Marina whispered.

"Helping out so you will be done faster."

"Don't," she hissed. "You're embarrassing me."

Now, that was rich coming from her after she'd accused him of being embarrassed about her spending the night with him.

He leaned to whisper back. "Are you afraid your people will find out about us?"

She stopped collecting dishes, took the plate he was holding, dropped it in the bin, and took his hand. "Come with me." She tugged him behind her out of the dining room.

When they were outside, she turned to him. "You are making everyone in there uncomfortable. They don't want their employers to help them clean up. They want the place devoid of immortals so they can joke and laugh and not worry about appearances."

He could understand that. "If you want me to leave, you'll have to give me something."

"What?"

"A kiss. A good one."

A smile spread over her lovely face. "I can do that." She wound her arms around his neck. "Kiss me."

He shook his head. "Nope. I want you to do it and make sure it's a good one, or I'll go back in there and keep on helping."

A giggle escaped Marina's beautiful lips. "That's the worst blackmail I've ever heard, but fine." She lifted on her toes and pressed a soft kiss to his lips.

Cupping her bottom, he lifted her and urged her to wrap her legs around his middle. He then turned around and pressed her against the wall.

"We can do it right here," she whispered against his lips.

That was a scandalous suggestion, but his kink didn't include exhibitionism. "Tempting, but no." He nibbled lightly on her lower lip. "Our first time is going to be the whole nine yards and not a quickie against the wall."

She leaned away to look into his eyes. "Why are you being so nice to me?"

That was an odd question. "Because I care about you."

"Why? We've just met, and you know nothing about me. What if I'm a horrible person?"

"You are not." He gave her bottom a squeeze. "And I know a lot about you. Probably more than any human male you will ever meet will get to know, and that's even if you spend the rest of your life with him."

Marina closed her eyes. "That's true. But it's also true that there is a lot you don't know about me."

He pretended to frown. "Are you really horrible?"

"No. I don't think so."

"Then that's settled." He transferred her weight to one hand to free the other and cupped the back of her neck. "Let me take care of you, Marina." He dipped his head and nuzzled the curve of her throat, then pressed a kiss to her wildly beating pulse. "Don't be afraid of me. My only wish is to give you pleasure."

"I'm not afraid." She lifted her hands and cupped his face. "I'm excited." She kissed him, and as he parted his lips, she swept her tongue into his mouth, and he let her even though his fangs were starting to elongate.

He allowed her to explore his mouth for a few seconds and then took over the kiss. She melted against him, her lips soft and pliable, her tongue dueling gently with his. He then coaxed her to taste him again, enjoying the freedom of letting her explore.

"Marina!" someone called from the door to the dining room. "*Gde ty?*"

The lights in the corridor had been dimmed, and they were standing in an alcove that wasn't visible from the door, so there was no chance that the human looking for Marina could see them.

She looked dazed when she drew back. Her lips swollen from his attention, she groaned quietly. "*Ya budu tam cherez minutu,*" she called out. Resting her forehead on his, she let out a breath. "I have to go."

He kissed her eyelids, planted one last soft kiss on her lips, and then, reluctantly, let her slide down his body. "Take this." He put a keycard in her hand. "I'm in cabin 305. Let yourself in."

She looked at the card and then lifted her eyes to him. "You trust me with this?"

He smiled. "I'm trusting you with my body and soul. The key is meaningless."

She gave him a crooked smile. "What if I'm an assassin, and I'll sneak up on you when you're asleep?"

"I'll risk it." He pulled her against his body and kissed her one last time before letting her go.

"Thank you." Marina lifted on her toes, planted a quick kiss on his cheek, and scurried away.

A stupid smile stretching his face, Peter stood in the shaded nook for a long moment before commanding his feet to move. He excused it by not wanting to compromise Marina, but the kitchen staff probably knew what she was doing and with whom. Maybe that's why that woman had called her back in? To give her a talking-to for fraternizing with the employers?

Would they make her change her mind about coming to his cabin later tonight?

The thought was too upsetting to be just about losing a night of pleasure with an attractive female. He liked being with Marina even though they hadn't spent more than a few minutes together.

What was it about her that made her special?

The answer to that seemed simple. Other than Kagra, she was the only female to share his bed, knowing who he was. He didn't need to pretend to be human, he didn't need to hide his fangs and glowing eyes, and after she passed out from the euphoric rush of his venom, he wouldn't need to thrall her to forget anything. He also didn't need to leave the bed and could wake up next to her and maybe even go for another round.

But it was more than that.

When she'd told him why she'd dyed her hair blue and put a ring in her brow, it had resonated with him. He had been at the mercy of another only once, and it hadn't been for long, but he had never forgotten how it had felt to be helpless.

Maybe he, too, should dye his hair some crazy color. Purple would look good on him. Or maybe bright red?

Regrettably, piercings were out of the question for immortals except for the fake ones that only looked like piercings and were held by a magnet. But those were for kids and posers, and he was neither.

30

MARINA

E xcitement thrumming in her chest, Marina removed her apron and added it to the laundry cart with all the linen collected from the dining room.

Mila eyed her with a knowing look as she dropped her own apron into the cart. "Are you going to indulge that immortal tonight?"

It was nobody's business who she spent the night with, but it irked Marina that Mila thought she was doing so under duress the way it had been in the Kra-ell compound.

"I'm going to indulge myself." She waggled her brows suggestively. "Have you seen the size of his shoulders?"

Not to mention that face, that mischievous look in those dark eyes, and the goatee that made him look devilishly handsome and a little dangerous. Peter was sex on a stick, and he also seemed like a nice guy.

Was he too good to be true?

Yeah, probably.

He was an immortal, and she knew nothing about their sexual practices. The rumor was that they were like human males, only better, but she didn't know what the rumor was based on. So far, none of the humans had admitted to having been with one of them. Well, other than Sofia, but she was part Kra-ell, and she had moved with her boyfriend to the village. Still, she might have been the source of those rumors.

As far as Marina knew, Sofia had never shared a Kra-ell's bed, so even if she was the one who had supplied those flattering rumors about the immortals' sexual prowess, she could only compare her lover to a human man and not the Kra-ell.

Losing her virginity to a Kra-ell had trained Marina to enjoy the sharper edge of sexual pleasure, so even if Peter was more like the Kra-ell males than humans, but not too much so, she would probably like being with him more than she'd enjoyed being with Nicolai.

That would be more than welcome. Having an amazing new lover was the best way to get rid of the specter of the old one.

A throaty laughter shook Mila's ample bosom. "I have to admit that these immortals are much nicer to look at than the Kra-ell." She sighed, and the smile slid off her face. "Be careful, Marina. You might think that you are just having fun tonight, but once the line is crossed, there is no going back. There are many single males on this cruise, and they are a lustful bunch. Others might get the idea that we are free for the taking, and things could get ugly. I don't want us to go back to the way it was with the Kra-ell."

"These immortals are nothing like the Kra-ell. They treat us with respect, and they don't expect us to serve them unless they pay us proper wages for our work."

"I'm talking sexually, Marina."

"They don't expect us to share their beds unless it's our choice, and they are also not as rough."

"And you know that how?"

"I kissed Peter, and he was very gentle with me." Too gentle. She hoped he would loosen up tonight.

Mila pursed her lips. "One kiss is not enough to judge."

"I'll tell you tomorrow how it was." Marina patted Mila's fleshy forearm. "If my experience is good, perhaps you can snag yourself an immortal lover as well."

Mila laughed again. "I'm too old for these immortals to look at with desire in their eyes. Those days are behind me. But even if they are wonderful lovers, don't fool yourself, expecting more than a night or two of pleasure with this Peter or any of the others. If you are smart, you will forget about these immortals and choose a nice boy to marry and have children with."

"I've tried that, but as you know, it didn't work." She gave Mila one last smile. "I'll see you tomorrow at lunch."

Thankfully, she wasn't on the breakfast roster, so she could afford a sleepless night.

It was nearly four in the morning, and Peter had been waiting for over two hours for her, but she didn't intend to head straight to his cabin as he'd suggested.

Her hair and her clothing smelled of cooking and cleaning materials, and even though he had promised her a bath, she didn't want to show up smelling and disheveled for their first time together, or what might be their only time if she disappointed Peter.

Marina really liked him and would have spent the night with him even if she didn't have an ulterior motive, but her plan was to have him like her enough to invite her to live with him.

It was an ambitious plan, and it might not work, but she desperately needed a change, and the village was her only option.

Nicolai was done with his studies and had settled into life at Safe Haven, making her life miserable every time he'd shown up in the staff dining hall with the fiancée that he had brought with him from the university. It wasn't that she still loved him, but he'd hurt her, and seeing him with another woman while she was lonely was like throwing salt in an open wound.

Marina opened the door to her small cabin as quietly as she could, careful not to wake up Alina, who had the morning shift, and tiptoed to the tiny bathroom.

There wasn't time to properly condition her hair and style it, and she knew it would be a frizzy mess the next morning, but she didn't want to make Peter wait any longer than necessary. Gathering it into a tight bun, she secured it with a couple of hairpins and examined her pale face in the mirror.

She was still attractive despite the age showing on her face, but she was a little washed out, and makeup was a necessity even though she was going to bed.

Some lip gloss, a blue liquid eyeliner, and a few strokes with a brown eyebrow pencil took at least five years off her face. A pair of low-cut leggings and a flirty blouse with short puff sleeves that left her midriff exposed made her confident enough to face the immortal, who was physically perfect in every way.

31

PETER

It was after four in the morning when Peter heard the front door to the cabin open.

Jay was already asleep when he entered the cabin earlier, and the door to his bedroom was closed, so he hadn't been able to warn him that he was expecting a visitor.

What if the door opening woke Jay up, and he thought that Marina was an intruder?

What if she couldn't see his open door and opted to go to Jay's bedroom?

The drapes were drawn closed, so not even moonlight could filter through, and the light he had left in his bathroom was enough for him to see clearly, but not for Marina.

Risking scaring her, Peter jumped out of bed and leaped into the living room. "Over here," he whispered.

Her hand flew to her chest. "You scared me," she whispered back. "It's so dark in here. I can't see anything."

As she took a step toward him, he closed the rest of the distance between them and lifted her into his arms. "I see perfectly well in the dark."

Marina smelled freshly showered so he could skip the bath he had promised her. There was always the next time and the time after that. With her, he didn't need to limit himself to just one night, and he didn't plan to.

Her fingers splayed over his bare chest for a brief moment, and she sucked in a breath. "I imagined how you looked without clothes, but the reality of you is so much better."

He never wore clothes to bed, and the only reason he had pants on was because he didn't want to jump her as soon as she came in.

"I'm glad you like what you can't see." He cupped her bottom.

"I see with my hands." She wrapped her legs around his torso and lifted her arms to his neck. "I want you," she whispered.

He could hear her heart racing and her breath hitching, and he hoped it was desire and not fear. Her scent indicated the former, but women often confused the two, which wasn't necessarily a bad thing, and a little fear could enhance their pleasure, but this wasn't a normal situation.

Marina knew that he wasn't human, and she'd had a bad experience with powerful aliens. He didn't want her to think that he was like them or that she would have to do anything she wasn't a hundred percent into.

"I want you, too," he murmured into her hair. "I ache for you. But I want you to know that with one word from you, everything stops. No matter how desperate I am for you, I'm never too far gone to stop. You have nothing to fear from me."

"I don't fear you." She leaned away and frowned. "Your eyes are glowing."

"That's what happens when immortals get excited."

A smile bloomed on her face. "I'm glad that I excite you." She brushed her lips across his and threaded her fingers in his hair.

He took it as a silent invitation, and as his tongue parted her lips, capturing her tongue, she moaned softly against his mouth.

Still kissing her, he carried her to his bedroom and held her up with one hand under her soft bottom so he could gently close the door behind them with the other.

If Jay hadn't woken up while they were in the living room, he didn't want him to be woken by the sound of the door slamming.

"I planned on bathing you and pampering you with a foot massage, but since you've showered already, I'll give you a rain check for the next time." He laid her gently on the bed.

Marina lifted on her forearms and looked at him. "You assume that there will be a next time."

He smirked. "I don't assume. I know." He crawled over her and straddled her legs. "You'll want more of what I will give you tonight."

"So confident," she murmured as he tugged her leggings down. "I need you to promise me something, though."

He paused. "What is it?"

"I want to remember everything precisely as it happened. Promise that you won't thrall me to remember delights that didn't happen."

"You offend me, Marina." He put his hand over his chest. "Do you think I would resort to cheap tricks like that?"

"I don't, but I want to hear you promise that."

"I vow to the Fates that I will not alter your memory of this night or any others that follow. But if the boss decides to erase the memories of this cruise from the minds of all the humans on board, there isn't much I can do about it."

She nodded. "That's good enough for me."

3 2

MARINA

As Peter started to slowly undress Marina, her insecurities flared. Her breasts were too small, her hips were too big, and she had cellulite. But he looked at her with so much hunger in his eyes that the pressure in her chest eased.

"Beautiful," he murmured as he lowered himself on top of her and kissed her.

She wanted to argue and tell him that he shouldn't lie to her, that she knew she was pretty but far from spectacular, but he didn't let go of her mouth, kissing her with so much passion that all she could do was moan and undulate her hips under him.

He still had his pants on, but they were made from thin nylon, and he wasn't wearing underwear, so she could feel the thick, hard bulge of his erection almost as if he was naked, and if she lifted her hips and moved them just right, she could get the friction she needed.

When he finally let her come up for air, she was too dazed to remember that she'd wanted to argue with his appraisal of her, and then he was sliding down her body, and she didn't need a working brain to know what his intentions were.

No one had pleasured her that way in ages, and Marina was surprised that she was allowing a stranger to perform such an intimate act.

"Beautiful," he murmured again as he spread her thighs to make room for his broad shoulders.

Was that the only word he could think of when he was with her? Or was it something he said to all the women he took to his bed?

Jealousy flared in her chest, but as his finger slid into her wet entrance and then another, filling her deliciously, she forgot what made her feel jealous and surrendered to the pleasure.

Moaning, she rocked her hips, chasing his pumping fingers and needing more.

He blew a breath over her moist petals, and then his mouth was on her, his tongue gently brushing against her clitoris. He was shockingly good at this, building up her pleasure gradually instead of trying to rush her. It was as if he was in her head, knowing exactly how to pleasure her. When she neared the peak, he closed his lips around her clit, sucking it in while his fingers kept pumping, but even though she was teetering on the edge, she couldn't tumble over it.

Was she so out of practice that she couldn't orgasm unless it were her own fingers working the magic?

"Peter," she breathed.

He didn't answer, probably because his lips and tongue were busy, but he lifted a hand to her breast and toyed with her nipple, alternating light pinching with gentle tugging.

The extra stimulation was amazing, and yet she couldn't dive over the edge. He was being too gentle, and she didn't know how to tell him what she needed.

"Please," she murmured instead.

"Please, what?" he growled.

"I need to come, and I can't." It was as close as she could come to admitting her need.

He lifted his head and looked at her with understanding in his glowing eyes. "Close your eyes," he ordered. "And don't move an inch."

A new surge of moisture gathered between her thighs as she obeyed his command.

She heard him open a drawer and then some rustling as he rummaged through it.

What was he looking for?

His hand pushed under her head, and a moment later, she felt a piece of cloth wrapping around her head.

A blindfold.

Was he reading her mind? She'd only made him promise not to change her memories of their time together. She hadn't said anything about him staying out of her head.

"Are you reading my thoughts?" she asked.

"I don't need to. You are an open book to me, Marina."

No one had ever told her that, but maybe this immortal saw her better than most.

When he gripped her wrists and pulled her arms over her head, she suspected that Peter hadn't told her the truth about not peeking into her mind.

The blindfold must have triggered memories of the games she'd played with Nicolai, but it must have been subconscious because she hadn't been aware of thinking about him.

The sad truth was that as much as Marina tried to forget about Nicolai, he was never far from her thoughts. He'd hurt her, eroded her confidence, and she'd spent months obsessing about all the things she might have done better to keep him from leaving her.

Pathetic.

Hopefully, Peter wasn't reading those loser thoughts. She would be mortified if he did.

He didn't say a thing, though, and then she felt another piece of fabric wrapping around her wrists. It wasn't tight, and she could get free if she really wanted to, but it was a reminder to keep her hands where he wanted them, just the way she liked it.

"I know you are reading my mind," she said.

"I told you I'm not." He lifted her legs and delivered a stinging slap to her bottom. "Don't ever doubt my word."

Great Mother, he was perfect.

"I won't make that mistake again." She couldn't help the smile that spread over her face as she planned to do it again as soon as another opportunity presented itself.

"You liked that, didn't you?"

"You know I did."

"Then you are going to like this." His mouth descended on her nipple, sucking and lightly pinching.

Too lightly.

Hadn't he figured out already what she liked?

Suddenly she felt something cold and metallic rub against the wet, turgid peak, and knowing what it was, she sucked in a breath.

As the clamp closed over the sensitive flesh, it stung, and she sucked in another breath, waiting for Peter to do the same to her other nipple.

From experience, she knew that both needed to be clamped for the euphoric rush to wash over her.

As Peter sucked and nipped her other nipple, Marina bit down on her lower lip, stifling the whimpering that threatened to derail this incredible experience. If Peter thought that she was in distress, he would stop, and that was the last thing she wanted.

She just needed that other clamp to even out the torment.

When it finally happened, she could no longer hold the whimper in, and she arched her back, silently begging him to continue what he had started.

"Tell me what you need, beautiful," he murmured against her nipple.

"I need to come," she said shamelessly.

At this point, she was beyond shame.

Peter had already discovered all of her dirty little secrets. If he chose to humiliate her with them, it was too late to do anything about it.

His mouth lowered to where she needed it, and as his tongue flicked against her clit, she detonated, screaming out her climax at the top of her lungs.

33

PETER

The lady was a screamer, which Peter normally loved in a woman. There was no higher compliment for a male than his lady enjoying an explosive orgasm, especially since his venom had nothing to do with it.

Still, it was a little problematic when he was sharing a cabin with another guy. He was sure that Jay had heard Marina scream despite the excellent soundproofing, but since he hadn't barged in, he must have figured out that it was passion and not pain or fear that had produced that sound.

What a sheer stroke of luck it was bringing the cuffs and the little clamps on the cruise.

He'd packed his modest sexual toys arsenal on the remote chance that he would find a suitable companion on one of the shore excursions, but until now, the opportunity hadn't presented itself.

It was as if the Fates had sent Marina to him, knowing that he would be just what the female had been looking for. After all, sex toys were not about the one wielding them. They were about the one on the receiving end, and he loved being the fulfiller of sexual fantasies and the deliverer of memorable sexual experiences that he didn't need to erase or change because they had to do with his fangs or venom.

Kagra had been the only female whose mind hadn't been blown by his masterful ministrations, and it had been a blow to his ego. Marina was the most wonderful antidote to that insult, and he was determined to show his gratitude the best way he could.

Lifting his eyes, Peter smiled at the blissed-out expression on her face. The blindfold, the cuffs, the clamps, she loved all of that, but he needed to see her eyes when he entered her, so the blindfold had to go.

When he removed the scarf he had tied around her eyes, Marina blinked up at him, her gaze unfocused as if she didn't recognize him, but it was all good. She was still riding the high of her orgasm.

"Beautiful," he murmured for the third time tonight.

She blinked again, and then a smile lifted the corner of her lips. "Is that all you can say to me?"

"The word beautiful encapsulates many meanings. Kind of like the word fuck, which is what's next on the menu."

She licked her lips. "Yum. My favorite."

"Is it, now?" He got rid of his pants and got between her legs.

"Are you hungry for this?" He slid his shaft over her slicked folds.

With his other hand, he removed the fabric cuffs holding her wrists.

He expected her to reach for the clamps, but as her arms remained over her head, he removed one, immediately closing his lips over the swollen nub to ease the sting of the blood rushing back in. When he repeated the process with the other, she sighed with relief.

He gave her a moment to catch her breath before pushing the tip of his shaft inside of her. Refraining from surging all the way in was a struggle.

She was tight, thankfully not like a virgin, but more like a woman who hadn't been sexually active in a while, and he wanted to go slowly and let her adjust to him.

Pulling out a fraction, he pushed back, and she lifted up, impaling more of her sheath on his length.

"Patience, beautiful," he said against her ear. "I don't want to rush it."

"Please do," she groaned. "I want you."

He growled and slid a little more of his length inside of her, then forced himself to remain still.

"Oh, Mother of All Life." Marina spread her legs wider to accommodate more of him.

As he rocked his hips, she lowered her arms and cupped her sensitive breasts for a moment before lifting her thumbs to stroke her swollen nipples.

Damn, that was so sexy.

Everything about Marina was so sensual, and if he didn't guard his heart, he could easily fall for her.

Kagra's words once again reverberated in his head. *You are a romantic. You are in love with the notion of love.*

Angry at the memory, he snarled and pushed into Marina until he was buried in her to the hilt, then realizing what he had done, he stilled, letting her adjust to his invasion.

When she started undulating under him, urging him to start moving, he obliged her, and soon he was pounding into her with all the pent-up need that he had been struggling to hold back.

"I...I...." She threw her head back and screamed even louder than before, her body shaking from the force of her orgasm.

Spreading her even wider, Peter pounded into her hard and fast. When he was about to explode, he gripped the top of her head and tilted it to the side.

In a moment of clarity, he saw her eyes widen in fear, but she didn't fight him or say anything, so he took it as consent and licked the spot before sinking his fangs into the smooth column of her neck.

She screamed, but he wasn't sure whether it was in pain or pleasure or a mixture of both. But then her sheath tightened around his shaft, and as she climaxed again, he exploded inside of her, coming so hard and so long that once he was depleted, he felt like he had transferred his life force to her.

It took Peter long moments to regain enough energy to pull out of Marina and then a few moments longer to go grab some washcloths to clean her and the mess their combined issue had made.

She was out, soaring on the blissful clouds of euphoria, and it would probably take her several hours to come down from the venom high, but when she did, he would be there, holding her in his arms, and she would remember every last bit of the immense pleasure they had shared.

It occurred to Peter that Marina hadn't mentioned protection, and neither had he. Hopefully she was on the pill, but if not, it wasn't a big deal.

He couldn't get her pregnant anyway.

34

MIA

Mia drove outside the dining hall and parked her wheelchair in a secluded corner to call Margo. When there was no answer, she waited for Margo's voicemail to kick in and left a message: "Hi, Margo. It's Mia. I guess you fell asleep after all. Call me as soon as you can. I have good news for you and also some instructions, so it's important that you call me."

She ended the recording and put her phone back in her purse.

It was late, so it wasn't surprising that Margo was asleep, and yet worry niggled at her.

Margo was a light sleeper, and the ringing should have woken her up. Perhaps she'd had too much to drink and was passed out?

It was possible.

Perhaps she should call Lynda and ask her to check in on Margo. Except, she really didn't want to do that, especially if Lynda was asleep. The woman was cantankerous when she was in a good mood, and if Mia woke her up, she would definitely not be in a good mood.

But someone needed to check on Margo, and she was the only one there.

Pulling out her phone again, Mia searched her contacts for Lynda's number and placed the call.

The phone kept ringing for a long time, and Mia was about to hang up and call again when it was finally answered. Given how loud the music playing in the background was, Lynda wasn't asleep, and Mia was surprised that she'd even heard the ringing.

"Mia?" Lynda yelled in her ear. "Did something happen? Why are you calling me in the middle of the night?" She sounded a little slurred, but she was still coherent, so she wasn't overly drunk.

Perhaps Margo was with her, and that would explain why she hadn't answered her phone.

"Is Margo with you?"

"No, she decided to stay in the hotel and read. Did you try to call her?"

"I did, and she's not answering. It's not like her. Did any of your friends stay in the hotel who can check up on her?"

"No. We are all here, but as soon as we get back, I'll go to her room and see what's going on. She's probably sleeping with the earplugs in or forgot to charge her phone." Lynda snorted. "Maybe the couple next door is making noises. Get it? Get it? Loud, sexy noises that made Margo jealous because she hasn't gotten any in ages." She snorted again.

Yeah, Lynda was definitely drunk. She never would have talked like that sober. Did Rob know that his fiancée was getting plastered in Cabo?

Whatever. It wasn't Mia's problem.

"Call me as soon as you check on her, okay? Don't forget."

"I won't. I promised Rob that I would keep an eye on his sister. Not that the prude needs a keeper. What could happen to her while she's reading next to the pool in the hotel? I would say sunburn, but she puts on a shitload of sunscreen and keeps reapplying it, so she will be going home just as pale as she left. No one is going to believe that she was in Cabo."

Mia rolled her eyes. "When are you heading back to the hotel?"

"I don't know. Maybe in an hour. This place is open until morning. Isn't that great? This is the most fun I've had in ages."

"Call me no matter what time it is, and if I don't hear from you in the next couple of hours, I'm going to call you."

"Fine. Good night, Mia." Lynda ended the call.

Mia tried Margo's number again, but the call went straight to voicemail. When the same happened the third and fourth time she called, a surge of panic constricted Mia's throat.

Something was wrong.

Driving back into the dining room, she didn't go to her table but straight to Kian's.

When Toven saw the direction she was going, he rose to his feet and headed toward Kian's table as well.

He intercepted her just as she reached her destination. "What happened?"

"Margo is not answering her phone." Mia shifted her gaze to Kian. "I called her four times and each time, the call went to voicemail, and it worried me. Margo was awaiting this call, and even if she fell asleep, she is not a heavy sleeper, and she would have heard the ringing. I called Lynda, her brother's fiancée, but she's at a club with the rest of her girlfriends and won't be back at the hotel for at least another hour, maybe longer. I don't know what to do."

"That's no reason to panic," Kian said. "Maybe Margo has gone to the Airbnb, and there is bad reception there?"

"It's only a fifteen-minute walk from the hotel. There is no reason for it to have worse reception than the resort."

"Can you see if she checked into the Airbnb?" Syssi asked.

"I can call the owner tomorrow morning, but I have a bad feeling that it's going to be too late." Mia lifted a shaking hand to her chest. "Margo suspected that Jasmine's boyfriend was a trafficker, and he wanted to sell her. What if Margo got taken along with Jasmine?"

Toven put a hand on her shoulder. "Let's wait for Lynda to return and check on Margo before we jump to conclusions. She might find Margo asleep in her room, and all this speculation was for nothing."

"I wish." Mia sighed. "I should call Lynda again and ask her to cut her outing short. I need to tell her what Margo told me about Jasmine and her scumbag boyfriend. Maybe that will get her worried enough to get back to the hotel."

Mia wasn't sure it would because Lynda was as selfish as they came, but she had promised Rob to watch over his sister, so there was that. At the very least, it was worth a try.

35

KIAN

Less than an hour later, Mia's phone rang.

"Oh, God." She lifted her shaking hand to her lips. "Did you check the pool bar? Maybe she's there?"

Kian tried to listen to what was being said on the other side, but the music was playing, and it was too loud to hear. Still, the expressions on Mia's face were enough for him to guess what she was being told.

Mia put the phone on the table with a shaking hand. "Margo is not in her room, and she's not in any of the resort's public places either. Lynda called hotel security, and they are searching for her." She trained a pair of teary eyes on Kian. "What do we do now?"

Amanda leaned over the table. "Is there a chance she found a guy to hook up with for the night?"

Mia shook her head. "Margo does not do hookups. She barely even dates. Besides, she was on a mission to save her new friend. She wouldn't have abandoned her to be with some guy. There is no way in hell she would do that."

"We need to send a search party," Toven said. "Perhaps Turner knows a private operator that works in the area. Whatever the costs, I'll cover them."

Kian considered his options.

If Margo was right, and her new friend's boyfriend was indeed a trafficker, and she had somehow got caught in the snare, they couldn't just abandon her to her fate. Mia would never forgive him, and the same went for Toven and Frankie.

The bottom line was that he had no choice but to get involved, which was a real pain in the rear, given that Doomers were lurking in the hotel, waiting for Guardians to show up.

Perhaps it hadn't been the boyfriend but Doomers that had taken Margo?

It was possible that she had talked about joining a cruise, and they had found out about it after interrogating some of the staff and guests.

Talk about a shit storm. That would also reveal that they were arriving by ship. Would the Doomers make the connection? There must be other guests in the hotel who were joining friends on a trip.

Right. That was just wishful thinking.

Kian's philosophy was to always prepare for the worst rather than hope for the best.

"I guess I'm not going to sleep tonight." He leveled his gaze at Toven. "And neither are you. We need to have another emergency meeting with Turner and Onegus and devise a strategy. Given that we suspect the hotel is crawling with Doomers, it's not as simple as sending a search party."

Toven nodded. "Of course. Whatever you need from me is yours."

"Do you need me to attend?" Dalhu asked. "I'll be happy to offer my assistance in any way I can."

The guy sounded excited about getting some action again. Evidently, disposing of the Doomers in Acapulco had just whetted his appetite for more.

"You are welcome to join." Kian pushed to his feet and offered Syssi a hand up. "So are you, but you can also stay and enjoy the rest of the festivities."

Syssi never joined the strategic meetings unless she had something to add, either an insight or a vision, but he needed to offer her the option to make it clear that he valued her opinions even though she was not a strategist.

"I'll stay," she said. "I guess you will be commandeering the suite again."

Kian nodded. "I'm sorry."

"You can use ours," Toven offered. "I'm part of the meeting, and Mia won't be able to sleep anyway."

"Thank you. I appreciate it." Kian was grateful for the offer so Syssi and Allegra could sleep undisturbed.

He leaned and kissed Syssi's cheek. "Are you going to be okay here by yourself?"

"Of course." She gave him a bright smile. "I'll go dancing with Amanda." She turned to his sister. "Are you game?"

"Am I ever?" Amanda rose to her feet. "Let's get Sari and Alena to join."

As the two left to get his other sisters, Kian's gaze followed them. He loved that they loved Syssi and thought of her like another sister.

After the ceremony, Okidu and Onidu had taken the little ones to his mother's cabin, and his mother was watching Allegra, Evie, and Darius with their help. That meant that the parents could enjoy the party for as long as they wanted to without having to worry about the kids, but regrettably, the party was over for him.

Oh, well. There was nothing new about that.

With a sigh, he headed toward Onegus's table with Toven and Dalhu at his side.

"What's going on?" The chief rose to his feet.

Kian explained as the four of them continued to Kalugal's table and got him and Lokan to join them. Then the six of them continued to Turner's table.

"Trouble?" he asked.

"Yes." Kian put a hand on his shoulder. "We need your help." He turned to Bridget. "Perhaps you want to join us as well. It's possibly a case of trafficking. Mia and Frankie's friend Margo is missing, and we suspect she was taken by a trafficker."

"Is there anything I can contribute?" the doctor asked.

"I'm not sure. It's up to you if you want to join the meeting."

The doctor shook her head. "I'd rather stay. If you need me for anything, call me. My watch will vibrate." She lifted her hand to show her smartwatch. "Nifty trick. Now I don't have to worry that I will not hear the ringing when it's noisy."

Kian had hoped that would be her answer. He hated disturbing Brundar's celebration and taking more guests out than was necessary. "Good. Enjoy the party. If we have any questions, Turner or I will call you."

Turner leaned over and kissed her cheek before getting up. "I just need to stop by my suite to get my laptop and notepad."

"We are using Mia and Toven's suite for the meeting tonight," Kian said. "You can meet us there after you get your stuff."

"Good deal." Turner buttoned his tux. "I will also gladly change clothes. Especially if we are going to pull an all-nighter."

"That's a good idea." Kian turned to the small group he had assembled. "We should all get changed. Let's meet in Toven's suite in ten minutes."

As the others nodded their agreement, Kian saw Anandur bee-lining for him.

"What's going on, boss?" he asked.

"Mia's friend is missing. I called an emergency meeting to discuss our options."

"I'm coming."

Kian put a hand on his bicep. "No, you are not. You are staying right here and celebrating your brother's wedding. We are not heading out to war, and I don't need a bodyguard on the ship. Stay with your wife and enjoy the party till it ends."

Anandur didn't look happy, but he knew that Kian was right. "You are the boss." He let out a breath. "Call me if you need me."

NEGAL

N egal twirled Gertrude around the dance floor, mimicking the moves of the immortals around him. The weddings were a wonderful opportunity to learn modern human dances and secure partners for the night, just not this time.

It wasn't Gertrude's fault that a pair of fierce eyes kept floating into his mind's eye, regarding him accusatorially when he held her in his arms or when she plastered herself to him during slow dances.

What the hell was wrong with him?

He had briefly glanced at Frankie's friend's picture, and he hadn't even found her all that attractive. She was pretty in a very human way, but not the kind of female poems would be written about. Those eyes, though, had imprinted themselves on his soul, and not because they were remarkably beautiful or uniquely colored. It was the spirit he had seen in them that haunted him, making him feel guilty for holding another woman in his arms.

Was it a psychosomatic response to Frankie's assertion that he was meant to be with her friend?

Had Frankie's conviction that she and her two friends were all destined to mate gods rubbed off on him?

Probably.

The question was what he was going to do about it. He couldn't disappoint Gertrude after promising her a night of passion, and he wouldn't. Somehow, he would power through those annoying fierce eyes and pleasure the immortal like she deserved.

"Something is going on," Gertrude said. "Kian is collecting members of his war council." She pointed with her chin at Turner's table, where Kian, Onegus, Kalugal, Toven, Dalhu, and Kalugal's brother were standing next to the strategist. Toven's mate, Frankie's wheelchair-bound friend, was with them, which made him suspect that it had something to do with the fierce-eyed blond haunting his psyche.

Oh, damn. He knew perfectly well what her name was, so he should stop referring to Margo as Mia or Frankie's friend and pretending that she was nothing to him.

Gertrude's eyes clouded with worry. "Are we being pursued by Doomers?"

"I don't think so. The ship slowed down. It didn't speed up." He watched as the group headed toward the exit. "But perhaps I should find out what's going on. They wouldn't be leaving Brundar's wedding and their mates behind just to smoke cigars. They could have done it right here out on the terrace."

Gertrude nodded. "Mia wouldn't have gone with them if they were going to smoke. She's regrowing her legs, and Bridget told her not to tax her body's healing ability by unnecessarily abusing it. Alcohol and tobacco are unhealthy, and even an immortal's body has to work at counteracting their influence. Please find out what's going on and let me know. My mind is racing with possibilities, and none of them are good."

"Same here. Good things don't necessitate a middle-of-the-night emergency meeting." Negal leaned to kiss Gertrude's cheek. "I'll be back."

He left the dance floor and rushed after the group, catching up to them just as they were entering the elevator. He squeezed inside before the doors closed.

"Hello, gentlemen." He smiled. "Is there an emergency I should be aware of?"

Kian nodded. "Mia's friend is missing. She could have been taken by the Doomers or by an unrelated player."

Negal felt his fangs elongate. "Did she meet someone at the hotel?"

"She met a woman named Jasmine, and the player was the woman's boyfriend. Margo suspected that the guy wanted to traffick Jasmine, and she was trying to help her escape. She might have been caught up in a game she shouldn't have butted her nose into."

Negal didn't know anything about Margo except for the fierceness he had seen in her eyes, but that was enough for him to believe that she would have gotten involved when she suspected that someone was in trouble.

As the door opened on Kian's deck, he followed the regent out. "Do you mind if I join the meeting?"

Kian frowned. "I don't mind, but why would you want to? You should get back to the party and enjoy yourself."

"I feel responsible for Margo." Negal blurted the first thing that came to his mind. "If she needs rescuing, I should be part of the rescue team."

Kian's frown deepened. "You don't even know her."

"I'm aware of that, but Frankie and Mia believe that their friend is destined to mate a god, and I'm the last one available. If they are right, Margo might be my fated mate."

Thankfully, Mia and Toven had already gone to their suite, so Mia wasn't there to dispute his claim.

It was Frankie's idea, not Mia's, to introduce him to Margo, and Negal was quite certain that Margo wasn't his fated mate, but he needed to rescue her, nonetheless. He had to meet her face to face and stop those eyes from haunting him. There was no way the effect could be as profound in person.

Kian regarded him for a long moment before nodding. "We might need your particular talents for this mission. We are meeting in Toven's suite in a few minutes. I'm going to change out of the tux, and I suggest you do the same. It's going to be a long night, and none of us is going to get any sleep any time soon."

"Thank you. I'll be there." Negal darted back toward the elevators.

Should he go down and tell Gertrude that their plans for tonight were not going to happen? Could he just send her a text?

It was bad form to send a text to cancel their plans for tonight, but he was in a rush, and this was a real emergency.

Gertrude would understand.

As the elevator doors opened, he got inside, pressed the button for his level, and pulled out his phone to text the nurse.

KIAN

"Whiskey?" Toven asked.

"Definitely." Kian pulled out a chair at the round dining table in Toven and Mia's cabin.

The cabins were equipped with only five dining chairs, so Dalhu brought the missing ones from his and Amanda's cabin. There wasn't enough room around the dining table for the eight of them, but there wasn't much they could do about that.

Mia had chosen to stay by the couch to give them room, but she wasn't going to last long, even though she was worried about her friend. Her eyes were closing, and from time to time, her head was lolling forward.

"You should go to sleep, love." Toven walked over to her and crouched next to her. "Your body is working hard on re-growing your legs, and you know what happens when you deprive it of rest. The growth slows down."

She shook her head. "I need to stay awake. There isn't much I can contribute to the battle plans, but I know Margo. She is resourceful and brave, and if she can find a way to communicate where she is, she will. That's why it's important for me to stay by the phone. And if I fall asleep, you need to answer it for me right away."

Toven nodded. "I'll bring a pillow and a blanket from the bedroom so you can lie down on the couch. Will that work for you?"

"Yes. Thank you."

Casting a sidelong glance at Negal, Kian noted that the god looked pleased by Mia's praise of Margo.

Could he really be feeling a connection to the girl even though he had never met her?

Doubtful.

He'd seen Negal dancing with Gertrude, and the two seemed very cozy. He had no doubt that the god would be later invited to the nurse's bed.

"So, what's the deal?" Onegus asked.

"Let's wait for Toven to be done." Kian took a sip from the whiskey. "I don't want to have to say everything twice."

Once Mia was comfortable on the couch and Toven had sat down next to the table, Kian told everyone what Mia had told him and then glanced at her. "Am I missing anything?"

"No. You've got it all right. I just got a text from Lynda that the hotel security didn't do much to find Margo. Her suitcase and her satchel are still in her hotel room, and Lynda says that they are both packed like Margo was ready to leave, but her purse and her phone are not there. The hotel security people assume she's either partying in one of the clubs or shacking up with a guy, and they are not concerned. They told Lynda to inform the police after Margo had been missing for more than twenty-four hours. Lynda and her friends have early flights tomorrow, and she doesn't know what to do."

"Tell her to go home," Kian said. "There isn't much she can do. She's just going to be in the way, but don't tell her that. I don't want her to know that we are coming. I suspect that the Doomers might have found out who Margo is. She probably talked about joining a cruise ship, and even if she didn't, Lynda or her friends might have talked about it and been overheard."

Mia frowned. "So, you don't think it's the boyfriend?"

"It might be him, but it could also be the Doomers, and in my opinion, they are the more likely suspects. With all due respect to Margo's theory about the boyfriend, it's a little far-fetched."

"I don't think so," Mia insisted. "He took Jasmine's passport, her driver's license, and her credit cards. Why would he do that if he didn't want to do something nefarious to her?"

"Why did she allow it?" Dalhu asked. "She should have refused and called hotel security."

Mia cast him a sad smile. "It's not that simple for women who think that they are in a loving relationship. Her boyfriend gave her a logical excuse, and at that moment, she didn't think it through. Later, she might have thought he was overbearing and that maybe she shouldn't be with him, but she didn't feel an urgency to act immediately until Margo planted in her head the idea of him wanting to trade her."

"Mia is right." Kian let out a breath. "Ella had a similar experience. She met a guy who seemed like a loving boyfriend. He invested a lot of time in her, and she agreed to go with him to visit his family in New York, thinking she was just going for a weekend. She had no idea that she was walking into a trap. Still, that was a very unique situation. The oligarch who ordered her delivery saw her picture in an advertisement and got obsessed with her because she was the spitting image of the love of his life, who had died when he was still a young man. I doubt Jasmine's story is the same."

Toven leaned back in his chair and crossed his arms over his chest. "You know the saying about great minds thinking alike? It's true whether those great minds are good or evil. Perhaps someone ordered Jasmine's abduction."

"That's possible," Kian agreed. "But then why would they also take Margo?"

"So she wouldn't spill?" Kalugal offered. "Margo was a witness. I assume that she's a good-looking young lady, so the perpetrator might have thought to kill two birds with one stone. He eliminated the only witness to Jasmine's abduction and made more money by selling another woman. Win-win for him."

"I still think it's the Doomers," Kian said. "We know that they are in the hotel and that they know we are picking up a woman from there. It's logical to assume that they asked around and heard that there was a woman who talked about getting picked up by a cruise ship." He grimaced. "That means that they know we are arriving by ship, and figuring out which of the ships that left Acapulco earlier today is ours won't be too difficult."

"I don't think the Doomers took her," Dalhu said. "Margo is useless to them as a hostage because they don't know how to contact us. If they could, they would have already done so and stated their demands. The best thing for them to do is to leave her be, watch who she interacts with, wait until she either leaves or gets collected by someone, and then let her lead them to us. My bet is on the boyfriend, although following that logic, the

Doomers should have intervened and freed her, so that's a hole in my theory."

"There is another possibility," Kian said. "The Doomers could have decided to do what their brethren in Acapulco did with Luis. Perhaps they wanted to set a trap for us and lure as many of us as possible into coming to search for Margo, expecting us to show up with a big search and rescue team."

38

NEGAL

"Does it matter who took Margo?" Negal asked. "In either case, none of your people can show up at the hotel. You will be immediately recognized by the Doomers. My teammates and I are best suited for this mission. We can enter the hotel shrouded in invisibility and search for Margo, going room to room."

What Negal was concerned about was what was being done to Margo in the meantime. If any of those maggots touched her inappropriately, he would tear the skin off their bodies one inch at a time.

Kian smiled indulgently. "No, you can't. Shrouding doesn't work on surveillance cameras, and I'm sure the first thing the Doomers did was to either take over the control room or hack into it. They will see you even if you shroud yourselves. That being said, you do have one advantage over us. You don't activate the built-in immortal alarm for some reason. You could go in disguise, and they won't know that you are not human."

That was true to some extent. He remembered meeting Magnus and the other immortals for the first time. He'd sensed that they weren't human, but they hadn't known what to think of him and Aru. Later, he had learned that their so-called built-in alarm hadn't been activated by the presence of gods. It only worked with other immortals.

Still, wearing a disguise seemed like such a primitive method. "Can't you do something about the surveillance? Your hacker can access it remotely and put it on a loop. By the time the Doomers figure out that they are watching the same thing over and over again, we will be done."

"That might be doable." Kian put his whiskey glass down. "But a disguise will be much easier to do and with less possible fuckups. You can shroud for only a limited time, and you will need to open doors to search rooms, which will not go unnoticed. I don't have a problem with the ghost stories that will start, but I'm sure the Doomers will figure out what's going on. On the other hand, if you disguise yourself as hotel personnel, let's say plumbers, no one will give you a second glance."

Toven chuckled. "Three extremely good-looking guys with plungers will not go unnoticed. I'm sure they will garner a lot of attention."

"Eva will have to work her magic on them," Kian said. "She can cover their faces with fake beards and pock-marks and whatnot."

"Guys," Mia said from the couch. "You are missing the most important part. If Jasmine's boyfriend took Margo, by the time we get there and Negal and his friends go to investigate, the scumbag could have gotten her and Jasmine very far away from the hotel, and there will be no clues left as to where he took them. Besides, you will need to question the staff and the guests if they saw anything, and how are you going to do that with the Doomers watching the hotel?"

"Good point." Kian sighed. "We need a diversion to draw them away."

Negal lifted a hand. "First, we need to determine that they don't have Margo. Otherwise, creating a diversion will be pointless."

"True." Kian drummed his fingers on the table. "So, you and Aru go in and search the rooms for Margo, pretending to be plumbers or service guys. I doubt Dagor will agree to leave Frankie's side while she's transition-ing, so he's not going to come. Once we are sure that Margo is not in the hotel and that the Doomers don't have her, we create a diversion to draw them away. The question is, what kind of diversion?" He looked at Turner. "If you have any ideas, please feel free to share."

"A group of Guardians can enter the hotel and openly start asking questions. The Doomers will not attack with so many human witnesses. They will wait until the Guardians leave and try to ambush them somewhere less public. Except, we will turn the tables on them and ambush them instead."

"Won't they be expecting that?" Kalugal asked. "They know that we know that they are there, or at least they suspect that we know."

"Rank and file Doomers are not that sophisticated," Lokan said. "They will assume that we are the stupid ones who didn't figure out that they are waiting for us. If we wave the proverbial red flag in front of their eyes, they will attack. My concern is the Doomers watching the harbor. I think we should still go ahead with the plan of pretending to be a regular cruise with humans on board and have several groups leave the ship in disguise. Cabo is a tender port, which means that we go ashore using water taxis that can take only a few passengers at a time. That works in our favor. It would have been much more difficult to pull it off in a regular port where everyone disembarks the gangway right onto the dock."

Onegus nodded. "The Guardians who go to the hotel will need to disembark before we get to Cabo by using the lifeboats like we did in Acapulco, and Turner will have to arrange for vehicles once again. When they arrive with cars to the hotel, the Doomers will assume that they drove from Acapulco, which would have taken just as long by land as it will take us by sea, even with the big loop around the Sea of Cortez. Cars can travel much faster than ships."

"I like this plan." Kian reached for the whiskey bottle and refilled his glass. "The force will split into three groups, each arriving separately. First, Negal and Aru will arrive in disguise and search the hotel. If they determine that Margo is not there, a large group of Guardians will continue to the hotel to create the diversion, while the third group will wait on the town's outskirts." He looked at Turner. "What do you think?"

39

KIAN

Turner tapped his pen on his yellow pad. "I think that we are tired and not considering all the possible angles."

The guy was probably referring to everyone other than himself and was just being polite. Turner hadn't said much during the meeting, and he had probably devised a dozen different strategies by now.

Kian wracked his brain, trying to figure out what he and the others might have missed, but he was coming up empty.

"Do you want to guide us through your thought process?" he asked Turner.

"Of course. I'm not saying that I have the answers, only that we weren't methodical in our approach."

Right. The guy was trying to spare their feelings so they wouldn't look dumb when he revealed those different angles they had failed to consider.

Toven pushed to his feet. "I'll brew us coffee. We definitely need the boost."

Turner flipped to a new page on his yellow pad. "Let's analyze the situation methodically." He lifted his eyes to Kian. "To figure out who took Margo, we can have Roni hack into the hotel's surveillance servers and go over the recordings from where Mia last talked with Margo and until she called her and didn't get an answer. The second thing we need to do is trace Margo's phone. The perpetrators probably dumped it somewhere, but even that can give us a clue as to where she was taken to."

What Turner had said sounded so obvious and logical that Kian couldn't understand how he hadn't thought of it. Was he really that tired? Or maybe it was the whiskey?

He pushed the glass away. "We should get Roni in here."

Turner smiled. "I've already sent him a text message. He's on his way. He's just stopping by his cabin to change and grab his laptop."

Kian hadn't noticed Turner texting either, so he really must be tired. "Okay, what else?"

"We need to watch the footage and see if we can identify Doomers. They are pretty easy to spot, so if they are there, ambling around the resort and asking questions, we will know."

"That's true," Onegus said. "They look military but with the added fluidity of movement that only immortals and professional dancers have, and Doomers definitely don't look like dancers."

Lokan chuckled. "If you want to enrage a Doomer, tell him that he looks like a dancer."

Dalhu winced. "Or a painter, a poet, a musician, or any other artistic form of expression. Most of the cultures in that region of the world are incredibly homophobic, and Doomers are among the worst. They think that being artistic is feminine, and if any member of the Brotherhood is even suspected of homosexuality, they are executed, so no one dares to express their creativity even if they possess any." He sighed and ran his fingers through his hair. "I'm ashamed to admit that I was close-minded and ignorant in that regard as well."

"That's illuminating but irrelevant," Turner said. "Let's get back to analyzing what we are likely to face in Cabo. We dealt the Doomers a big blow in Acapulco. We eliminated an entire team of immortals and a large number of cartel thugs. By now, their superiors in the Brotherhood know that, and they also know we are coming to Cabo. They will have a much larger force waiting for us there." He looked at Lokan. "Am I right?"

Lokan nodded. "If they had several teams in the area, they will have called all of them to Cabo. They probably also recruited the help of the local cartel and all the officials they could bribe and extort, including the police, the military, the harbor control, etc."

"Great." Kian groaned. "I really don't want to engage with all that. I hope that Roni can find out what happened to Margo."

Turner regarded him with a sad smile. "We have to deal with them whether we want to or not. They will figure out which ship we are on sooner or later, even if we deploy the disguised teams. Look at it this way—they have no reason to believe that all the ship's passengers are immortal clan members. They are more likely to assume that several immortals are vacationing among humans. So, seeing humans disembark at Cabo and do touristy things will not remove suspicion from the *Silver Swan*."

Turner was right. The Doomers would question people at the hotel or just thrall them to check their recent memories, and someone would remember talking to Margo, who had mentioned joining a cruise that got delayed several times. From there, it would be easy to find out which ship fit that profile, and it was game over. The Guardians might be able to eliminate the local forces that had arrived there, but then more would be waiting for them in Long Beach.

This called for a drastic change of plans, but he wasn't sure what he should do. Turn back to Acapulco? The Doomers wouldn't be expecting that. He could get everyone off the ship there and fly them to Los Angeles.

The *Silver Swan* would have to stop emitting signals, so it couldn't be easily tracked.

As the doorbell rang, Toven walked over and opened the door.

"So, what are we dealing with now?" Roni walked over to the crowded table and put his laptop down.

"I'll get you a chair," Toven offered.

Roni looked around with a sour expression on his face. "This looks like a command post in a playground sandbox. We need another table. Whose cabin is the closest?"

40

MARGO

Margo's head pounded, and she felt nauseous. She turned on her back and tried to open her eyes, but her eyelids felt as if they weighed five pounds each and refused to open.

Was she in her room?

Was it her head that was swaying, or was it the bed?

Wait, two men were talking in hushed voices on the other side of the room, but she couldn't understand what they were saying. Were they inside her room, or was she hearing voices from the outside?

She must have left the windows open.

Wait, she didn't have windows that opened in her hotel room, just balcony doors, and she never left them open so bugs wouldn't get in.

Trying to focus, Margo listened to the voices until she could discern the words. They were talking in Spanish, which she could understand to some extent, but she was far from fluent.

One of the voices belonged to Alberto or someone who sounded like him. The other one sounded much older and more authoritative, and the two were arguing.

"What did you want me to do with her, *señor*? I had to bring her. She's beautiful in her own way. She is no Jasmine, but then, not everyone is as discriminating as you are, *señor*. I'm sure many men will find her alluring."

Was she dreaming? If she was, this was a nightmare, and everything she had suspected about Alberto was true.

"The hair color is fake. Anyone can be a blond," the older voice said.

"It's not fake. It's real, which is rare and in high demand."

"How do you know that it's real?"

Margo wanted to know that, too. Had Alberto checked her pubic hair?

"It's obvious. She has no dark roots, and the shade is not one that can be achieved with artificial coloring. Just look at it. It looks like spun gold."

"She's too old," the one Alberto called *señor* said. "But she is passable. I can gift her to Carlos. He likes blonds."

Someone exhaled a relieved breath, and she heard a door open and close, but she was still afraid to open her eyes. Heck, she was afraid to breathe.

Listening intently, Margo heard breathing that didn't belong to her and wondered whether Alberto was still in the room. It wouldn't be *señor* because he had sounded impatient and pissed.

Long moments passed as she listened to every sound and registered every sensation. She was swaying, but she wasn't sure whether it was her bed or her head. Was she on a water mattress? It kept moving.

Finally, after what seemed forever, she cracked her eyelids open just a little and peered at the ceiling. When no one said anything and no one moved, she dared to turn her head slightly and look at the room.

The first thing Margo noticed was that there was another woman sleeping on a bed only a few feet away. She was lying on her side with her back facing Margo, but given the black hair spilling from behind her and the hourglass outline of her body, that was Jasmine.

Above her was an oddly shaped window, and Margo tried to figure out what it reminded her of, but her mind was fuzzy. It was dark outside, so it was still night, and she could see the stars and the moon, but they were also swaying.

It finally dawned on her where she was.

The stars and the moon weren't moving, but she was because she was on a boat, and the swaying she'd felt meant that it was moving.

Great. How the hell was she going to escape from a boat in the open sea? Did yachts have lifeboats that she could steal?

Groaning, she forced herself to sit up, then lowered her feet to the floor. She was still wearing the same clothes she had on yesterday, but someone had removed her shoes.

Thank goodness for small mercies. No one had removed her clothing, so she hadn't been violated while she was asleep.

Not asleep.

She'd been drugged.

That's why her head felt so heavy and why her eyelids were not fully cooperating with her brain's demands.

Trying to stand up was a no-go, and she resorted to dropping down to her knees and walking on all fours toward Jasmine's bed.

There couldn't have been more than six feet separating the beds, but she was so badly uncoordinated that it took her several tries until she made it across.

"Jasmine," she whispered while shaking her friend's shoulder. "Wake up, Jaz. We are in big trouble."

She got a groan in response, but that was it. Jasmine must have been even more out of it than she was, and there was no waking her up.

Margo was on her own.

Sitting on the floor by Jasmine's bed, she tried to reconstruct the events that had landed her in this crappy situation.

The second bottle of wine must have been laced with something. Was it the infamous date-rape drug?

Jaz had drunk more than she had, so maybe that's why she seemed more out of it. Margo remembered Alberto filling up his glass from the bottle and lifting it to his lips, but he must have only pretended to drink.

What the hell was she going to do?

Taking another look around the room, or rather cabin, she saw her purse on top of the dresser and almost cried with relief. Her phone was in there. If they weren't too far away from shore, maybe she could call for help.

Crawling to the dresser, she used the handles to hoist herself up and reached for the purse. She pulled it down, catching it before it could hit the floor, and cradled it to her chest as she caught her breath.

The little movement she'd made had exhausted her, and she was so nauseous that she almost threw up. Maybe it was the drugs that were still affecting her like that, or maybe it was the fear she was trying to shove into a corner of her mind so she could think instead of panic.

After resting for a moment, Margo opened her purse and reached inside. Her heart sank. The phone wasn't there.

Of course, it wasn't. That was the first thing they would have gotten rid of, probably tossing it overboard or even before that into a garbage bin.

With a sigh, she closed her eyes and leaned her head against the dresser. How the hell had Alberto managed to carry two unconscious women out of the hotel?

Someone must have helped him.

Margo imagined being stuffed into a laundry cart like she'd seen in the movies, one cart for her and another for Jasmine. A van had probably waited for them next to the service exit, and Alberto and his accomplice had loaded them inside.

Or perhaps it happened some other way. Maybe she and Jasmine had walked out on their own two feet, the drugs making them pliant and obedient like two automatons. She'd seen that in movies, too.

Tomorrow, Mia and Frankie would arrive on the Perfect Match cruise ship, and when they couldn't find her, they would call the police. But what good would that do?

She'd heard about the local police and how corrupt they were. But perhaps it would work to her advantage. Tom could bribe someone to actually make an effort to find her.

Mia would beg him to do that, and Tom didn't refuse Mia anything, so maybe there was hope she would be rescued before Carlos, the guy that *señor* wanted to gift her to, could put his hands on her.

41

NEGAL

Now that they had two tables pushed together, there was plenty of room for everyone, and Roni got to work while the rest of them drank coffee and tried to stay awake.

As Negal peeked at what the kid was doing, he saw that Roni was watching footage from several cameras at once and at ten times the speed. It was difficult for Negal to follow, and given that his senses were superior to the immortals', it was very impressive that the kid was able to take all of that in.

"I'm going to move Mia to the bedroom," Toven said quietly as he walked over to the couch.

She had fallen asleep and didn't wake up when Toven lifted her into his arms and carried her to the bedroom.

Negal was glad that she managed to fall asleep before Turner gave them his assessment. According to him, the situation was much worse than what the rest of them had considered, and he wasn't wrong.

They were all hoping that Roni would find a clue as to Margo's whereabouts, but that would only solve half of the problem. Even if they could retrieve her without engaging the Doomers, the entire ship was at risk, and Kian was thinking about aborting the rest of the cruise and flying everyone home, but not directly to Los Angeles.

He and Turner were discussing sending people to different airports around the country and having them fly to Los Angeles from there.

The question was what to do with the rescued women who had no passports.

"The remaining couples that were supposed to be married on the cruise will be disappointed," Onegus said. "I wish there was a way we could continue as planned, but even taking out all the Doomers in Cabo won't help. That will only make the Brotherhood more rabid about retaliation."

Kalugal smoothed his hand over his short beard. "There must be some way to turn this around, but my brain is too sluggish this late at night to come up with anything."

"I've got something," Roni said when Toven returned to the living room. "I'll slow it for you." He turned the screen around so most of them could see it. "Here is Margo leaving her room last evening."

The camera was in the corridor, and Negal saw one of the doors open, and a woman walk out. She wore a sleeveless dress that was somewhat shapeless and looked like nothing special at first glance, but then she lifted her head and looked straight at the surveillance camera, and Negal's heart lurched into his throat. There was that fierce look that had been haunting him, and it seemed like she was looking at him and challenging him to come to her aid.

"I ran the footage until two other women rushed in. I assume that was her sister-in-law and one of her friends. That means that Margo never returned to her room. She told Mia that Jasmine and her boyfriend were staying in the presidential suite, so I watched that feed next. Margo and Jasmine entered the suite a little over an hour after Margo had left her room, and a few minutes later, the boyfriend walked in." Roni rewound the feed and slowed it down so they could see the boyfriend walking out of the elevator, pulling out his card key, and entering the suite.

"He's a good-looking guy," Onegus said. "But he's not immortal. He's not military, either. He looks too soft."

Negal memorized the maggot's face. If he harmed Margo, he was going to pay.

Roni sped up the recording. "Room service arrived about forty minutes after the boyfriend, and given how packed the cart is, they ordered dinner. There is also a bucket with two bottles of wine."

The waiter entered the suite, and several minutes later, he left. Roni sped up the recording again. "Now things start to get interesting." He slowed the feed again. "About two hours later, the same waiter arrives with a laundry cart, and behind him, another guy is pushing a second one. It's a two-bedroom suite, so two laundry carts wouldn't have been too out of place if it was daytime, but in the middle of the night, I'd say that's suspicious as hell."

"One for each woman," Dalhu said, sounding slurred, not because he was tired or drunk but because his fangs had elongated. "That's how he got them out."

"Correct." Roni sped up the recording until the suite doors opened again, and the two men exited with the carts.

"Where is the boyfriend?" Toven asked.

"Let's see." Roni sped the feed up, but not as fast as he had done before. "Here he comes." The guy left the suite, rolling two suitcases. "That's why he stayed behind. He needed to pack." Roni smirked. "Now we will follow him from camera to camera and find out the vehicle he used. My bet is that the so-called waiters have already loaded the content of the two carts into his car."

42

KIAN

R oni followed the boyfriend through the different surveillance cameras all the way to the service entrance of the hotel, where a Ford Explorer waited for him.

He loaded the suitcases into the back, but given the camera's angle, it was impossible to tell whether the women were inside. They might have been laid out on the back seats, or they might not have been there.

"Let's hope that he's delivering them in person," Turner said.

"Let me check." Roni started clicking with his mouse, flipping from one recording to the next. "Got them," he said triumphantly.

An earlier recording showed the two guys with the laundry carts next to the same SUV. They had been smart about unloading their cargo without leaving recorded evidence, though. Aware of the location of the surveillance camera, they had gone to the other side of the vehicle, which wasn't in the camera's view, and a few moments later, they walked away with their carts.

"They definitely loaded the women into the car," Onegus said. "The vehicle dipped slightly from the added weight."

"I noticed that," Kian confirmed. "Now the question is how we will find out where he took them?"

"Street cameras," Roni said. "I need a little time to hack into the city's network."

While their super hacker got busy, Kian pushed to his feet and walked over to the kitchenette. "Anyone want more coffee?"

A chorus of voices answered in the affirmative.

Dawn was already on the horizon, and the light filtering through the glass doors bathed the cabin in soft hues. It was such a surrealistically tranquil moment, given the storm of their reality, that it gave Kian pause.

Doomers, traffickers, two missing women, and a ship full of his clan that he would probably need to evacuate.

"All in a day's work," he murmured under his breath as he waited for the fresh pot of coffee to brew.

When it was ready, he brought it to the two combined tables and refilled everyone's mugs. "Did you get anything?" He leaned over Roni's shoulder.

"Not yet. I'm working as fast as I can, but it's a lot to go through."

The kid was whizzing through the footage, switching from one camera to the next with dizzying speed, but it seemed that it would take him some time to find the Explorer.

"Got him." Roni zoomed in on a license plate. "He's entering the harbor and heading to the yacht club." Roni kept clicking around for several minutes before lifting his head from the laptop. "I need to hack into the harbor surveillance server, and that will take a while. They have better security than the hotel and the street cameras."

"Take your time." Turner clapped Roni on the back before getting up. "I need to stretch my legs. I'm going to the balcony to watch the sunrise."

"That's a great idea." Toven followed him out.

It was also a great opportunity to light up a cigarillo. Kian patted his pockets and pulled out the small tin box.

Out on the balcony, Kian leaned over the railing, lit his cigarillo, and looked at the horizon where the golden orb cast a pathway of shimmering light across the water's surface. The water rippled gently, disturbed only by the ship's passage.

As his companions talked in hushed voices, Kian turned his face toward the sun, enjoying the warmth, the gentle breeze, and the smell of salt in the air.

Nearly an hour later, the door behind him opened, and Roni poked his head out. "I've got it, guys. You can come back inside."

Kian flicked his cigarillo into the water and followed Roni. "What did you find out?"

"Do you want the good news first or the bad?"

"Makes no difference to me." Kian sat down and took a sip from his coffee, which had cooled down in the time he was outside enjoying the sunrise.

"So, I know where they were taken, but the guy was smart and avoided the cameras. I don't know how they loaded them onto the yacht, but I saw him boarding it with his luggage, so I assume they were either brought there before or after, but it's not on camera."

Kian groaned. "All we have is circumstantial evidence. We have no solid proof that Margo and Jasmine were taken from the hotel, loaded into the SUV, and then transferred onto the yacht."

"We don't need proof," Onegus said. "It's enough that we suspect they are there. Even if we are wrong about them being on the yacht, we need to get the boyfriend and interrogate him about Margo and Jasmine and what he did with them, so in either case, we are storming that boat."

"I think we can be sure they're on the yacht," Roni said. "I checked in with Frankie and got Margo's phone number. I was able to track the phone to the harbor, but that was as far as it went. He probably dumped both of the phones there."

Turner nodded. "He probably took their purses with him and either brought them to the yacht or dumped them as well."

"As far as storming the boat is concerned, there is one problem," Roni said. "It sailed a little over three hours ago, and it's heading south at a very leisurely pace. It's not in a rush to go anywhere. The good news is that it has a helipad, so if we can get a chopper, we can land it on the boat."

"I can get us one," Turner said.

Leaning back in his chair, Roni crossed his arms over his chest. "We might not need to avail ourselves of your services because I think I know where we can find the helicopter that goes with that boat. The question is whether it will still be there when we get our forces to the mansion of the cartel boss who owns that yacht and the chopper."

43

NEGAL

Turner was quiet for a moment. "Where is the cartel boss's mansion located?" he asked.

"He has many properties." The hacker didn't lift his head from his laptop. "The one I'm talking about is about thirty miles south of Puerto Vallarta, and it has a private bay with a dock for his enormous yacht, so that's where he's taking her."

"Then we are in luck," Kian said. "We are less than an hour away from there." He pulled out his phone. "I'd better tell the captain about our change of plans. We need to stop the ship."

"Don't." Turner lifted his hand. "You can tell him to slow down, but don't tell him to stop. We need to keep up appearances, remember?"

"Right." Kian put his phone down. "So, what do we do? Do we send Guardians in lifeboats to take over the cartel boss's compound and wait for the yacht to arrive? Or do we keep going and intercept it?"

"Give me a moment to think." Turner tapped his pen on his yellow pad. "We know where the yacht is and at what speed it's going." He turned to Roni. "Can you calculate how long it will take it to reach Puerto Vallarta?"

The hacker didn't seem to need time to calculate, answering right away. "About twelve hours if it continues at its current speed."

"We can't wait that long," Negal said. "Fates only know what those thugs are doing to Margo while we wait."

Kian shook his head. "If we want to intercept the yacht instead of going to Puerto Vallarta, we can do that in about six hours at the current speed or faster if we increase it."

Turner leaned back in his chair. "And then what? The yacht is probably crawling with cartel thugs, and it might even have Doomers on board. Not that I think it's very likely that the Doomers are involved in the kidnapping given what we saw, but we need to be prepared for the possibility that they are."

Kalugal raised his hand. "Compeller here. With a megaphone in hand, I can take care of anyone on that yacht."

"True," Turner admitted, "but then we will have the cartel chasing after us in addition to the Doomers."

"What do you suggest we do?" Kian asked.

Negal was losing his patience. Turner obviously had come up with a plan and was dragging it out instead of just spitting it out, so everyone would appreciate how smart he was, and in the meantime, Margo was suffering.

"We kill several birds with one stone," Turner said.

When the strategist was done explaining his plan, Kian nodded. "We need Andrew to access information about the cartel boss. I'm sure the US government has collected information about him, and Andrew can access it." He looked at Roni. "What's his name?"

"Julio Modana. His brother Carlos is his second in command," the hacker said. "They manage to put up a legitimate front, but everyone knows what they are really about."

Negal wondered whether Roni had found all of that just now or was that cartel boss so well known that he'd heard about him before. If Modana was such a big name, would Turner's simple plan work against what could be a large force?

As Kian pulled out his phone, Negal thought of ways to poke holes in the strategy, but when he couldn't, he had to grudgingly admit that Turner was indeed as brilliant as everyone said he was.

"Hi, Andrew," Kian said as his call was answered. "I need you to check what information the US government has on the Modana cartel. Specifically, I need information about their compound in Puerto Vallarta, if you can find it."

"I'm on it," the guy on the other side said. "Is that where they are holding Frankie and Mia's friend?"

Kian was forever amazed by how fast rumors traveled within the clan.

"It looks like they are being taken there via Modana's yacht." Kian explained in a few words what Roni had found out and what Turner's plan was. "We are most interested in finding out the number of helicopters on the property."

"Give me half an hour or so," the guy said.

"I can give you that, but no more. Our teams are heading out in an hour."

"I might need longer than that."

Kian looked at Turner. "Can we wait?"

Turner shrugged. "It is what it is, and it will take as long as it has to take. We can make changes to the plan while the teams are deployed, improvising as needed."

"Call me whenever you have something," Kian told Andrew.

"I will." The call ended.

"I'm going," Negal said.

"I'm joining as well," Toven said. "You need a strong compeller for this plan to work."

Kian shook his head. "Kalugal will do. With all due respect, you don't have any military training, and this is a military operation."

Toven glared at him. "You didn't mind me going into Kra-ell territory and risking both Mia and myself."

"That was different. You were not part of the assault team. This operation is a commando attack, and you will be a liability instead of an asset."

Toven looked like he was going to strike Kian dead with his eyes, but fortunately for Kian, he didn't have that ability. "The last time Kalugal was part of an active operation was eighty years ago. He's no better equipped to be part of this mission than I am."

"Let's flip a coin." Kalugal pushed his hand into his pocket. "My pockets are empty. Does anyone have a quarter?"

Toven crossed his arms over his chest. "I'm not going to flip a coin over this. I'm going, and that's the end of this discussion."

Kian let out an exasperated breath. "One of you needs to stay on the ship to defend it in case of an attack. Decide between you who will do what."

Negal pushed to his feet. "I'll talk to Aru and Dagor. Hopefully, both will agree to come."

Onegus got up as well. "I will assemble the team. We will meet in forty-five minutes on the promenade deck. Those who intend to join the mission, get dressed to be ready for deployment." He turned to Toven. "I prefer for you to stay on board and defend the ship. Kalugal is more than capable of taking care of a bunch of humans. There is a remote possibility that Modana is hosting Doomers or that one of the thugs is immune, which is why we are taking precautions and assembling a force. If not for that, Kalugal could achieve our objectives all by himself with a megaphone in hand. But since we are leaving the ship with just one-third of the Guardians, we need the stronger compeller to stay here, and that's you."

After a long moment, Toven nodded. "Very well. You are the chief, and if you want me to stay on board, I will bow to your authority."

"Thank you." The chief dipped his head.

Negal was glad that Onegus hadn't objected to his and his two friends' participation in the mission, but he wasn't surprised that neither the chief nor Kian wanted Toven to be in the line of fire. He was a royal, and even here on Earth, where there were supposedly no different classes of gods, Toven was deemed more valuable than three commoner gods.

Not that the royal seemed happy about it. Toven would have preferred to participate, and Negal appreciated that.

Once outside, he typed a long message to his teammates, explaining what was going on and asking whether they were willing to join.

Hopefully, they would respond to the text despite the early hour. If not, he would go to their cabins and ring the bell until someone answered the door.

44

MARINA

Marina woke up after the most wonderful dream. It hadn't lasted long enough, though, and she wished she could return to floating over the beautiful alien landscapes with colors that didn't have a name in any of the languages she spoke.

She was no stranger to the effects of a venom bite, but compared to the Kra-ell, the immortal's was much more potent and delivered twice the euphoric experience.

She was warm and deeply satisfied, but most of all, she felt safe. Peter had his arms wrapped around her, his leg draped over her thighs, caging her in as if he was afraid she would escape while he slept.

Or at least that was what she imagined, what she hoped for.

The night with Peter had been revelatory. Marina had experienced passion and connection that she hadn't expected, and as she looked at Peter, a wave of sweet affection washed through her. He looked so peaceful, his features relaxed in his slumber, and she wanted to believe that it was because he felt as contented as she did.

Lifting her hand, she feathered her fingers over his cheek, the slope of his nose, his forehead. His skin was perfect. There wasn't even a hint of a wrinkle anywhere, not a blemish or even a freckle. It was good that he kept some facial hair, or he would have looked like a boy.

Marina chuckled softly.

Peter was all man, or rather all male, one who knew a hell of a lot about pleasing women. She didn't want to think about the number of bed partners he'd had over his long life.

How old was he?

For all she knew, he could be thousands of years old. All those immortals looked to be in their twenties and early thirties, and they didn't volunteer their age.

Asking was out of the question, and not just because it might be considered rude. It was an unspoken rule for humans to be seen but not heard and to be as unobtrusive as possible.

She'd broken that rule by going to the Lido deck and ordering a drink at the bar like she was a guest. The truth was that she'd expected the robot barman to refuse to serve her and had been surprised when he'd served her with his fake but oddly endearing smile.

She also hadn't expected to find Peter there, sitting alone at the bar.

Marina had taken it as a sign that she should approach him. It couldn't have been a coincidence that the one time she'd gathered the courage to go to the bar, the immortal she'd been watching from the first day of the cruise was there.

Observing Peter during every meal she served, she'd noticed him glancing her way a few times, but as soon as his eyes met hers, he would shift his gaze away, pretending that he was just looking in her general direction but not directly at her.

Sometimes, she was certain that he was watching her, but other times she thought that she imagined it, and approaching him had been difficult.

She was glad that she had. If he hadn't lied about reading her mind, he was perfect for her. Then again, he wouldn't have restraints and nipple clamps on hand if he wasn't into the same kink she was.

"Why are you awake?" he murmured with his eyes closed.

"Am I supposed to be asleep?"

"Definitely." He lazily lifted his eyelids. "You are supposed to be out for hours after a venom bite, soaring on the wings of euphoria."

She smiled. "I was. You forget that this wasn't my first time getting bitten. My body is familiar with the effects, and I don't black out for as long."

His lazy smile wilted. "The Kra-ell?"

She nodded. "Their venom is not as potent as yours, but it still delivers the fun stuff along with the blackouts."

"Were you forced?" he growled.

"Forced is too strong of a word. I was coerced and bribed, but I was given a choice. I could have said no."

He looked skeptical. "Could you really?"

"Rape was not condoned in the compound, but everyone knew that saying no carried consequences. Besides, we all knew that it was impossible to say no to bloodsuckers who could take hold of our minds and convince us that we desired them."

"Was that what happened to you?"

"I don't know for sure. He might have thralled me to think that he was sexy and that I wanted him. He was a nineteen-year-old hybrid whom I found attractive. I was seventeen at the time, but I was born in the compound, and I didn't think that I was too young. I grew up knowing that one day I would be summoned, and when I was, it felt almost like a rite of passage. I was so glad that my first was a hybrid and not a pureblood. I was terrified of them, and I heard that they were brutal. Yogun did his best to be considerate of my inexperience, but with his Kra-ell strength and natural proclivities, he wasn't all that gentle. Not that it was bad. His own natural lubrication and the bite helped make it a good memory."

That had been the first time Marina had realized that she craved some pain with her pleasure and that she enjoyed being dominated.

Perhaps it had been a survival mechanism because that had been her reality, and even if she didn't enjoy that sort of thing, she would have to endure it anyway. Whatever the reason was, the need hadn't gone away when she was with Nicolai, who was technically a human like her, even though he was one-quarter Kra-ell.

Peter's eyes were fully open now, and they were glowing. His fangs were down as well, but not because he was aroused. He was angry, and she regretted telling him too much.

"I assume that there were others," he slurred through his elongated fangs.

"Of course." She affected a smile. "I'm a thirty-two-year-old woman, and other than the last year, I haven't been celibate." It had been probably a little less than a year, but she still couldn't remember when the last time she'd been with Nicolai was.

Peter frowned. "You were liberated only two months ago."

"The Kra-ell stopped inviting me to share their beds when I was approaching thirty. I've never conceived, for which I was grateful, so they must have realized that I was not good for breeding and left me alone. I had a human boyfriend for a while, but we broke up some time ago, and I haven't been with anyone until now." She let out a breath. "Why are we talking about that? It's in the past, and I want to live in the present." She put her hands on his chest and pressed a soft kiss to his sternum. "You fulfilled your promise last night."

"You mean this morning."

She shifted her eyes to look at the scant light the drapes were allowing to filter through. "Okay, this morning, you made good on your promise. You pleased me so well that I want more."

The grin that spread over his handsome face was like warm sunshine despite the enormous fangs protruding over his lower lip. "Right now?"

"Why not? The venom bite is like taking a shot of energy and vitality. I'm rejuvenated, revitalized, and ready for more."

45

PETER

"Is that right?" Peter brushed his fingers over Marina's taut nipple and then drew a circle around it.

Her eyes became hooded. "It is."

He dipped his head and kissed the underside of her breast, lazily making his way to her needy little nub.

He wasn't in a hurry, and neither was she, and he could take his time exploring her with gentle touches and soft kisses.

"I forgot to ask." He slid a hand down her back and cupped her bottom. "Are you on any kind of contraceptives?"

"I've got the shot, and I'm clean. I haven't been with anyone in a long time."

He chuckled. "I'm immortal. I don't get diseases, and I probably can't get anyone pregnant either, but on the remote chance that the impossible happens, you should be protected." He slid a finger down the seam between her ass cheeks, eliciting a hiss and a wiggle.

"Why can't you get anyone pregnant?" she asked.

"Immortals' fertility is incredibly low."

"I'm sorry." She shifted closer to him, so her nipples were rubbing against his chest.

"Nothing to be sorry about. It's just the way it is. Nature makes sure that we don't overpopulate the planet."

"Makes sense."

Gently, he pushed her on her back and lay on his side, his head propped on his forearm, facing her. "I love your breasts." He gave her nipple a little tug. "They are so responsive."

She hissed. "They are still a little tender from what you did to them. The venom didn't take care of that."

"I'm sorry." He dipped his head and gently laved one stiff peak and then the other. "Better?"

"Yes." She smiled. "Don't stop."

"Yes, ma'am." He resumed his tender care for a few more moments and then cupped one breast. "Do you want me to stay away from them?"

"No. Just treat them gently."

It pleased Peter that Marina was instructing him. It meant that she felt comfortable with him and given what she'd been through and who he was, that was no small accomplishment.

He ran his thumb over her nipple and then kissed it and took it between his lips, gently sucking on it.

Marina moaned. "That's good."

He smoothed a hand down her belly, and as he reached the apex of her thighs, she spread them for him, and as he feathered his fingers over her moist slit, he reached behind her with his other hand and did the same to the seam between her ass cheeks.

"You're so bad," she breathed, her face reddening either with excitement or embarrassment or both.

"On the contrary. I think I'm so good." He pressed his thumb against her rear opening and at the same time rubbed his finger over her clit. "Tell me this feels bad."

She bit down on her lower lip and shook her head.

"I didn't hear that. What did you say?" He applied a little more pressure to the small rosette.

"It's bad." She smiled sheepishly.

He laughed. "Liar." He slapped her bottom. "Liars get spanked, Marina. So, let me ask you again? Does it feel bad?" He returned his thumb to her rear entrance.

"It feels good." She worried her lower lip. "But if I say that it feels bad, would you spank me again?"

"You like that, don't you?"

"I hate it."

He laughed and slapped her bottom again, then leaned and sealed her lips with his own.

Working her front and back at the same time, he had her writhing in no time. "Come for me," he commanded as he plunged three fingers into her wet heat and pushed the thumb of his other hand against her rear opening.

She gasped and writhed, and as he added the heel of his palm, pressing it against that most sensitive bundle of nerves, her body arched, and she came, screaming silently this time.

Watching her come apart from just his fingers was satisfying as fuck, and she was so beautiful to him at that moment that he wanted to pull out his phone and take a picture.

Instead, he kept pumping and massaging until her tremors subsided.

Wrapping his arms around her, he pulled her on top of him, and for a long moment, she just lay there, exhausted by her climax, her cheek resting on his chest and her breath fanning over his throat.

He was as hard as a rock, but he didn't want to rush her. Caressing her back, he murmured words of praise, and if she fell asleep on him, it would have been fine as well. But after several minutes, she lifted her head and gifted him with a lazy, satisfied smile.

"I might never want to leave this bed."

"Then don't."

She wiggled, rubbing herself against his hard length. "I owe you an orgasm."

"You don't owe me a thing." He squeezed her bottom. "But if you want to avail yourself of my pleasure stick, you are more than welcome."

She laughed. "Pleasure stick. I haven't heard that one before." She pushed up until she was straddling his thighs and took his erection in her hand. "I want to take a taste."

He lifted his arms and tucked his hands under his head. "Be my guest."

She bent forward and was about to take him into her mouth when his phone rang.

He frowned. It was never good news when he got a call so early in the morning, and the timing sucked. "I hate to interrupt your tasting session, but I have to take it."

Pouting in disappointment, she leaned over to the nightstand and retrieved the phone for him.

"It's my boss." He lifted her off him and sat up. "What's up, Onegus?"

"Meeting in fifteen minutes at the promenade deck. We have another situation."

"On my way, chief."

"See you there." Onegus ended the call.

"What's going on?" Marina regarded him with worried eyes.

"I don't know, but I'm going to find out." He leaned over and kissed her on the lips. "Stay here and get some sleep. I'll let you know what this is about, provided that I'm allowed."

MARGO

Margo woke up from a needle prick in her forearm. "What the hell?"

Alberto smiled down at her. "You'll feel amazing in a moment."

What was he talking about?

Margo was still sitting on the floor, propped against the dresser with her purse in her lap. She must have fallen asleep like that, but she couldn't remember why.

For a moment, she tried to concentrate, but then she was flooded with a rush of euphoria, and warmth spread throughout her body. The relaxation was so complete that she let her arms flop by her sides, and her legs extend in front of her. "Wow," was all she managed to say.

She felt relaxed and happy.

Why had she been scared before?

This was amazing.

"I'll get you some food," Alberto said before leaving the cabin.

"I'm floating," Jasmine said from the bed. "Why am I floating?"

Margo giggled. "Because we are on a boat, silly."

In the back of her mind, she knew that this was all wrong and that the happy floating feeling was artificial. She'd been drugged, and if she had her phone, she would search the internet for the kind of drugs that could produce an immediate reaction like that. How long was it going to last?

What would happen once the drug wore off?

Would she start shaking all over like she had seen in the movies?

And why did Alberto do that to her?

It was difficult to think, and even more difficult to worry about anything when she was feeling so amazing. Margo couldn't remember ever feeling so good. No wonder people were willing to do anything for this feeling.

Except, it felt foreign. She was a glass-half-empty type of person, and all this happiness and euphoria felt like an artificial sweetener. It was a good approximation of the real thing, but not quite.

"I need to pee." Jasmine dropped her legs to the floor. "Where is the bathroom?"

"I don't know, and I need to pee too."

Suddenly the urge became overwhelming, and Margo had no choice but to try to stand up and find the bathroom. Using the dresser for support, she managed to haul herself up and then stumbled toward the other door in the cabin, the one Alberto didn't use.

Thankfully, Jasmine was moving even slower than her, so she got to the bathroom first, and barely managed to lower her panties and sit on the toilet when her bladder started to empty itself in a gush.

The door opened before she was done, and Jasmine lurched in. "I'm going to pee in the shower."

Margo laughed, her shoulders heaving as if that was the best joke she'd heard all year. "I don't know you well enough for that, but go ahead. I can't get up from this toilet even if I tried to."

She kept laughing as she watched Jasmine struggle with her underwear, pee on her feet, and then wash it off with the handheld shower head.

"It's not funny." Jasmine grabbed a towel to dry off and then started laughing too. "I take it back. It is funny."

The bathroom door opened, and Alberto poked his head in. "Food is here."

Margo tried to put on an indignant frown. "Can't you see I'm on the toilet? Get out!"

When he closed the door, she started laughing again. "We are so fucked, Jasmine. He drugged us, and it feels so good, but it's so bad. Do you know what he injected us with?"

Jasmine's puzzled expression was comical. "He injected us? I didn't feel anything. I thought he drugged the wine."

Margo had no energy to explain. It took a lot of concentration to just wipe herself clean, flush the toilet, and pull her panties back up.

Somehow, she made it to the sink and washed her hands. "Are you hungry?" she asked Jasmine.

"No. Are you?"

"I'm thirsty." She used the wall to get to the door and open it. "Come on, Jaz. I smell coffee."

Alberto put a tray on the nightstand between the two beds. There were two glasses of orange juice, two cups of coffee, and two plates of fruit, cheese, and crackers.

He waved a hand over the tray. "Five-star service for five-star ladies."

"Where are we?" Margo sat on the bed and reached for the orange juice.

"You are on a yacht." Alberto helped Jasmine to the other bed and then sat on the single chair in the cabin.

The orange juice helped clear some of the cotton candy stuffing Margo's head. "I figured that one out already. Why are we on a yacht, and where are we going?"

Alberto crossed his legs. "You are the guests of Julio Modana, and we are going south to Señor Modana's compound."

"Who is Julio Modana?" Jasmine asked.

"Your new owner."

Jasmine shook her head. "What are you talking about?"

Alberto let out an exasperated breath. "You are so dumb, Jasmine." He glanced at Margo. "You get it, right?"

"Yeah, I think I do. You drugged us, and neither of us can think straight, but I'm a little less affected than Jasmine, who is not dumb at all."

He snorted. "Oh, yes, she is. Dumb as a brick. Otherwise, she wouldn't be here. But she's beautiful, and that's why Señor Modana wants her. He told me to bring her to him, and you just stuck your nose in where it didn't belong, which is why you are here too." He grimaced. "Carlos agreed to take you because you are pretty enough and a natural blonde."

Bits and pieces of the conversation she'd overheard before were floating around in her addled brain. Margo remembered the name Carlos being mentioned.

"Who is Carlos?"

"Julio and Carlos Modana are brothers. Carlos is the younger one."

Margo smiled. "Oh, goodie. I get the young one."

Alberto shook his head. "There is nothing good about it. Julio Modana might be older, but he treats his women well. I can't say the same about Carlos."

"Why did you do that?" Jasmine whispered.

Was she finally sobering up?

Alberto shrugged. "I do what the boss says. He told me to bring you to him, and I did. It was much easier than I thought it would be because you are so fucking stupid."

"I'm not sure who's the stupid one," Margo said. "If your boss wanted Jasmine for himself, he won't like it that you sampled the merchandise." She waggled her finger at him and then burst out laughing. "You are in so much trouble, *Alberrrrto*." She rolled the Rs. "He's going to kill you."

"Shut up." The jerk pushed to his feet. "Modana is not an idiot. He knew what I needed to do to make her come with me voluntarily. Besides, he doesn't care. When he tires of her, which won't take long once he realizes what a bore she is, he will give her to me anyway."

4 7

PETER

When Peter made it to the promenade deck, many of his fellow Guardians were already there. The sea breeze was cool this early in the morning, which was welcome. He wasn't a fan of the humid heat.

"So here is the situation," Onegus said once everyone gathered around him. "We were supposed to get to Cabo and collect Mia and Frankie's friend from a resort hotel there. Turns out that Luis, the tour guide who was kidnapped by the Doomers, overheard his passengers talking about it, and Kalugal didn't erase that memory. Long story short, we believe that the Doomers are waiting for us there in force."

Crap, that wasn't good.

Onegus waited until the murmurs subsided before continuing, "As it turns out, we don't need to go to Cabo because Margo was abducted along with another woman by someone working for a cartel boss named Julio Modana." The chief continued to explain how Margo got snared in a web that hadn't been meant for her and how Roni had found out what had happened. "They are currently on his yacht, traveling south toward Puerto Vallarta, where his mansion is located. Naturally the place is well guarded by cartel members, and even though Kalugal will join the mission, we need to provide him with backup and support and get him within hearing distance of the guards. I need fifty volunteers to go on this mission. Everyone who wants to join, please step forward."

Fifty guardians were about two-thirds of the force, which meant that Onegus was leaving the ship with skeleton protection.

Peter raised his hand. "Isn't the force left to defend the ship too small?"

Onegus shook his head. "Not with Toven staying behind with a megaphone in hand. Thirty Guardians are enough to man all the battle stations, and if anyone tries to board the ship, he can turn them against each other or tell them to jump overboard and swim ashore."

As some of the Guardians chuckled and joked about all the possible things Toven could command the infiltrators to do, Peter thought about all the other dangers that Onegus hadn't mentioned, like a torpedo attack, or a military drone, or maybe even a military jet. Toven could do nothing to protect the ship from those, but then all the Guardians together couldn't do much either. They had hidden cannons and torpedoes of their own, but they also had very limited experience of operating these weapon systems.

As much as Peter felt bad for Margo and the other woman, his priority was protecting the ship, and while his friends eagerly stepped forward, he stayed behind.

Once the two groups were finalized, Magnus took the group of defenders to one side while Max took the group going on the mission to another.

Magnus divided guard duty among the twenty-seven Guardians staying behind, and Peter got assigned to the Lido deck, where twelve defenders were to be stationed. The others were assigned to man the ship's defensive equipment.

"Is everyone clear on their assignments?" Magnus asked.

"We need to get armed," Jay said.

"Of course." Magnus waved a hand. "Follow me to the armory."

They had to wait their turn until the assault team was done, and then each of them was given a machine gun and a Kevlar vest.

"After you are done, go get something to eat," Magnus said. "Report here in half an hour."

Peter rushed out of the armory first, but instead of heading to the dining room, he headed back up to his cabin. He hadn't asked permission to tell Marina what was going on, but he assumed it was okay.

"Hold up," Jay ran out after him. "Is the woman still in your room?"

"Yes. Why?"

Jay shrugged. "Just checking. Who is she?"

"One of the humans from Safe Haven."

"I know that. Which one?"

"Marina. The girl with the blue hair."

Jay smiled. "She's a looker. How did you get her into your bed? I tried flirting with some of the others but got the cold shoulder. They just pretended not to understand English, but I think they did."

"It's called charm, my friend." Peter clapped Jay on the back.

"Lucky bastard," Jay said. "She's one hell of a screamer."

Peter briefly closed his eyes. "Please don't mention that again. Not to me and not to anyone else. She would be mortified if she found out that you heard her."

Jay put two fingers over his lips and mimed locking them and throwing out the key. "Do you want me to move to another cabin?"

"You can if you want to, but as long as you keep your mouth shut and treat Marina with respect, I have no problem with you staying. If you are nice to her, she might mention you to her friends."

She probably wouldn't, but that would ensure that Jay was on his best behavior around her.

His cabin mate grinned. "I'll keep that in mind."

MARGO

After pacing the small cabin while rubbing the back of his neck, Alberto cast Jasmine another disdainful look and sat back down.

Was he being mean to Jaz because he felt guilty for tricking her?

Margo suspected that it was easier on his conscience to shift the blame to Jasmine. In his mind, if Jaz was stupid enough to fall for his lies, then she deserved what he had done to her.

It was convoluted logic, and Margo was surprised that she figured it out despite her drugged state. Perhaps the effect was wearing off, and she could think more clearly?

Thankfully, Jasmine was still riding the high, so Alberto's insults didn't seem to bother her. Staring at the window with a grin on her gorgeous face, she looked oblivious to her fate.

Margo put down the toast she'd been eating and took another sip of coffee. "Who is Julio Modana? What does he do?"

"He's a businessman," Alberto said.

"Right." She snorted. "A businessman. Where is he now? Doing business from his posh cabin? Or sleeping?"

"He's not here."

Alberto cast a sidelong glance at Jasmine, that Margo thought was full of guilt, but she didn't trust her judgment in the state she was in.

"I heard him talking with you earlier, so how can he not be here? We are on a yacht in the middle of the ocean."

He looked at her down his nose. "First of all, we are not in the middle of the ocean. We are not far away from the coastline. And secondly, this yacht has a helipad. Señor Modana flew back home after inspecting the merchandise."

Margo grimaced. "You are an asshole, Alberto, but then I'm not telling you anything you don't know. You care for Jasmine, and yet you handed her over to your boss."

"I don't care for her." He shook his head a little too vehemently. "She's just a woman." He pushed to his feet. "I don't know why I'm wasting my time in here with you."

That wasn't good. Margo needed him to stay and keep talking. The more she could learn from him, the better her chances of escape.

"Don't go." She plastered a smile on her face. "Jasmine is half catatonic from the drugs you injected us with, and I need someone to talk to."

He cast another dark look at his former girlfriend and sat back down. "I'll finish my coffee and then go."

"Good." Margo sipped on her coffee for a few moments before firing another question. "So, when is Señor Julio coming back?"

"I don't know. He doesn't tell me his plans. But he will probably want to take another look at her, so he will return sometime later today."

"Why her?" Margo asked. "Was it Jasmine specifically, or would any stunning brunette do?"

He regarded her with suspicion in his eyes but then shrugged. "It doesn't matter what you know. You are not going anywhere." He took another sip from his coffee, and Margo thought that he wasn't going to answer, but then he said, "Señor Modana wanted Jasmine specifically. He'd seen her in a commercial, and he pointed at the screen and said, I want her. Bring her to me, and I'll make it worth your while."

"Did he make it worth your while?"

"He will." Alberto put his coffee cup on the tray and rose to his feet. "I'll come later to give you another dose. You are sobering up too quickly."

Damn, she should pretend to be more out of it than she was. "I'm not. If I were sober, I would be throwing stuff at you or trying to escape or both."

"You can try, but I promise you will regret it." He gave her a salute before opening the door and closing it behind him.

Margo waited to hear the lock engage, and when that didn't happen, she waited a few more moments before getting up and trying the door.

It wasn't locked.

"I'll be damned. We can just walk out of here." She turned to Jasmine. "Do you want to go exploring?"

Jasmine kept staring out the single window in the cabin.

"Come on, Jasmine." Margo snapped her fingers in front of her eyes. "Are you pretending, or are you really out of it?"

"I'm so dumb, but I don't care. I don't care about anything."

Margo sat on the bed next to her. "It's the drugs talking, sweetie. You are not dumb. Alberto was just saying that because he felt guilty for doing this to you."

She shrugged. "Julio Modana might be an improvement over Alberto. Instead of being a small-time crook's girl-friend, I will be a big-time crook's pet."

Margo chuckled. "That's a very smart observation. You see? You are not dumb."

"Why did he drug us?"

"To make us more compliant. But it's not going to work." Margo gave her hand a reassuring squeeze. "Do you know why?"

Jasmine shifted her big brown eyes to her. "Why?"

"Because I am so contrary that even drugs can't make me agreeable. That being said, from now on, I'm going to pretend to be drugged out of my mind, and you keep doing what you're doing. Perhaps it will buy us more time between injections."

KIAN

After most of their war council had left, only Kian, Roni, Toven, and Turner remained.

Kian ran his fingers through his hair. "Why do I have a feeling that we are missing something?" He briefly closed his eyes. "I hate making hasty plans, but it's not like we have a choice."

"Your gut feeling is correct," Turner said. "We are missing something, or rather someone." He looked at Roni. "I didn't want to bring it up in front of everyone, but we need Sylvia to join the mission. Without her disabling the surveillance cameras along the way, Modana's people will see our teams coming from miles away. We don't know what kind of firepower they have on the premises, but we need to assume that they have the latest and most advanced weapons at their disposal. Also, the compound is likely to be surrounded by explosives buried in its perimeter, ready to be detonated from the control room inside the compound. It's crucial that we take them by surprise and get Kalugal within hearing distance, and regrettably, shrouding is just not going to cut it."

Great. Kian didn't want a civilian on a mission that involved explosives and machine guns. "You should have mentioned that before. Perhaps we should abandon this ambitious plan of yours and simply continue on an inter- cept course with the yacht. We will face fewer opponents and retrieve Margo and her friend with little to no effort."

Turner arched a brow. "Did you forget why I came up with this idea in the first place? Doomers and cartel thugs chasing after us?"

"Right." Kian let out a breath. "We need Sylvia." He looked at Roni. "Are you okay with that?"

"Of course, I'm not, but what can I do? Turner is right, and it's not going to work without her. Besides, I can't speak for Sylvia. It's up to her whether she wants to go."

"We need her," Turner said. "If she says no, we have to abort or come up with another plan."

Roni let out a sigh. "Sylvia will say yes. She's too brave for her own good, and she knows what this is about. If we tell her she's needed, no one will be able to stop her from coming."

"Call her," Kian said. "Explain what's going on and have her come to the promenade deck in half an hour."

Roni winced. "Why don't you call her and explain? Sylvia is a sweetheart except for when someone dares to wake her up, but she won't be yelling at you."

Kian stifled a chuckle. "Fine, I'll call her."

Scrolling through his contact list, he found Sylvia's number and placed the call. The first attempt went to voicemail, but he called again, and this time she picked up.

"What?" Sylvia barked, probably without looking at the caller ID.

Or so Kian hoped. He wasn't big on protocol, and he didn't expect deference from his people, but he expected basic courtesy.

"Good morning, Sylvia. This is Kian. I apologize for the wake-up call, but we need your services, and the teams are heading out shortly."

"To rescue Margo?"

"Yes. I'm glad that you know what this is about. The guys can fill you in on the plan on the way, but the gist of it is that we need your special talent for disabling surveillance equipment. It's a dangerous mission, but I will make sure that you are protected. Still, you are a civilian, and you are not obligated to go. If you'd rather not take the risk, we will come up with another plan."

"Of course, I'll go. When and where?"

He chuckled. "I was hoping that would be your response. Half an hour on the promenade deck. Dress like a hiker. You know the drill."

"Someone better bring me coffee," she grumbled.

"I'll prepare a thermos." Roni rose to his feet. "Tell her that I'm on my way."

"I heard that," Sylvia said. "He'd better make it fast."

"Thank you, Sylvia. I appreciate it."

"Yeah, yeah. I need to get ready." She ended the call.

Roni winced. "I told you that she's grumpy in the mornings."

"That's okay." Kian pushed away from the table and walked over to the kitchenette. "I'm grateful for her help, so I would have forgiven her even if she had cussed me out."

"It was a close call." Roni closed his laptop. "I'm going to leave it here and come back after I say goodbye to Sylvia."

Kian nodded. "I'll join you on the promenade in half an hour. I hope that by then, Andrew will have information for me."

NEGAL

"Here we go again." Dagor wiped the spray of ocean water from his face.

The lifeboat was going as fast as a speedboat which made the ride bumpy, but Negal didn't mind. The faster they made it to Modana's estate, the faster they would get to Margo.

Naturally, they couldn't go straight to his private bay and just dock there. They needed to land a couple of miles away and make the rest of the way on foot. The clan's techno disruptor was with them, and hopefully, she could disable the surveillance cameras around the cartel boss's compound.

Negal had never heard of an innate talent like Sylvia's, and he was wondering how it came to be. If it was unknown on Anumati, then the gods hadn't coded their genetics for it. It was either a fluke of nature, or she was the descendant of a god who had been given experimental genes.

He and his teammates were tasked with keeping her safe, and Negal had given Roni his word that he would personally ensure her safety.

He didn't like the idea of putting Roni's mate in danger, and he'd even told Turner that they could get a helicopter elsewhere, but Turner rebuffed him by explaining that taking the cartel boss's helicopter was just one objective of the mission and that the others were no less important. Negal had argued that the two objectives didn't have to be achieved simultaneously, but then Turner's winning argument had been that it would take too long to get another helicopter, reminding Negal that they couldn't waste time.

For all they knew, Margo was being subjected to terrible torment and degradation on the yacht, and Negal couldn't think about that without his vision turning red and his fangs punching over his lower lip.

The fastest route to freeing her was getting Modana's helicopter and flying it to the yacht. Negal would have been content to leave the rest of the plan to Kalugal and the Guardians and rushed to save Margo, but he needed Kalugal to do his thing first for the rest of the plan to work. He also needed the clan's helicopter pilot because neither he nor his teammates knew how to operate one.

"I'm surprised that you were willing to leave Frankie," Aru said to Dagor. "That must have been a difficult decision to leave her alone in the clinic during her transition."

Dagor snorted. "Are you kidding me? Frankie commanded me to go and save her friend. On my part, I know that she has Mia and Toven to keep her company, and she's doing great, so I'm not worried. Bridget said that she's not likely to take a turn for the worse."

"Interesting." Aru smiled. "Gabi wasn't happy about me leaving, and she tried to convince me to stay. I guess Frankie cares a lot about Margo."

Dagor shrugged. "She also knows what I'm capable of and trusts me to bring her friend home."

As the two kept talking, Negal turned to Sylvia, who was sitting next to him. "Are you okay?"

"Yeah, why wouldn't I be?"

"I thought that it might be a little scary for a civilian to join a military mission."

She smiled. "This is not my first, nor will it be my last operation. Kian tried to convince me to join the Guardian force and do this full time, but the truth is that there aren't enough missions like this, and I would be wasting my time and sweating through training. I prefer to be an outside consultant, so to speak. He can call on me whenever my talent is needed, but I'm free to do whatever I want with the rest of my time."

"Makes sense," Negal agreed.

It was difficult to keep talking over the noise of the engine and the rush of the waves, and they soon gave up, riding the rest of the way in silence. When the lifeboat hit the sand, Negal and the other males jumped out and hauled the boat to the shore with Sylvia sitting inside it like a queen.

"Thank you." She took his offered hand and stepped out of the lifeboat onto dry sand. "I appreciate not getting wet."

He smiled. "I promised Roni to take care of you."

"This is becoming familiar," Dagor said as they dragged the boats further up until they reached greenery that could act as camouflage.

Unlike the other time, when they had taken a second lifeboat just for appearances, this time the two lifeboats were full of personnel. Not everyone was going to storm the cartel boss's stronghold, though. Most would remain behind as backup in case Doomers were encountered. Given their experience in Acapulco, it seemed that the Brotherhood had close ties to the drug cartels, so it wasn't such a stretch to think that they could be found in Modana's compound.

"Okay, people." Max lifted his hand to get their attention. "Break up into groups of three to five members. Your weapons need to stay hidden in your backpacks. To anyone sighting you, you need to look like backpackers."

They had gone over all of that before boarding the lifeboats, and the clan's disguise expert had done her best to make them look human. Negal wore a bandana around his head, and his jeans were torn and frayed in places. The backpack he was carrying was made from a large potato sack that he had attached straps to, and the machine gun inside was padded by a blanket, so its shape wasn't evident.

Eva had painted a five-o'clock shadow on him and added a large birthmark on his upper left cheek. It might fool people from afar, but not up close. Dagor and Aru had received similar treatment, and so had the other Guardians. There hadn't been much time, so only the bare minimum was done to make them appear more human and less perfect, but hopefully, it would be good enough to fool those watching the feed from the surveillance cameras.

Aru adjusted his earpiece. "Are the three of us on our own?"

Max shook his head. "Kalugal and Dalhu are with you. You worked well together in Acapulco. You are the spear team."

Aru adjusted the straps of his makeshift backpack. "I thought that the plan was for Kalugal to be behind us with another team."

"There was a change of plans." Max tapped his earpiece. "They are still working on the details."

"I just hope the boss and his helicopter are on the premises," Negal said. "I would hate to go to all this trouble for nothing." Especially since they could have sailed ahead and intercepted the yacht.

Max touched his earpiece. "Roni says that the compound has more than one helicopter. If the boss is not there, we can commandeer the other one."

"What if both are gone?" Negal asked.

Max repeated the question to Roni.

"He says that's not likely. Andrew got back to Kian with the information the government has collected on the Modana brothers. One of them is always on the premises, and it's safe to assume that whoever stays behind has a helicopter on standby at his disposal."

MARGO

It had taken Jasmine a long time to finally agree to go exploring, which in a way was a blessing. Margo's mind was clearer now, the fog of the drug slowly lifting.

Jasmine was still struggling though, unsteady on her feet, so Margo took her hand and led her to the door. Stepping outside, they found themselves in the lower deck corridor of the yacht.

It didn't look like much, but as they ascended a simple staircase to the next deck, the decor changed drastically, and the contrast to the cramped space they had been confined in made it clear that they had been put in the crew quarters.

This deck was super luxurious, with sleek lines and minimalist decor dominating the space. High-gloss surfaces and metallic accents reflected the light, and the walls were covered with modern art pieces in bold colors. Some were abstract, others depicted faces or objects, and each was signed by the artist.

"It pays to be a drug lord," Margo murmured. "The art alone must be worth a fortune."

Jasmine shrugged. "I don't like any of it. I like pictures of beautiful landscapes or ordinary people doing fun things, like children on swings or people sitting in cafés."

Margo could understand that. In an ugly world where so many suffered, it was important to surround oneself with depictions of peace and tranquility, of happiness.

Margo sighed.

The drugs must really be wearing off if she was once again seeing the glass half empty, but if she wanted to avoid another needle jab, she needed to retain the appearance of still being heavily drugged.

They passed through a lounge area, where floor-to-ceiling windows offered breathtaking views of the sea. Just like in the previous rooms, the furniture was sleek and modern, with clean lines and a monochromatic palette, interrupted only by occasional vibrant throw pillows.

Further exploration brought them to the dining area. A long glass dining table stood at the center, surrounded by high-backed chairs upholstered in white leather. The floor was dark wood, and the simplicity of the design was elegant.

"Look at this." She pointed to a stunning glass staircase that led to the upper deck. The steps were made of clear Plexiglas and seemed to float in the air.

"I'm afraid to step on them," Jasmine said. "What if they break?"

Margo laughed. "They look like a piece of futuristic art, but they serve a function. I'm sure they will not break."

"You go first." Jasmine waved a hand.

"No problem, but I want you right behind me. I don't want us to get separated."

"Okay." Jasmine eyed the staircase as if it were the maw of a leviathan.

When they got to the deck, the expanse of the yacht was revealed in its full glory. The deck was an open, airy space with pieces of contemporary furniture arranged in comfortable groupings. Some of them were under a roof, shaded from the strong sun beaming down on the deck; others were exposed, the sun casting a sparkle across the glass surfaces of the side tables and deck railings.

Beyond the railing, the ocean stretched to the horizon, its surface rippling and shimmering.

Laughing and stumbling to perpetuate the impression of being drugged, Margo looked around the deck and counted six men. They were armed with machine guns that were casually slung over their shoulders, but there was nothing casual about their demeanor.

They looked dangerous and alert, but they seemed to be paying little attention to her and Jasmine.

Evidently, their captors were more concerned with threats from the outside than with them escaping.

Margo's eyes fixed on the vast ocean stretching out before them. They were sailing south from Cabo San Lucas, and in the distance, the shore was visible as a sliver of land. It could have been an illusion, or perhaps the drugs made her see things that weren't there, but seeing the shore gave her hope.

The sun hung low in the sky, casting a warm, golden light that danced on the water's surface. A gentle breeze carried the salty tang of the sea, and as it brushed against her skin, it offered a fleeting sense of freedom.

"We could grab a life vest and swim for it," Margo said, only half jesting, her eyes gauging the distance to the shore. "We can just float, and the tide will bring us in."

Jasmine looked out at the expanse of water between them and freedom. "Are you sure the tide will bring us to the shore?" she whispered.

Their quiet plotting was abruptly shattered by a laugh. Alberto approached with a sneer, the sun casting sharp shadows across his face. "You think you can swim ashore?" he mocked in a derisive tone. "It's much farther than you think. And even if you made it, the men would pick you up before you could shout 'help'." He turned his scornful gaze to Jasmine. "So dumb," he spat.

Anger surged like a wildfire inside Margo, burning away the last vestiges of the artificial good mood the drugs had induced. She wanted to slap the jerk and wipe the smirk off his face, but her brain wasn't addled enough to think that it was a good idea.

Her fists clenched at her sides, she forced herself to take a deep breath and put a stupid smile on her face. "It was my idea. So, I guess I'm dumb, too."

"You said it." Alberto ambled away.

"Don't mind him," Margo whispered. "He's an asshole."

"I know." Jasmine leaned her forearms on the railing and looked at the waves created by the yacht's passage.

Margo leaned on the railing next to her friend and returned her gaze to the line of land that symbolized the life they were being torn away from. With a sigh, she lifted her face to the gentle caress of the sea breeze. It felt as if nature itself was trying to soothe her anger and make this terrible day somehow better.

Well, on the positive side, she got to see how the crooked rich lived, and if she ever got free, she would have one hell of a story to tell Mia and Frankie.

To be frank, it was partially her fault. If she hadn't tried to help Jasmine, she wouldn't be in this mess, but she wasn't the type who could walk away when there was something she could do.

Now, she was trapped at the mercy of a ruthless cartel boss, and escape was a fantasy. She and Jasmine were prisoners in this floating palace, and every moment brought them closer to their terrible fate.

NEGAL

Negal handed his backpack to Aru, bent down, and tapped his shoulder. "Come on, Sylvia. Hop onto my back."

"No." She put her hands on her hips. "I can walk."

She and her hacker were a match made by the Fates. She was just as stubborn and contrary as Roni was.

"We can move faster if you ride on my back, and if you are not preoccupied with where your next step should go, you will pay more attention to your surroundings and locate the damn surveillance cameras."

So far, they hadn't encountered any, and Negal was starting to worry that they were missing them. They were less than a mile away from the cartel boss's compound, going through rough terrain that was so steep that the immortals were having difficulty traversing it without injury.

Perhaps that was the reason for the lack of cameras. The cartel boss didn't think anyone would come at him from this side of the estate.

"Fine," Sylvia relented. "But if Roni gets mad at us for getting too close for comfort, I'll point my finger at you."

Negal suppressed an eye roll. "You are a mated female who is faithful to her mate. You smell like Roni, and that's very unattractive to me. I'll have to keep my nose closed the entire time I'm carrying you."

"Then I won't do it." She shrugged and kept going, stumbling and twisting her ankle. "Ouch. Damn it."

"Please, Sylvia," Kalugal said. "If you don't take Negal's offer willingly, I'll have to compel you to take it. You are slowing us down."

"You should be thankful that I'm here," she muttered under her breath as she put her hand on Negal's shoulder. "Crouch lower. I'm injured now. And don't you dare say that you told me so."

"I'm saying nothing." He put his arm under her butt and hoisted her over his back. "Wrap your legs around my middle and hold on like a monkey."

"Great visuals you are giving me," she murmured.

They kept going for another hundred feet or so when her arms tightened around his neck. "Slow down. I see a camera." She lifted a hand and pointed at something high up in the tree, but he couldn't see anything.

"What are you pointing at?"

"It's right there, but don't worry. I've already taken care of it. Keep going."

He did as she said. "How did you see it up there?"

"I sensed it, so I looked for it."

"I didn't know you could do that," Kalugal said. "What does it feel like?"

She chuckled. "Like what you would expect it to feel if you could. It's like a buzz of electricity. When there is a lot of tech around, it's more difficult to isolate the cameras, but there is nothing here, so it's easy."

"We should stop and put our Kevlar vests on," Dalhu said.

"Yeah, good idea." Negal let Sylvia slide down his back. "Especially you, young lady."

She tilted her head. "Are gods bulletproof?"

"Almost," Dagor said. "Our bodies expel bullets so fast that you could say so. That's why we are not putting them on." He waved at Kalugal and Dalhu. "You two, on the other hand, should wear them. The heart and the head should be protected."

"We don't have helmets," Dalhu pointed out. "The vests will have to do."

After the immortals got their vests on, Sylvia hopped onto Negal's back, and the six of them continued at a much slower pace.

"There are not many of them," Sylvia said. "That's just the second one so far."

"What are you doing to them?" Aru asked. "Are they disabled for good?"

"Usually, I would just fritz them out for a few seconds so it would look like a glitch, but because the rest of the force is moving behind us, I'm changing the cameras' angles and getting them stuck in one position instead of fanning out. Whoever is watching the feed sees the canopy of the next tree over."

"Won't it look suspicious?" Dagor moved a branch out of their way.

"Hopefully, they will think that there was a gust of wind that moved the camera. It happens. Like antennas that fall out of alignment in a strong wind."

"Oh shit." Dagor stopped. "Do you hear that?"

Negal heard it a second later. "Dogs barking." He turned around to look at Kalugal. "Please tell me that you can compel animals."

The immortal winced. "They don't understand language, so I can't compel them, but I can try to thrall them. I suggest the rest of you climb up the trees."

As Sylvia released her grip on Negal's neck, he caught her hands. "What are you doing?"

"You can't climb a tree with me on your back."

"Hold on tight and watch me."

Negal rushed to the nearest tree and climbed it effortlessly until he reached a branch that looked strong enough to hold him and Sylvia. "Don't let go."

"I won't." She clung to him so hard that she was choking him.

"You can ease your hold on my neck a little. I promise not to let you fall."

"Sorry." She lowered her arms to wrap them around his chest.

When three large dogs cleared the bushes, the only one remaining on the ground was Kalugal, but the dogs ignored him, and their barking stopped. They put their noses to the ground and sniffed around, but Kalugal must have taken hold of their minds because they whimpered, tucked their tails under their bellies, and ran off.

In the distance, someone cursed in Spanish, and the dogs whimpered some more, and then it got quiet again.

"You can get down now," Kalugal said.

Aru was the first one on the ground. "What did you tell the dogs?"

Kalugal snorted. "I didn't tell them anything. I put an image of a snarling cougar in their pea-sized brains."

KALUGAL

"You are clear to proceed," Kalugal said into his earpiece. "The threat has been neutralized."

"You mean the dogs?" Max said in his ear.

Was that a condescending tone that he detected in the Guardian's voice?

"Yeah, the dogs. I thralled them to think I was a cougar. Could you have done that?"

"Not likely," Max said. "I didn't know you could do it."

"Neither did I." Kalugal tapped the earpiece to indicate that he was done.

It had been a neat trick with the dogs, and Kalugal was damn proud of himself. He had never been a dog person, so he'd never bothered trying to get into the brains of dogs or other pets, but apparently, he could do anything he put his mind to.

He chuckled softly at his own pun.

"That was impressive," Negal said. "When we are done with this mission, I would like you to teach me how to do that."

Kalugal tilted his head. "Have you ever tried to get into the mind of an animal?"

The god shook his head. "We have weapons that can neutralize an animal without killing it. Regrettably, we've left them behind."

Kalugal was very interested in those weapons, but given how the gods safeguarded their technology by making it impossible to reverse engineer, it wouldn't have done him much good to get his hands on one of them. Still, he would have liked to hold the weapon and get to use it at least once to get a feel for it.

"Would it be possible for me to play around with your toys?"

Negal cast a sidelong glance at Aru, who shook his head.

"Kian got to see how our tiny spy drones work," Aru said. "So, I can let you play around with one of those, but not our other tech."

"That's a shame. I'm an entrepreneur, and my main interest is in cutting-edge technology. Sometimes, seeing something extraordinary can spark ideas for new products."

Dagor nodded. "I get it. I have ideas for new products all of the time."

Kalugal's interest was piqued. "Perhaps we can get together once this is all over and play around with ideas."

Dagor smiled. "I would like that."

"We should get moving." Negal adjusted Sylvia on his back. "The longer we take, the longer Margo suffers."

Sylvia cast Kalugal a sidelong glance. "I was wondering about something. Kian keeps referring to me as a civilian, but you are a civilian too, and yet he has you going on one mission after another."

"I'm a civilian now, but I have military training, and I'm the only compeller the clan has who knows how to operate modern weapons." He chuckled. "Toven might be a powerful god, but he was never a fighter, and I doubt he can shoot a rifle."

"I see." Sylvia returned her gaze to the canopies. "That's another camera," she said quietly. "We are very close to the compound now, so I expect more of them. We should proceed at a slower pace."

Kalugal reached into his backpack and pulled out his weapon of choice. He didn't carry a semiautomatic like the others in his team.

His weapon was the megaphone.

Sylvia disabled eight more cameras before they reached the backyard fence.

Kalugal motioned for the others to crouch low and hide behind the fence while he peeked over the block wall and noted the positions of the guards.

There were two stationed next to the French doors, and one more was on the roof, but the guard was looking toward the front, not the back. There were probably many more at the front of the house, but hopefully, the megaphone would carry his voice to those guards as well.

"We are in position," Max said in his earpiece.

Kalugal waited until Max informed him that the Guardians were in position before lifting the megaphone to his mouth. "Lay down your weapons," he commanded in Spanish. "Kick them away from you, go down to your knees, and put your hands on your heads."

The two guards next to the French doors complied, their rifles clattering to the ground first and then their knees hitting the soil, followed by their hands going over their heads. The one on the roof took a little longer, but he too was on his knees within seconds.

Thankfully, he didn't fall off the roof. Not that Kalugal cared whether he lived or died, but in case those at the front had not been affected by his command, he didn't want them to be alerted by the guard's fall.

"We are moving in," Max said in his earpiece.

"Stay here," Negal told Sylvia. "The Guardians will come get you once we have the compound secure."

She nodded. "Good luck, Negal. Bring Margo safely to the ship."

As the gods and the Guardians rushed by him, Kalugal proceeded at an easy pace toward the first guard. "Keep your hands on your head, get up, and lead me to your boss, Julio Modana," he commanded the guy.

The strength of his compulsion had the human drooling and glassy-eyed, but he complied with the command and walked toward a pair of French doors.

As soon as the guard opened the doors, Kalugal lifted the megaphone to his lips and repeated the command for everyone to lay down their weapons and go down on their knees in case someone hadn't heard his first command.

All the Guardians and the gods were wearing the specialty earpieces that William had developed especially to filter out his compulsion, so he didn't have to worry about them dropping their weapons in response to his commands.

"Get up," he told the guard who had dropped to his knees once again. "Take me to your boss."

As the guy started walking, the three gods entered through the glass doors and joined Kalugal. "The front of the house is secure."

Kalugal smiled. "Did my compulsion affect everyone?"

"So it would seem," Negal said.

"Excellent. Let's go talk to Señor Modana."

NEGAL

As the guard shuffled ahead, Negal followed Kalugal, with Aru and Dagor flanking him.

The place was lavish, and as they passed a pair of grand ornate doors, they entered a living room that was filled with expensive furniture and artwork that was probably original. The soaring ceilings were adorned with detailed moldings, and a large crystal chandelier was suspended from its center. The plush sofas and armchairs, though inviting, were a reminder of the comfort and security that Modana had built at the cost of so many lives.

It was ironic that such a beautiful space hid such ugliness. The money that paid for all that grandeur was tainted with blood and suffering.

As they passed a bar that was as big as that of any hotel, Negal's gaze was drawn to the array of spirits. He could use a drink, but he wouldn't touch anything in this place.

The journey through the house was a silent one, the only sound being the soft tread of their steps on the polished hardwood floor. The dining space they briefly passed was another display of excess, with its large, ornate table that was set up as if expecting a grand feast at any moment.

Finally, they reached the boss's office.

The transition was almost jarring. From the open, airy rooms to a space that was decidedly more utilitarian but no less luxurious. It was a command center, with a large, imposing desk dominating the center of the room. The walls were lined with bookshelves and portraits of Modana and his family, posing like royals in their finery, and cruel expressions on their faces.

At first, Negal thought that the guard had tricked them and that his boss wasn't there, but then he heard the rapid heart rate and shallow breathing coming from somewhere behind the enormous desk.

Peering over it, he was surprised to find a small-sized human kneeling on the hardwood floor, his balding head peeking from under his splayed fingers.

"There you are," Kalugal said in English as he sauntered to the chair Modana must have occupied when he had issued the command for everyone to lay down their weapons and go down on their knees.

"Julio Modana," Kalugal drawled. "What a lovely home you have." He shifted his eyes to the portraits on the walls. "Is that you over there?" He pointed. "You don't look that good from where I'm sitting. The artist did you a favor." He leaned down to look into the man's terrified eyes. "How does it feel to be helpless, Julio? Not so good, eh?"

The guy shook his head.

Kalugal's gaze shifted to a small statue of the Christian goddess, the Madonna. "She would be so disappointed in you, Julio. You've been a very naughty boy, and I'm here to deliver your punishment."

"Who are you?" Modana mumbled.

Kalugal smoothed a hand over his goatee. "Who do you think I am?"

"El Diablo," the boss muttered with a trembling lower lip. "The devil. But why does the devil speak English?"

Kalugal laughed, his laughter booming through the office. "What else would the devil be speaking?"

Negal stifled a chuckle. Kalugal was enjoying this, and he hated to spoil the guy's fun, but they were in a rush.

"El Diablo, forgive me for interrupting." Negal bowed his head mockingly. "But we don't have time for this sinner."

Kalugal laughed again and then leaned down to look Modana in the eyes. "I am indeed in a bit of a rush today, and I'm feeling merciful. I'll give you another chance at redemption, Julio. You will stop selling drugs and cease all of your illegal activities. From now on, you will be a philanthropist dedicated to the betterment of your people. There are several villages near Acapulco that suffered terribly from Cartel activity lately. Do you know anything about it?"

Modana nodded. "I had nothing to do with it. It was Carlos. He's not right in the head. He's dealing with these foreigners who are telling him to do bad things."

They had almost forgotten about the brother.

"Where is Carlos?" Kalugal asked.

"He's in Cabo, meeting with those foreigners. They are bad news, but he made a deal with them, and now it's too late."

"Too late for what?" Kalugal asked.

"Too late to get out of the deal."

Kalugal looked up at Aru. "I hoped we wouldn't have to do this, but we need to take out Carlos and those bad foreigners."

Negal shifted on his feet. "Later. We need to move out."

"Right." Kalugal returned his focus to Modana. "You will give money to these villagers that your brother wronged. You will build a school and a hospital, and you will give out scholarships to kids that do well in your new school and send them to college." He leaned even closer to the man. "I will be checking up on you, Julio. And if I find out that you were a bad boy, I won't give you another chance. Do you understand?"

"Yes, El Diablo. I do." The guy bobbed his head in gratitude.

"There is one more matter we need to settle, Julio. You're holding two women on your yacht against their wishes. I don't approve."

"I will let them go. I promise."

"Yes, you will, and you will do it right now. Where is your helicopter, Julio?"

"On the helipad."

"Get up slowly and lead us to it. We will retrieve the women." Kalugal tapped his earpiece. "I need the pilot."

55

MARINA

As Marina moved around the kitchen, the clink of cutlery and the soft rustle of packing materials was a relaxing soundtrack to her thoughts.

The lunch shift in the dining room was over, the tables were clean, the floor had been vacuumed, and all the dishes had been loaded into the dishwashers. The cooks were already starting to work on dinner, but she had an hour-long break until she needed to be back, and she wanted to spend it with Peter.

He hadn't come to the dining hall for lunch, so she assumed that he was still on duty. She also realized that she didn't have his phone number and he didn't have hers.

Her simple flip phone was a far cry from those fancy smartphones that were like mini-computers, but she could send and receive messages as long as it was with other people on the ship. Communication with the outside world was not permitted, but that was nothing new to her.

The same rules applied at Safe Haven.

The human former members of the Kra-ell compound knew too much to be allowed to roam free or communicate with whomever they pleased on the outside whenever they pleased. No one could erase a lifetime of memories, and the compulsion they were put under to keep the aliens a secret needed periodic reinforcement to stay effective.

Marina understood, but she still hoped that they would one day be allowed more freedom. After all, the students were allowed to attend universities, and to reinforce their compulsion, they had been required to return to the compound once a month. Now that their new home was Safe Haven, they only had to come back every three months.

If she were allowed the same freedom, perhaps she could've done something more with her life than being a maid.

The thing was, Marina had no idea what she would have done if she were free. She hadn't been exposed to enough experience to know what that thing was.

Perhaps the lack of communication had been one of the reasons that her relationship with Nicolai had fallen apart. They had exchanged letters, but knowing that they were being censored precluded any romantic declarations and made the entire thing awkward.

Besides, she wasn't good at expressing herself in writing, and neither was he, and seeing each other for one or two days a month just hadn't been enough to keep the flame alight.

Nicolai had hung in there for a long while, but eventually he'd replaced her with someone who was readily available to him at the university.

Why was she still thinking about him, though?

She'd managed to block thoughts of him for weeks, but now that she was entering a new relationship, she was examining all the ways in which things had gone wrong in the previous one.

But that was stupid.

Peter wasn't human, there was no future for them, and even if she figured out where things had gone wrong with Nicolai, it wouldn't teach her anything useful about keeping Peter.

In a way, it was liberating.

All she had to do was be herself, and if it worked, great, and if it didn't, then it wouldn't be a failure.

She couldn't fail without knowing the rules of engagement, right?

Except, her pragmatic nature refused to just let go and allow her to enjoy the moments of intimacy with Peter until the end of the cruise. Marina had a hard time accepting that she had no control over the situation and was powerless again to direct her own future.

Now that she thought about it, her plan to have him fall in love with her and invite her to live with him was like wishing for Prince Charming to come bearing the glass slipper or some other fairytale combination that even young girls didn't believe in.

She was supposed to be her own savior, and she was working on it. Significantly improving her English skills had been the first step, and the next was to enroll in an online school that would teach her something she could do online, like website design or maybe even translation work, but that was still far in the future.

With a sigh, she finished packing lunch into two cardboard boxes, put them inside a paper bag, and added two cold bottles of water before remembering that Peter was stationed on the Lido deck and could get all the drinks he wanted from Bob.

As she recalled their first meeting at the outdoor bar and how nervous she'd been, a smile lifted the corners of her lips.

Marina hadn't expected things to progress so quickly, but she didn't regret spending the night with Peter, even for a moment.

The sex had been phenomenal, but the memory she cherished the most from last night was how he had looked at her. It was as if he could see beyond the façade she was putting up for the world. How could a male she'd just met see her so clearly when the guy she'd dated for nearly two years hadn't?

It was also possible that she had imagined it.

Peter had figured out her kink without her having to tell him anything, but that wasn't difficult to do, and he also knew that she'd been held by the Kra-ell, but that was the extent of it.

Hefting the bag, she stepped into the elevator and leaned against the side wall. The thing stopped nearly on every floor as it ascended to the Lido deck, and more people got in until she was pushed to the very back of the cab.

Some of the immortals were casting her curious looks, but no one said anything to her or inquired why the human was riding the passenger elevator and not the service one.

Still, she couldn't help but feel like a trespasser, and as the elevator reached its final destination and all of its occupants spilled out, she took her first deep breath since the first stop.

When she walked out through the glass doors, the humid heat enveloped her, and for a moment it felt pleasant after the cool air-conditioned environment inside, but as she made her way through the deck searching for Peter, sweat gathered on the top of her lip and the back of her neck, and she used her hand to wipe it away.

Thankfully, a light breeze began, brushing against her face and cooling it.

When she spotted Peter, her heart skipped a beat, and as he turned to look at her and smiled, the beat accelerated.

"Hey," she greeted, extending the bag with the lunch she'd packed. "I didn't see you at lunch, and I thought we could eat out here."

He surprised her by pulling her to him and planting a kiss on her lips in front of everyone. "Thank you." His eyes danced with mirth as he took the bag from her. "Let's find a table."

PETER

No one had ever packed lunch for Peter before, and Marina's gesture warmed his heart. It was such a thoughtful thing to do.

Not even his own mother had done that for him.

Back when he was a kid they had been still living in the Scottish Highlands, and schooling was done by the mothers, who had taken turns teaching the clan kids. Classes had never lasted for more than a couple of hours a day, so there had been no need to pack lunch for school.

"Are you allowed to sit down?" Marina asked as he put the paper bag on the table.

"Of course."

The truth was that Peter had forgotten to signal Mathew that he was taking a break, so he pushed to his feet and waved at the guy. When he got a nod of approval back, he pulled out a chair for Marina and then sat down himself.

She glanced at Mathew, who was standing next to the railing on the other side of the pool. "I should have thought about bringing lunch for all the guards. Now I feel bad." She frowned. "I can give him mine, but then it wouldn't be fair to the others."

"Relax." Peter put a hand over hers. "They all ate already. They packed lunch during breakfast."

"Did you?" She looked embarrassed.

He shook his head. "I'm one of those dumb guys that never plans his meals ahead. If I'm full, I'm not thinking about getting hungry a few hours down the line."

"Good." Marina released a relieved breath. "I mean, it's not good that you don't plan ahead, but it's good that you haven't eaten yet." She smiled. "I was looking forward to sharing lunch with you."

He gave her hand a gentle squeeze. "You have no idea how much that means to me. No one has ever done that for me."

Her eyes widened. "No one has ever brought you lunch?"

"Nope." He opened the cardboard box and took out a beautifully wrapped sandwich. "Did you wrap it, or was it one of the cooks?"

"I did, why?"

"It looks like a present, including a red string for a ribbon."

Marina shrugged, but he could see that she liked his praise. "It's just parchment paper."

"I know. But how did you fold it like that?" He turned the sandwich this way and that, making a big deal of admiring the folds.

She chuckled. "If you start eating it instead of just looking at the wrapping, I'll teach you how to do it."

"You've got yourself a deal."

He carefully peeled the parchment away to reveal what was inside, and it was just as carefully prepared as the outside. The crust had been removed, and the slices were shaped into a perfect square and cut into two perfectly symmetrical triangles. In between was a thick layer of cold cuts, lettuce, tomato, and pickles.

Did she prepare all her sandwiches to look like that, or was it her way to show him that she cared?

"Take a bite," Marina encouraged.

He lifted one of the triangles to his mouth but didn't bite. "You said you will teach me how to do it. Start, and I'll bite."

"Fine." She rolled her eyes and pulled the paper he'd just removed toward her. Pulling out a napkin from the bag, she placed the remaining triangle on it to clear it. "You set the sheet of parchment paper in front of you and place the sandwich in the center."

She stopped and waited for him to take a bite. When he did and moaned his appreciation, she smiled and continued. "Bring the top and bottom edges to the center of the sandwich, line them up, and fold them by half an inch. Make a sharp crease and continue folding while creasing each time until the fold is flush with the sandwich."

Enjoying the dance of her slender fingers on the paper and the sound of her voice explaining what she was doing, Peter kept chewing and humming his approval.

Marina could have been talking about the snow melting in Karelia, and he would have found it fascinating.

She lifted her eyes to his, and seeing how rapt his attention was, continued her tutorial. "Use your fingers to press the opposing edges into the center. It will form a triangle, and you need to press down and crease its edges before tucking them underneath." She lifted the neat square she'd created. "That's it. The whole complicated process."

He finished chewing the last bite of the second triangle and took out a napkin to wipe his mouth. "That was delicious. Thank you for the sandwich and for the lesson, although I doubt I would do as nice of a job as you."

"I don't doubt it at all." She leaned to retrieve another container from the bag. "I knew that one wouldn't be enough for you. There are two more in there, each one different, and there is also dessert."

He pulled out the second sandwich and motioned at the one in front of her that she hadn't touched yet. "I kept you from eating your lunch."

"That's okay." She waved a hand. "I kept snacking on cold cuts and sliced veggies as I was making these. I'm not really hungry."

"You should eat." He leaned closer to her ear. "A woman can't survive on venom alone. You need to replenish your energy stores so we can enjoy ourselves again tonight."

He was surprised when a blush colored her cheeks.

"When does your shift end?" she asked.

"When the others return. I hope it will be in time for tonight's wedding. I want another dance with you."

She cocked a brow. "Just one dance?"

He took her hand and brought it to his lips for a kiss. "I want to dance the night away with you, but I know that you need to work."

"I can switch shifts," she murmured hesitantly.

"Then I'll be honored if you'd agree to be my date at the wedding tonight."

Marina's eyes widened as if she hadn't expected that. "I was just joking. I have nothing nice to wear to a wedding."

He had lived for long enough to know how to respond to that, but this time, he wouldn't be lying. "Anything you wear will look beautiful because it's you. You could make a burlap sack look chic."

Marina laughed. "You are such a charmer, Peter, but I like it. And I can probably do better than a burlap sack. I'll put something together."

"I have no doubt."

57

MARGO

"This is not so bad." Jasmine lifted her martini glass to her lips. "I don't mind lounging on the deck of a luxurious yacht and being served drinks and food."

Drinking while drugged was probably a bad idea, but they needed to pretend to still be under the influence, and the drugs were wearing off.

They had been served a delicious lunch cooked by the yacht's chef and delivered by one of the guards. Everyone was cordial to them, but Margo had caught the sneers.

The only reason no one was molesting them was that they now belonged to the cartel bosses, and the men were afraid to touch them.

Margo leaned back in the ridiculously comfortable armchair and closed her eyes. "It's so peaceful out here. I wish this voyage would never end, and we would never reach our destination, wherever it is."

"Puerto Vallarta," Alberto said. "That's odd." He looked up. "He wasn't supposed to come back. We were supposed to come to him." He cussed in Spanish under his breath. "He will be mad that you were just drugged." A new litany of curses spilled from his lips.

"Who is coming?" Jasmine asked.

"Señor Modana," one of the guards said. "Maybe he's impatient and wants to play with his new toy now."

Jasmine shuddered.

Margo followed Alberto's gaze and looked up at the sky. In the distance, a shape was steadily growing, but she was too loopy to focus her eyes. It wasn't until it was only a few hundred feet away that she realized it was a helicopter.

"Darth Vader arrives," Margo murmured. "Dah, dah, dum," she hummed an ominous sound.

"Come on," Alberto said. "He will be pleased if you are there to welcome him when he arrives."

He probably meant Jasmine, but Margo rose to her feet out of solidarity and walked toward the helipad with her friend.

Alberto stopped them from climbing the stairs to the level above. "That's close enough."

The landing pad was only a few feet higher than where they stood, so they could watch the arrival of the cartel boss. Not that she or Jasmine were looking forward to it, but Margo had never seen a helicopter up close, and she was curious.

The craft cut through the sky, its rotors churning the air and sending a powerful gust across the deck, causing Margo's hair to whip around her face.

It looked like a high-end model, its glossy black exterior gleaming in the waning sunlight. There was some insignia on the side, but she didn't know what it meant.

The pilot skillfully maneuvered the helicopter towards the helipad, making the descent smooth, and then it hovered for a moment above the helipad before gently touching down. The rotors slowed, their deafening whirr diminishing to a low hum, and then, finally, there was silence.

Margo held her breath as the door to the helicopter opened. She knew that whoever was about to step out would hold the key to her and Jasmine's fate.

The setting sun cast long shadows across the deck, adding a dramatic flare to the unscheduled arrival, and as one of the men rushed to open the door, Margo held her breath, praying it was Julio and not Carlos.

So yeah, it was selfish of her, but Alberto had said that Julio treated his women well, and Carlos didn't, so there was that.

The figure emerging from the helicopter matched what she'd imagined the elder Modana looked like. He was short, pudgy, and balding, but instead of wearing a fierce and intimidating expression, he looked like he was either scared or confused.

Margo frowned. She hadn't seen Modana when he'd been in her and Jasmine's cabin, but she'd heard him, and he'd sounded haughty and condescending. Perhaps he'd gotten some bad news?

Would it be too much to hope for that the bad news was the demise of his cruel brother?

Her musings came to an abrupt halt when the next guy stepped out of the helicopter. He was one of the most gorgeous men she'd ever seen, and he had a megaphone in his hand.

That was odd. What did he intend to do with it?

"That's not Carlos, right?" she whispered.

Looking stunned, Alberto didn't answer.

The hottie lifted the megaphone to his lips. "Lay all of your weapons down, get on your knees, and put your hands over your heads."

The command reverberated through her body, and in the next moment, Margo found herself kneeling on the deck with her hands on her head. Next to her, Jasmine and Alberto were doing the same, and so were all of Modana's men, including Modana himself.

"You can get up." The gorgeous man tapped Modana's shoulder. "Tell your men to relax and obey my commands."

Was that magic?

Or was the megaphone some kind of a new weapon that took people's will away and made them obey orders? If so, it was a very dangerous weapon but also very useful in the right hands.

As the megaphone wielder moved aside, another man jumped out of the helicopter, and if she thought that the previous guy was the most gorgeous man she'd ever seen, she now had to revise her assessment because the tall blond was the stuff of fantasies come to life.

"How can you be so stunningly perfect?" she murmured under her breath.

As if he'd heard her, the man turned to look at her, his intense blue eyes boring straight into her soul.

Margo couldn't breathe.

The world tilted, and she was falling, and then there was nothing.

58

NEGAL

Negal recognized Margo right away. She had obeyed Kalugal's command like everyone else on the yacht and was kneeling on the spot, but there was something wrong with her. Her expression indicated shock, and she was swaying on her knees.

When she started to topple sideways, he used his incredible speed to jump from the helipad down to the deck below and catch her before she could hit the deck.

Lifting her into his arms, he walked over to one of the armchairs and sat down.

She was so much smaller than what he'd imagined, and her scent was off, but she was also much more beautiful than the picture he'd seen on Frankie's phone.

Her paleness worried him, and so did the dark circles under her eyes. Some of it was the fault of old, smeared mascara, but the wrongness of her scent indicated disease.

Kalugal walked over and crouched next to him. "What's the matter with her?"

"I don't know, but her scent is off. Can you smell it?"

Kalugal leaned closer, sniffed, and grimaced. "Drugs." He looked at the human male kneeling a few feet away and snarled, "I bet it's his doing." Kalugal pushed to his feet and walked over to where the other woman was kneeling and sniffed her. "She was drugged, too."

Negal tensed. "Is Margo in danger?"

Kalugal returned and crouched next to them again. "Margo's heart rate is normal, and she is breathing fine. Perhaps the drugs combined with the surprise of our arrival were too much for her after all she's been through. She probably just needs a few moments."

Negal didn't know anything about human physiology, but Kalugal's wife used to be a human before she'd transitioned, so he must be knowledgeable on the subject, and he didn't look concerned.

Kalugal shifted his gaze to the other woman, still kneeling with her hands over her head. "Jasmine, you are free to move as you wish."

The woman got to her feet and trained a pair of large brown eyes on him that were a little unfocused and glazed over. "How did you know my name?"

Kalugal smiled. "A little birdie told me." He turned to look at the human male kneeling a couple of feet away. "Is that your scumbag boyfriend?"

"He's not my boyfriend," Jasmine said. "But he is a scumbag." She giggled. "Why am I not mad at him? I should be fuming. It's the damn drugs." She giggled again. "Who are you?"

Kalugal smiled. "If I were single, I would tell you that I'm your knight in shining armor, but I'm taken, so you can think of me as the nice guy who came to rescue Margo and you. You can call me Kevin."

Negal didn't know why Kalugal was bothering with a fake name. In a few hours, Jasmine would board the ship and hear everyone calling him Kalugal.

"Nice to meet you, Kevin." She gave him a dazzling smile. "Are you with the ship that was supposed to pick up Margo in Cabo?"

"Yes, we are."

"Then I'll happily take your offer and hitch a ride back home with you." She turned her eyes to the chopper. "But I don't know whether I want to get there in that."

"You will not." Kalugal patted her shoulder. "We are staying on the yacht for now."

"Why?"

"Because I have work to do." He pointed his finger at Alberto. "You, get up and follow me."

The scumbag rose to his feet like his body was obeying Kalugal's commands and not his own, which was precisely what was happening.

Compulsion was such a useful tool. No wonder the Eternal King hoarded it for his family. The excuse was that compulsion ability couldn't be genetically engineered, but that was just one more lie in the many lies the king was spreading. Everything could be boiled down to genetics, including intelligence and even sexual proclivities.

Jasmine turned to look at him. "Where is he taking Alberto?"

"Don't worry. He's not going to kill him."

"I'm not worried. I'm just curious."

Negal had a feeling that Jasmine was incapable of worrying about anything in her drugged state. "Kevin is going to have a talk with all the men."

"Oh." She walked over and sat down on one of the other outdoor armchairs. "You and Kevin are such gorgeous men. You could play the roles of knights in movies." She crossed her long, tanned legs.

Was she flirting with him? Usually, when women commented on his looks, it was to hint that they were interested.

"I'm taken too," he said.

"I wasn't trying to flirt with you." She giggled. "That's a lie. I totally was. She's a lucky girl, but she might get jealous when she finds out you were holding another woman in your arms like she was your most precious possession."

What in the seven hells was he supposed to say to that?

He wasn't really taken, was he?

And if he was, it was by the woman in his arms, who didn't even know that he existed.

Negal swallowed. "It's fine." The expression covered a lot of different situations, and he hoped it was good enough for this one as well.

Jasmine shifted her eyes to Margo. "Is she okay? Maybe you should take her to see a doctor?"

"Kevin said that she would be fine. She just needs a few moments."

Jasmine tilted her head. "Is Kevin a doctor?"

"No, he's not." Negal tightened his hold on Margo.

What if Jasmine was right?

"Do you have a doctor on the cruise ship?" she asked.

"Yes, we do."

"Then maybe you should take Margo there in that helicopter," Jasmine suggested. "Or you could take her to a nearby hospital, whichever is closer."

She sounded much more lucid than she appeared, so maybe the drugs were wearing off already.

He had to admit that her suggestion had merit.

The helicopter was a four-person small craft that could possibly squeeze in one more, but they had decided to stay on the yacht until it reached the *Silver Swan*.

Negal had negotiated hard to be the only one other than the pilot and Kalugal to accompany Modana to the yacht. The rest of their team had stayed behind to deal with Modana's men and put them through a crash re-education course that was supposed to put them on the right path to assist their boss's new humanitarian endeavors.

He wondered whether it would work, but he couldn't fault the clan for trying to minimize bloodshed. Modana's men were all seasoned killers, but they hadn't committed the kind of atrocities that their counterparts in Acapulco had, so perhaps they were still capable of salvation.

Margo stirred in his arms, and a moment later, she opened her eyes and stared up at him. "Am I dead?"

59

MARGO

Margo was looking at the face of an angel, which meant that she was dead.

Evidently, she'd been wrong about there being no heaven or hell, and she had somehow ended up in heaven.

She hadn't been a bad person, but she hadn't been a very good one either. Or had she? If being good meant volunteering in homeless shelters or donating money to charity, then she hadn't been particularly good because she had done neither. But if being good meant not doing evil, then she qualified.

But wasn't she supposed to go through a trial before being admitted to heaven? There was supposed to be a review of all the bad and good deeds she'd done throughout her life.

The angel frowned. "Why do you think you are dead?"

He sounded a little hoarse as if he had been shouting, or maybe he was thirsty, but angels did none of that. He also smelled of seawater and clean male sweat, and that, too, was something angels didn't do.

"You're not an angel, are you?"

The smile he gave her was so bright that it was blinding. "You thought that I was an angel?"

She lifted her hand to shield her eyes. "You are bright like an angel, but you don't sound like one, and you smell a little sweaty. Not in a bad way, but not in an angelic way."

He laughed, and now she was convinced again that he was an angel because the sound was so beautiful that it stirred something in her soul.

Margo had always believed that music was a portal to the divine, the one thing that made humans superior to animals, and the guy's laughter sounded like the best melody.

Frowning again, he dipped his head and sniffed at his armpit. "I do smell a little. But I assure you that I'm not bright, and I don't have a glow. I'm not a royal."

That was such an odd thing to say. "Royals don't glow."

"They do where I come from."

"And where is that?"

"Portugal."

He said that with a straight face, but it must have been a joke, something about Portugal being a monarchy? Margo had never heard it before, so she didn't laugh. She also suddenly realized that she was staring into his impossibly gorgeous face because he was holding her in his arms.

"Why are you holding me?"

"You fainted."

Somewhere nearby a woman laughed, and as Margo shifted her eyes toward the sound, she recognized the olive-skinned beauty on her left. "Jasmine."

"Yeah, that's still me, and Mr. Angel over there flew like he had wings all the way from the helipad down here to catch you before you fell. I've never seen anyone move that fast." She leaned closer so her face was hovering a few inches above Margo's. "Maybe he has invisible wings that only other angels can see."

"My name is Negal, and I'm not what you call an angel. You only think that you saw me moving so fast because of the drugs. You've both been drugged."

"How do you know that?" Margo asked. "Is it that obvious?"

"I can smell the drugs on you."

"Oh." Jasmine's lips twisted in distaste. "I didn't know they had a smell."

Margo hadn't known that either, and she was mortified that the stunning stranger was smelling her foul smell. "You can let go now. I'm okay."

"Are you sure?" Instead of loosening, his grip on her tightened. "You look very pale."

She wasn't sure of anything, and being held by him felt heavenly even if he wasn't an angel, which she still wasn't convinced was the case.

Could angels lie?

It didn't seem right, given that lying was bad and angels were supposed to be good, but if they were sent to save people on Earth and needed to conceal their identity, lying would be necessary, right?

Except, there was one more thing that angels weren't supposed to do, and the one holding her was definitely doing. She could feel his erection hardening beneath her, and as she shifted a little in his arms, it got harder still.

"What kind of a name is Negal?" Jasmine asked. "I've never met anyone with that name. Is it Portuguese?"

"It's an old name that runs in my family." He didn't even look at Jasmine when he answered her, which pleased Margo.

In fact, it would have pleased her even more if Jasmine had gone away and left her alone with Negal. She was suddenly very possessive of her naughty angel, and she wanted to find out more about him.

"I'm a little warm." Margo put a hand on her forehead. "And I still feel a little faint. Is there a chance you could take me to the salon below? They probably have water in the bar's refrigerator." She lifted a finger to Negal's lips. "You seem thirsty."

His eyes flared with a glow that was for sure heavenly. "You are correct. I am a little thirsty." He pushed to his feet with her still in his arms, effortlessly as if she weighed nothing, and started walking but then stopped. "Where am I going?"

"I'll show you," Jasmine said.

Margo stifled a wince. Her plot to be alone with Negal hadn't worked. Was she a bad person for wanting him all to herself?

Was it a test, and she was failing it because she wanted Jasmine to go away?

Jaz was her friend, and Margo got herself into this mess to help her. So maybe she was allowed a little selfishness.

Winding her arms around Negal's neck, she looked at his glowing eyes and wondered whether it was the drugs' fault. If it wasn't, then all she'd believed about angels had been wrong, and the romance books she'd read about naughty angels who seduced human women or were seduced by them had been right.

60

NEGAL

The salon turned out to be occupied.

That was where Kalugal had taken Modana and his men, including the boyfriend. Negal still planned to punch the guy in the face for kidnapping Margo, even if he had done them all a favor by distancing her from the Doomers.

Worrying about what was being done to Margo had cost Negal a few centuries of his immortal life, and he thanked the Fates that she was mostly unharmed.

It was a miracle that the cartel bosses who had claimed both her and Jasmine had been busy and that no one had forced themselves on the women.

As the three of them passed through the room, Kalugal smiled at them and waved them on before returning his focus to Modana and his men.

The immortal was using his compulsion to reeducate Modana's men and continue his education of the cartel boss himself. The idea was to turn the ruthless killers into do-gooders and to spread misinformation that would reach the ears of the Brotherhood and get them off the clan's tracks. Both were lofty goals, but if anyone had a chance of achieving them, it was Kalugal.

Negal was glad that Onegus had chosen Kalugal to accompany them on the mission and asked Toven to remain on the ship.

He doubted that Toven would have been able to do what Kalugal was doing. The royal was too much of a straight shooter and an idealist. Kalugal, on the other hand, was a creative storyteller who didn't concern himself too much with the truth.

"Is there anywhere else we can go?" Negal asked Jasmine.

She shrugged. "Margo and I went through several areas on our way to the top deck, but I don't remember much of it." She lifted a hand to her forehead. "It was hard to think straight. Let's just keep walking until we find somewhere comfortable to sit." She cast him a sidelong glance. "Unless you are tired of carrying Margo. She must be getting heavy."

"Not at all." He hoisted his precious cargo higher on his chest so her face was closer to his, and he could feel her breath fanning over his skin. "She's practically weightless."

Margo giggled softly. "Thank you. That was the right answer."

He looked down at her. "I didn't know that I was being tested."

She lifted her face to him with a sweet smile. "Don't you know that you are judged on every word you say?"

"By whom?"

"Women," Jasmine said. "We try to determine a man's worth by testing him in every way we can, but I totally suck at it. I fell for Alberto's fake charm."

"He was a scam artist," Margo said. "You should stop beating yourself up over this."

"No, he was right about that. It was stupid of me." Jasmine kept walking, with Negal following.

"The blind leading the blind," Margo murmured into his chest. "She has no idea where she's going."

"Yes, I do." Jasmine looked at them over her shoulder. "If we can't find a good place, we can go back to our cabin."

"It's cramped and crappy." Margo shifted so she could look around. "Let's find the master bedroom suite. I bet it's amazing."

Jasmine snorted. "Do you have naughty ideas for the three of us?"

"Dream on, girl. Negal is mine." She gasped, and her cheeks reddened. "Did I just say that?"

"You certainly did." Call him a peacock and give him glorious tail feathers to spread because that's how he felt right now.

"I'm sorry." She buried her face in his chest. "It's the drugs talking. Don't pay attention to anything I say."

"I liked what you said."

"You don't know me, and I don't know you. You are not mine any more than you are Jasmine's."

"I'll take him," Jaz said.

"We are both drugged." Margo cast her friend a glare. "Her inhibitions are also compromised. You shouldn't listen to either of us."

"What's over here?" Jasmine pushed a door open. "Oh, look. It's the kitchen."

As Negal followed her inside, the smells assaulted his senses, and his stomach growled, reminding him that he hadn't eaten anything since the wedding last night.

"Someone's hungry." Margo laughed. "Put me down, and let's get something to eat."

There were two barstools in the large kitchen, but Negal had no problem eating while standing. He gently lowered Margo to one of the stools and held on to her until he was certain that she wasn't going to tip over.

As Jasmine walked over to the stove and started lifting lids and sniffing the food, a door opened, and a guy in a white coat brandished a gun at them.

"Put up your hands," he said in heavily accented English.

Wondering how the guy had managed to evade Kalugal's compulsion, Negal reached into his mind and changed his perception of what was happening.

They weren't intruders or hostiles taking over his boss's yacht. They were distinguished invited guests, and what was happening in the salon was an important business meeting. Negal also added that the cook should feed them.

"I'm so sorry." The guy lowered his gun and bowed. "I've made a terrible mistake, *señor y señoras*. Let me serve you dinner."

"I'll take that gun." Negal extended his hand.

"Of course, *señor*." The cook rushed over and put the gun in his hand. "Please, make yourself comfortable in the dining room. The kitchen is not the proper place for the distinguished guests of Señor Modana."

61

MARGO

"How did you do that?" Margo asked as Negal lifted her into his arms again. "And I can walk."

"Not yet." He carried her out to the dining room. "I don't want you falling over and hurting yourself."

"That's very kind of you, but you didn't answer my question. How did you make the cook lower his gun and give it to you?"

"I didn't do anything." Negal lowered her into the chair that Jasmine had pulled out for her. "He must have realized that he knew the two of you, and you were Modana's guests."

"What about you? He didn't know you."

"I was with you." Negal treated her to a brilliant smile that took her breath away.

"So, Negal." Jasmine unfurled a cloth napkin and spread it over her lap. "How did you know where to find us?"

It seemed that Jasmine was doing better with the narcotics. She didn't seem as loopy as she was before. Margo still didn't know what kind of drugs Alberto had used on them, and even if she did know, she didn't have her phone with her to search the internet for advice about shaking off the effects.

Negal hesitated for a long moment, then looked around the dining room and shook his head. "I'd better not say. There might be hidden cameras or voice recorders in here."

"Is it such a great secret?" Jasmine said in a teasing tone that grated on Margo's nerves.

She'd really liked the woman until Negal showed up, and suddenly Jasmine started acting like a floozy and flirting with him.

Well, Jasmine wasn't really acting like a floozy, and Margo wasn't sure that she was even trying to flirt with him, but she suddenly felt very possessive over a guy she had no business feeling possessive over.

He was a gorgeous stranger, chivalrous, kind, and intelligent, but that was no reason to act as if he belonged to her.

The thing was, Negal was like one of the supernatural heroes in her romance novels, and he checked all of her boxes and then some, but it must be a fantasy that she was creating in her head.

He was just a good-looking guy who'd saved her, and she was having a damsel in distress moment, fawning over her savior.

"Perhaps I can tell you some of it." Negal reached for the napkin and mimicked Jasmine's move, unfurling it and draping it over his lap. "Mia called Margo, and when Margo didn't answer, Mia got worried and called the sister-in-law, who was partying at a club at the time. When she returned to the hotel, she checked Margo's room, and when she didn't find her, she called hotel security. Hotel security performed a perfunctory search and informed the sister-in-law that she should contact the police after Margo had been missing for more than twenty-four hours. Mia suspected that your so-called boyfriend had something to do with Margo's disappearance, and she told us what Margo had suspected him of. She also remembered that Margo told her that you were staying at the penthouse. We used the services of a hacker to hack into the hotel's surveillance server and check the footage from the camera across the penthouse door. We saw a waiter deliver dinner, and a couple of hours later, the same waiter returned with a laundry cart and another staff member with an additional cart."

"I knew it," Margo exclaimed. "I knew they would use a laundry cart. It's just like in the movies."

Negal nodded. "The two left the penthouse with the laundry carts, and a short time after that, the boyfriend emerged with two pieces of luggage. The hacker followed him from one camera to the next until he saw him get into a large SUV. He didn't see you being loaded into the vehicle because they were careful to do it out of sight of the camera at the loading dock, but we assumed that you were there. The hacker followed the vehicle through the street cameras until it stopped at the yacht club. From there, it was easy to find out who the yacht belonged to, where he lived, and therefore where the yacht was heading to."

Jasmine shook her head. "It's like a James Bond movie. How did a bunch of computer nerds know to do all that?"

Margo chuckled. "Don't you know that geeks and nerds rule the modern world? And these particular computer nerds make the most amazing virtual adventures, which means that they have great imaginations. No wonder they solved the mystery. We are so incredibly lucky." She shivered. "I expected the worst. Alberto said that Carlos was cruel to his women, and I was to be his pet. If not for the drugs keeping me feeling like I could conquer the world, I would have probably thrown myself overboard and drowned. Death would have been better than that fate."

NEGAL

At Margo's words, fury washed over Negal, and as his fangs started elongating, he slapped a hand over his mouth. "Excuse me," he mumbled as he shot to his feet.

"What happened?" Margo lifted a pair of worried eyes to him.

Knowing that his eyes were probably glowing, he averted his gaze. "I need to find the bathroom." He rushed out of the dining room.

Finding the bathroom was easy, and after ducking inside, Negal locked the door and leaned against it.

Damn. This hadn't happened to him in a long while. He'd been trained to control his reactions, and he didn't allow his fangs to act on their own accord among humans. Perhaps it had been the time he had spent among immortals where he hadn't needed to hide his godly features that had weakened that mental muscle.

Walking up to the sink, he didn't bother looking into the mirror as he turned on the faucet and gathered water in his palms to splash over his face. After taking a few long breaths, he managed to retract his fangs, and when he finally looked at the mirror, his eyes didn't glow.

He took the opportunity to empty his bladder, washed his hands, and after several additional long breaths, opened the door and returned to the dining room.

While he'd been gone, the chef had served dinner, but neither Jasmine nor Margo were eating. They were waiting for him, he realized.

"I'm sorry. Something must have disagreed with my stomach." He lifted the napkin that had fallen on the floor when he'd made his hasty exit.

Margo smiled. "Now I know for sure that you are really a man and not an angel. Angels don't get upset stomachs."

Neither did he, but he couldn't tell her that. "Thank you for waiting for me." He draped the napkin over his lap. When neither of the women picked up their forks, he frowned. "Is there a special blessing over the meal that needs to be said?"

"Not unless you want to." Margo looked at Jasmine. "Do you want to say anything?"

Jasmine shrugged. "Thanks to the chef?" She waved a hand at the bottle of wine. "We should make a toast to our savior." She smiled at Negal. "We were waiting for you to uncork the wine. The chef just put it on the table without opening it. Usually, whoever serves the wine does the honors."

Margo chuckled. "Not on a yacht owned by a cartel boss. He probably doesn't drink anything that he didn't open himself."

"Good point." Jasmine let out a breath. "I didn't suspect Alberto of anything, so I didn't watch him open the wine bottle, and that was how he got us. He put something into the wine. Probably a roofie."

"What's a roofie?" Negal reached for the bottle, found the opener, and uncorked the wine.

"It's a drug that makes the victim sleepy," Margo said. "It's usually tasteless, and unscrupulous men spike unsuspecting women's drinks to take advantage of them."

Negal commanded his fangs to stay dormant and poured the wine into their three glasses. "I will kill him for you."

Margo's eyes widened. "Are you serious?"

He wasn't sure how he was supposed to answer that. "I want to kill him, but if it will displease you, I won't."

"He's just a maggot." Margo lifted her wine glass. "He's not worth tainting your soul for." She put the glass down without drinking.

Negal took a sip of the wine to refrain from saying that getting rid of vermin would by no means taint him in any way. Margo and Jasmine might have been through a terrifying ordeal, but thankfully, they hadn't seen true evil. If they had, Margo might have had a different view on things.

"Let's make a toast." Jasmine lifted her glass. "To our saviors, who arrived in the nick of time."

That reminded Negal that he hadn't arrived alone, and that the clan pilot and Kalugal were probably hungry as well. "I should tell Kal—I mean Kevin to join us."

Margo put her fork down. "He seemed busy." She frowned. "I wonder how he made all those tough guards obey his command. Come to think of it, why did Jasmine and I drop to our knees as well? We knew that he wasn't talking to us, and yet it was like my body was under his control, obeying his commands and not my own."

"Hypnosis," Negal said the first thing that came to his mind. "Kevin is a powerful hypnotist."

He would have to thrall both women and muddle their memories of what they had witnessed.

Margo grimaced. "That's a very dangerous trick. I'll stay away from that one." She picked up her fork. "Let's eat."

Negal cut a piece off the fragrant roast. "Kevin is a good guy. He only uses his hypnotic power for good."

"Well, thank you." Kalugal walked into the room with the pilot by his side. "I could smell this roast all the way from the salon, and I was salivating. The last meal I had was at the wedding last night."

63

MARGO

The drug must have further worn off, and Margo was starting to feel more like her old skeptical self again.

The third guy who had come with Kevin was nearly as good-looking as his two friends, and that just didn't make sense. What kind of an outfit employed only gorgeous guys?

Frankie had said that her guy looked like a god, and Margo had thought that she was exaggerating, but if he looked anything like these three, then Frankie was right.

"What did you do with Modana and his men?" Negal asked Kevin.

"I left them to contemplate their past and their future." Kevin lifted the small bell that Margo hadn't noticed before and shook it a couple of times.

The chef emerged from the kitchen and frowned at the new guest.

"Please be a good chap and bring out two more plates for me and my friend."

He'd said please, but Margo noted the hypnotic undertones in his voice. Except this time, she hadn't felt compelled to do his bidding as she had the first time. Perhaps it was because he'd addressed the chef as chap, which was obviously not directed at her.

The chef wrung his hands. "Of course, *señor*. Will Señor Modana be joining you?"

"No. He and his men will be dining later."

As the chef dipped his head and scurried into the kitchen, Kevin shifted his gaze to Jasmine and then to Margo. "You two seem to be a little more alert. Are the drugs wearing off?"

"I think so," Margo said. "I know that Alberto was trying to get us addicted, but I hope one dose is not enough to do that. I don't know anyone who's had to go through withdrawal, but if it's as bad as they portray it in movies, then it's nasty."

Jasmine nodded. "I hate to admit it, but I miss the euphoria. Now all I feel is sad." She pouted prettily, and Margo gritted her teeth.

What was happening to her?

She'd never been the jealous type, and she liked Jasmine, but now she was getting angry every time the woman flaunted her superior beauty and allure.

Thankfully, Negal seemed indifferent to her charms, and Kevin seemed amused. The only one who was affected was the third guy, whom no one had bothered to introduce.

Jasmine must have noticed the same thing because she turned her dazzling smile on the guy. "Your friends were remiss and didn't introduce you."

"Edgar, or Ed. I'm the helicopter pilot."

"Nice to meet you, Ed."

"It's a pleasure to make your acquaintance." Ed inclined his head.

Jasmine affected a gasp and put her hand over her chest. "Such beautiful manners you have, Ed."

He laughed. "I would make a Little Red Riding Hood joke, but given the circumstances, I shouldn't."

"Yeah." Jasmine's smile wilted. "I've already met the big bad wolf."

As the two continued talking, Margo was glad that Jasmine was focusing her attention on the pilot instead of flirting with Negal.

The door to the kitchen opened, and the chef came out carrying a tray with two more plates and place settings. While he served the two new dinner guests, Margo thought about what Kevin had said a few moments ago in regard to Modana and his men.

What had he meant by them contemplating their past and future? Had he hypnotized them?

She'd heard that hypnosis was a powerful tool that could be used in therapeutic ways. Was that what Kevin had meant?

Margo waited for the chef to be done and return to the kitchen before turning to Kevin. "Did you use hypnosis on the cartel boss and his men?"

Kevin shot Negal a glance, and Negal nodded, confirming that he had told them about it. "Margo wondered how you were able to make the guards obey your command so readily. I told her that you are a powerful hypnotist."

"Yes." Kevin draped a napkin over his pants. "I am. Hypnosis can be used to address various psychological and medical issues. It can help manage pain, reduce anxiety, treat phobias, and address other behavioral or emotional concerns." He smiled. "In this case, it addressed criminality, which is a deviant behavior. After a couple of sessions, Modana and his men will become the good men their mothers had hoped they would be."

Negal chuckled. "Who said that their mothers wanted that? Perhaps they wanted their sons to be the meanest, baddest criminals around?"

Margo thought about that for a long moment. "In some societies, that might be true. Not everyone has the same values that we hold sacred. Some mothers encourage their sons to become murderers."

Jasmine looked incredulous. "What mother would wish for such a thing and why?"

The woman was really naive or just uninformed. "Religion for one, social pressure for another. Some religions glorify death, and as it happens, those same religions discriminate against women and deprive them of basic rights that you and I take for granted. One of the few ways women can get respect in these societies is to encourage their children to become murderers for the cause."

Across the table, Kevin groaned. "Let's change the subject before I lose my appetite." He smiled at Jasmine. "Tell us a little about yourself. What do you do for a living?"

Ugh, why had she had to open her big mouth and spout depressing stuff?

Margo cast a quick look at Negal, but he smiled at her with affection, so perhaps he didn't mind that she was the glass-half-empty kind of girl.

"I'm an actress," Jasmine said. "I've been cast in a few commercials, and I even got a nice chunk of money for it, but since the roles are unreliable, I continue working in customer service to pay the bills, and what I get from the occasional commercial, I put in my savings account."

"That's smart." Kevin shifted his gaze to Margo. "And you?"

"I work at an advertising agency and hate every moment of it. I can't wait for Mia's boyfriend to get me the job he promised Frankie and me at Perfect Match Virtual Studios. For starters, I'll work at beta testing the new adventures you guys come up with, and then I hope to get promoted to the advertising department. They are doing amazingly well with their commercials, but I have a few ideas on how to improve on that."

Jasmine's eyes widened. "Can you get me a job there as well? I mean in the commercials. I'm not sure I would be good as a beta tester, but I can be a spokeswoman or a participant who describes her experience."

Kevin lifted his hands. "I'm not affiliated with the Perfect Match Studios. You will have to talk to Mia's fiancé."

Margo frowned. "I thought everyone on board was a Perfect Match employee."

"Not everyone." Kevin cut off a piece of the roast. "Some of us are just friends and family."

Very capable friends and family who had managed to take down a cartel boss and rescue two kidnapped women.

Margo regarded the three men.

They looked like models or actors, and if not for what Kevin had just said, she would have assumed that they worked on the production side of Perfect Match. They could have been former Navy SEALs or some other commando unit turned actors.

But according to Kevin, they didn't work for Perfect Match.

Mia had told her and Frankie that the owners of Perfect Match were very reclusive and lived in a secluded compound. She'd also said that they had security on board, which was what these men most likely were.

But why would Kevin say that they were friends and family instead of admitting that they were security?

And what was the deal with how gorgeous they were? Had they been chosen for their good looks or their combat skills?

Something was fishy about these men and about the cruise.

64

KIAN

"Good evening, Mother." Kian leaned to kiss his mother's cheek.

She shifted on the couch, motioning for him to sit beside her. "Thank you for coming over to give me an update in person."

He'd considered calling her, but there was no justification for that, given that her cabin was just down the hallway from his.

"I'll have to make it short because there is still much to do."

"Of course."

"As you have probably guessed, we are not heading to Cabo. We are making a detour and stopping at Puerto Vallarta instead. Hopefully, that will confuse the

Doomers, and they won't figure out which ship we are on."

She tilted her head. "You will have to explain your logic, my son, because I do not understand how changing ports will achieve that."

"From what they got out of the tour guide, they learned that he collected his passengers at the port, so they might suspect that we are traveling by ship. They also learned from him that we were supposed to collect a woman from the hotel in Cabo. Margo didn't keep it a secret that she was joining a cruise, and she probably told a number of people about it. The Doomers no doubt interrogated some of the staff and guests and learned who she was. When Margo went missing, we were afraid that they had taken her and were holding her hostage like they did with Luis, but that wasn't what happened. In a way, we were lucky that she befriended a woman in the hotel and got caught up in a plot to kidnap and deliver the other woman to a certain cartel boss, who happened to reside in Puerto Vallarta. I don't want to go into all the details, but thanks to Roni's hacking, we were able to find out what happened to her, and since we were close to Puerto Vallarta, we were able to storm the boss's mansion, get him on his helicopter, fly to the yacht where the women were being held and rescue them." He smiled. "Kalugal compelled the boss to change his ways and become a philanthropist, and he's re-educating the boss's men as we speak. The killers will become do-gooders."

Annani's smile was hesitant. "I love it, provided that this boss and his men were not involved in the atrocities. People like that do not deserve a second chance."

"I agree. None of them are nice people, and they have killed plenty, but there are degrees of evil, and they didn't cross that line." He raked his fingers through his hair. "I'm not a vigilante, and it's not my job to get rid of every thug there is. I limit myself to the worst offenders."

She nodded. "I taught you well, my son."

"I wish I could take credit for this plan, but it was Turner's idea. If we killed Modana and his men, the rest of the cartel would have chased after us, and that was in addition to the Doomers. This way, they won't know what hit them. Kalugal used a combination of compulsion and thralling to convince Modana that the Madonna herself had spoken to him and his men and demanded that they change their ways. Nothing will connect Modana's religious awakening to us. Once Kalugal's done, he will erase the entire episode from their memories, and they won't even remember having Margo and her friend on board."

"That is very smart, but what about the Doomers? They might access the same surveillance cameras that Roni did and follow the breadcrumbs to Modana. They will know what caused his so-called religious awakening."

"Even if they had a capable hacker like Roni, which they don't, they wouldn't have thought to check the penthouse surveillance camera feeds, which is where Margo and Jasmine were when they were drugged and kidnapped. They would have only searched those next to Margo's room. But just in case they do get smart, Roni took care of that footage. He replaced those sections of the recordings with the nothing special footage from before and after."

His mother shook her head. "I have a feeling that we are missing something. It cannot be as easy as that."

Kian sighed. "I know. I was contemplating evacuating the ship and flying everyone home, but that would have been so disappointing for the rest of the couples who were planning a cruise wedding. We will stay in Puerto Vallarta for the night and stay on high alert, watching out for the Doomers." He smiled. "Vlad and Wendy will have their wedding tonight after all."

"I am pleased." His mother patted his hand. "Vlad did not know whether he should have his bachelor party, but his friends convinced him to have it even if the wedding was canceled. Wendy is with the girls and her mother, getting pampered just like the other brides."

"Good. I should let them know that it looks like their wedding is happening." Kian pushed to his feet. "The wedding will have to take place late at night, though. We still need to collect Margo and her friend from the yacht, along with Kalugal, Negal, and Edgar. Once we reach Puerto Vallarta, we will pick up the rest of our people."

He rubbed the back of his neck. "Edgar flew Modana, Kalugal, and Negal to the yacht in Modana's helicopter. I could have asked him to fly the women over here and go back, but I don't want anything connecting us with the yacht or the helicopter. We will send a lifeboat to collect our people from the yacht, so if the Doomers or anyone else is watching the signals the vessels are broadcasting, they won't see us stopping next to one another."

Annani nodded sagely. "Very well. What time should I tell Amanda to plan Vlad and Wendy's wedding?"

"Ten-thirty should be fine."

NEGAL

Negal spent the rest of dinner in silence, pretending to listen to the others gushing over the wonders of Perfect Match. It was old technology on Anumati, and every interstellar ship was equipped with several chambers that were used for training as well as for entertainment.

No special helmets or wiring were required, and it was as simple as choosing a scenario and walking through a door.

He had done hundreds of those if not thousands, and if these people needed ideas for new adventures, he could provide them with plenty. The problem was that they would have no reference for the different worlds and creatures that he had seen firsthand and then experienced virtually.

Casting a sidelong glance at Margo, he wondered if she would have been brave enough to join him on those adventures. She was brave, as evidenced by her jumping in to help a woman she had just met. But on the other hand, she was reserved, almost shy around him, especially as the drugs she'd been injected with against her will were wearing off.

Negal missed those first moments of their interaction when she'd seemed so uninhibited, so free with her admiration and her attraction to him. But now, she was pulling back and retracting into herself, as if she was inexperienced with males or even fearful.

Perhaps her experience on the yacht had been more difficult than what she and Jasmine had admitted to?

What if those scumbags that Kalugal had attempted to turn into decent people had done bad things to the women?

Across the table, Kalugal cleared his throat quite loudly, drawing Negal's attention. "As I was saying just a few moments ago, it's important to stay calm and not let strong emotions hijack your mind." He stared pointedly at Negal.

Finally, he got the hint and closed his eyes, which were probably glowing. "Excuse me." He pushed away from the table. "I need to use the bathroom again."

"What's the matter?" Margo asked. "Are your contact lenses bothering you? Do you need me to help you get to the bathroom without bumping into anything?"

Kalugal chuckled. "I told Negal that he shouldn't wear them today, but he didn't listen."

The guy was such a resourceful liar.

Negal didn't dare open his eyes, so he had to accept Margo's help. Hopefully, she wouldn't insist on coming into the bathroom with him.

"Thank you for the offer, Margo. It's very kind of you."

"It's the least I can do for the man who leaped to catch me when I fainted and then carried me across the boat like a princess."

He heard her push her chair back, and then her hand clasped his, and his throat went dry.

What the hell was that reaction?

He'd held her in his arms for long moments, and she had put her head on his chest. Their breath intermingled. Why was the touch of her hand making him lose his composure?

"Come on, big guy." She tugged on his hand. "I've had my share of torment with contact lenses, and eventually, I gave up on them. I just use glasses for reading. You should do the same. You are so incredibly good-looking that glasses aren't going to take away from your attractiveness."

A smile tugged on the corner of his lips. "You think that I'm good-looking?"

She snorted. "I might be nearsighted, but I'm not blind." She leaned closer to him, her cheek grazing his forearm. "Did you and Kevin have plastic surgery?"

Gabi had asked Aru the same thing, so maybe he should just say that he had? But he didn't want to lie to Margo more than he already had. "No. I'm just fortunate to have been made with very good genes."

In his home world, they were nothing special, average genes that most commoners were given, but on Earth, they were superior.

"There is no shame in admitting that you had work done. Many men do that these days." She stopped next to the bathroom. "It's a competitive world, and everyone is trying to get a leg up." She opened the door. "Do you need me to help you in there?"

He looked at her from under lowered lashes, admiring the way the light from the windows made her hair look golden. "No, thank you. I'll be fine. I'll just take them out."

"Throw them away." She patted his arm. "I'll be outside the door if you need me."

"Thank you." Negal walked into the bathroom and gently closed the door behind him.

When he looked in the mirror, his eyes were still glowing, but not so intensely that the glow couldn't be explained away as a reflection from misty eyes.

He had sunglasses in his pocket but wearing them inside would be weird. Then again, he could say that the contact lenses irritated his eyes, and that's why he needed to shield them.

Splashing his face with cold water for the second time in less than an hour, he took a few deep breaths, dried his face with a towel, and pulled his sunglasses out.

When he exited the bathroom, he found Margo leaning against the wall right next to the door, just as she had promised.

"Sunglasses?" she asked.

"I know it looks strange, but my eyes are so irritated that even a little bit of direct light is painful."

"My poor hero." She took his hand again. "What did you do with the contact lenses?"

"I threw them away as you suggested."

"Good. Do you have more on the ship?"

He didn't know how to answer that. Did people usually have more than one pair?

"I'll have to check," he hedged. "I might have forgotten to pack the spare pair."

She regarded him with a frown and then shook her head. "Let's get back to the table. The chef is probably serving coffee and dessert."

"Hold on." He tugged on her hand to keep her from walking away. "I hate to do this, but I have to know whether anyone did anything inappropriate to you or to Jasmine."

"You mean other than slip us roofies and then inject us with God knows what?"

Nodding, he let go of her hand. "You know what I mean. Please, don't feel embarrassed about telling me. I just need to know."

Margo let out a breath. "The only one who interacted with us was Alberto, and as far as I know, he didn't touch me that way. But I was out of it for hours, so I don't know that for sure, but I don't think so. He might have taken a peek at my assets, and he jabbed me with a needle, but not with anything else if you know what I mean. I believe that I would have known if he, you know, did that."

MARGO

 egal looked confused, as if he wasn't sure what she was implying. Was it a language barrier?

His English was perfect, including a general American accent that wasn't regional, but he'd said something about being from Portugal, so maybe English wasn't his native language, and he didn't get some of the phrases and idioms.

It was either that or he was naive, but that couldn't be the case. The guy looked to be in his late twenties or early thirties, was as gorgeous as a god, and moved like one, too. There was no way he was inexperienced.

He was also very clearly attracted to her, so it wasn't like he didn't know what she'd been talking about.

"So, no one touched you sexually," he said. "You are sure of that?"

"Yes." She smiled and took his hand. "Let's go, or the others will think that we are doing something inappropriate."

He didn't need her to lead him back to the table, but it felt good to hold his hand, and she wanted more of the contact.

"What do you mean?"

She shook her head. "Never mind."

It must have been a language thing.

He looked down at where their hands were conjoined and then back up at her, but his eyes were hidden behind the dark sunglasses, so she didn't know what he was thinking.

Maybe it was not something he was comfortable with?

"I'm sorry." She let go of his hand.

"No, don't be." He reached for her hand and clasped it. "I like it. It's just that I don't know the local customs all that well, so I'm not sure if it's common for strangers to hold hands."

"We are not strangers." She started walking to hide her embarrassment. "You saved me, and I'm grateful. That's how I show my gratitude."

That was such a load of baloney, but if he really wasn't familiar with American culture, he might take her word for it.

"It's nice," he said.

"You sound so American. Are you really from Portugal?"

"I've lived there for a while, but I also travel a lot. My friends and I are flea market bargain hunters."

"No way." She stopped and looked up at him. "How does a bargain hunter become a cartel mob buster?"

"I was a soldier back in the day." He resumed walking.

That explained so much.

He could be from a military family that had traveled all over the world, and then he had become a soldier himself. Negal's English was good, and he sounded like a native because it was his first language, but because he had traveled and lived all over, he hadn't learned all of its nuances.

"Were you homeschooled?" she asked when they entered the dining room.

Frowning, Negal pulled out a chair for her. "I don't know what that means."

"Your mother teaching you to read and write," Kevin said. "I was homeschooled. First by my mother and then by tutors."

There was a buzzing sound and Kevin pulled out his phone. "Oh, good. We should get ready. Our pickup is on its way."

"What pickup?" Jasmine asked. "I thought we were leaving in the helicopter."

"A lifeboat was sent for us from the cruise ship, and it's going to be here in twenty minutes." He looked at Margo. "Is there anything you need to pack?"

"All Alberto brought was my purse and my phone wasn't in it. That was the first thing I checked when I came to on the boat. The rest of my stuff is still at the hotel." It suddenly dawned on her that Lynda was probably worried sick about her. "Oh my God, I need to call my sister-in-law and tell her that I'm okay. She probably has the entire family in an uproar. Can I use one of your phones?"

Kevin shook his head. "I'm sorry, Margo. Just for now, we need to keep a low profile. There is more going on than just the cartel, and we can't let anyone know that we have you."

She turned to Negal, who she had a feeling was the weakest link in the chain and easier to sway. "What's going on, Negal? What are you guys not telling us?"

He swallowed, looking like he wanted to be anywhere but there. "It's complicated. Kalugal is the boss, so you should ask him."

"Who is Kalugal?"

Kevin cleared his throat. "That's me, but you have to keep calling me Kevin for now." He turned to look at Jasmine. "Same goes for you. Call me Kevin."

"Yes, sir." Jasmine saluted him.

Now that Margo knew what to listen for, she'd heard the hypnotic tone and realized how it affected her. She and Jasmine were lucky that he was one of the good guys. Kevin didn't need drugs to make them compliant. All he needed to do was to say the words, and they would obey.

Margo shivered. What if all she'd been told by Mia and Frankie had been lies? This guy could have made them say anything he wanted.

She narrowed her eyes at him. "I have to let my family know that I'm okay, and you didn't give me a reason why I shouldn't do that. You have the cartel boss, and all of his men hypnotized to believe that the Virgin Mary revealed herself to him and commanded him to be good. Who else could be interested in me and whether I've been found, other than my family?"

He let out an exasperated breath. "Can you hold off your questions until we are on the ship? Everything will become clear once you talk to Mia and Frankie."

Yeah, right. Unless he had them and everyone else on that ship under his spell.

"Can I call either of them? Because I'm starting to think that maybe I shouldn't trust you."

If he readily agreed, then she would know that she couldn't trust her friends' words.

"They can't tell you anything over the phone. Besides, we don't have time for that." He rose to his feet. "We need to get ready for the lifeboat. Let's collect your purses and get out of here."

NEGAL

As the women left to collect their purses, Kalugal regarded Negal with a raised brow and amusement in his eyes. "What's going on with you?"

"What do you mean?"

"I mean the flashing of fangs and glowing eyes. You need to better control your reactions. These women have been drugged and thralling them while they are experiencing withdrawal might be harmful. I would hate to have to do that to them on top of everything else they have been through."

"You're right." Negal rubbed a hand over the back of his neck. "I'm usually very good at this. It's considered bad form on Anumati to reveal strong emotions, and we are trained from a young age to control our fangs and glowing eyes. But every time I imagine what could have been done to Margo and Jasmine, I get so consumed by rage that I lose hold of my responses."

Kalugal tilted his head. "Do you have a sister?"

"No, why?"

Kalugal shrugged. "I often wonder about Kian's over-protectiveness for females, and I think it stems from him having sisters. Don't get me wrong, it's our duty and privilege to protect the females in our lives and our communities, but Kian often crosses the line by stifling their right to choose. The clan has a very capable female Guardian, but Kian refuses to allow her to participate in missions against Doomers because they are known for their lack of honor, to put it in gentle terms."

Negal scoffed. "You don't need to use gentle terms with me, Kalugal. I've been a soldier for much longer than you have been alive, and I know what you refer to. Regrettably and shamefully, some of the Anumati colonies have succumbed to lawlessness, and females were the first to suffer when they lost the equalizing benefit of culture and technology when brute force became law."

Kalugal tilted his head. "I thought that gods revered females."

Negal let out a breath. "There are deviants in every society, and some manage to convert the weak-minded to their philosophy. From there, it doesn't take long for a few thugs to destroy thousands of years of progress and turn the entire place into a hellhole."

"I know what you mean." Kalugal shifted his weight to his other leg. "My own grandfather was such a deviant god. He abhorred the matrilineal tradition of the gods, and he wanted females to be deprived of all rights. In his insanity, he obliterated nearly all of the gods and plunged humanity into darkness. And don't start me on humans, but that's too lengthy a conversation for now. We should have it over whiskey and cigars when we are not pressed for time."

Negal dipped his head. "Gladly. I'm honored by the invitation."

Kalugal smirked. "Given that I don't have my own cigars, we will have to include Kian, but I'm sure he would enjoy a philosophical and historical discussion. In fact, we should include him regardless of the cigars, or he will think that I'm trying to pump you for information." He leaned toward Negal. "Which I totally am. I'm very curious about those colonies, the law-abiding and the lawless, but I don't mind Kian hearing about it, too." He frowned. "I hope it will be okay with your boss."

"I don't see why not. Aru would most likely love to join."

"Excellent." Kalugal clapped him on the back. "If my former brethren leave us alone, and we are not under attack tomorrow, I will organize a get-together in my cabin."

"Thank you. I would also love to hear about how you escaped the Brotherhood and what motivated you to do so."

"Oh, yes." Kalugal's eyes clouded over. "That's not nearly as interesting as your tale." He turned toward the staircase. "I should check on Modana and his men before we leave."

Talking with Kalugal had an oddly calming effect on Negal. Or maybe it was the fact that Margo wasn't near. He was different around her, and he didn't like that mindless version of himself.

It could be the protector in him that had surged to the surface because of the potential crimes that might have been perpetrated against Margo and Jasmine. It was hardwired into every male god to treat females with the utmost respect and never assume their favors, but even gods sometimes deviated from their genetic programming because not everything could be determined genetically. Free will existed, and fortuitous accidents happened, for better and for worse.

The other thing that could be responsible for this psychosis was the thought that Frankie had planted in his mind about Margo being his fated mate. Logically he knew it wasn't true, but a small part of his heart, a remnant from his youth, hoped that she was right and that he could have his happily ever after like Aru and Dagor.

It was just the placebo effect.

Margo was pretty but not exceptional, and the fierceness he'd seen in her photo was not as evident in person. He'd caught glimpses of it, but it was by no means as potent as he'd imagined.

Still, he couldn't ignore the fact that he wasn't attracted to Jasmine, who was as beautiful as any of the immortal females and could even rival some of the commoner goddesses, especially since her type of beauty was unusual on Anumati. Normally, he would have zeroed in on a stunning beauty like her, and the fact that he hadn't was significant.

Taking one last look at the opulent dining room, with its glass-top table, white leather chairs, and a chandelier that looked like a glass sculpture, Negal turned on his heel and headed toward the staircase. He was glad to leave the symbol of wealth purchased with blood money, but he wasn't sure he was glad to return to the cruise ship. To preserve his sanity, he might be better off renewing his trek through Tibet on his own.

MARGO

When Margo and Jasmine entered the cabin, Jaz walked over to the bed and sat down. "I miss the rush of euphoria. I've never felt so good in my life." She sighed. "It's going to be rough, you know. Have you ever seen anyone withdrawing from heroin? It's brutal."

"How do you know it was heroin?" Margo collected her purse and checked that everything was there.

Jasmine shrugged. "I don't, but what else would he use? I had a friend who got addicted, and she went through hell trying to quit."

"We will get through this together." Margo walked over to her and offered her a hand up. "We should tell Kevin to search Alberto's pockets and his cabin for your passport and credit cards."

Jasmine's eyes widened. "Of course. Why didn't I think of that? If I can get my stuff back, I can book a flight from Puerto Vallarta back home, and I don't need to hitch a ride on your cruise ship."

Margo should have been happy to get rid of the competition, but she wasn't. She'd grown attached to Jasmine, and she didn't want her to go. "Are you in such a rush to get rid of me?"

"Of course not." Jasmine wrapped her arm around Margo's middle. "You are my best friend." She leaned her head on Margo's shoulder, which couldn't be comfortable because she was half a head taller. "You have your besties waiting for you on board the cruise ship, and I know that I'm going to be jealous because you will no longer be mine."

It was probably the drugs talking because they hadn't known each other long enough to become best friends, but Margo was touched, nonetheless.

"Oh, Jaz." She patted Jasmine's head. "I will always be your friend. You can be the fourth member of our group."

Jaz lifted a pair of hopeful puppy eyes at her. "Do you mean it?"

"Of course. Imagine how much fun we are going to have when we are not being drugged by Alberto the scumbag or about to be sexually assaulted by vile cartel bosses."

A shiver rocked Jasmine's body. "It's just now starting to sink in. I didn't have much of a life to leave behind, but it was infinitely better than what was waiting for me with Modana. In a way, I'm grateful for the drugs. This would have been harrowing without them."

Margo had a feeling that Jasmine was starting to crash after the high.

She was feeling some of that, too, but it hadn't hit her as hard yet. It just felt like a low after a high, kind of like the way she felt before and after attending her favorite rock group's concerts.

Maybe that was why she'd been so taken by the pretty-faced guy. She had been still riding the high, and now that she was starting to come down, Negal would no longer look as beautiful and angelic to her.

When they got to the top deck, Negal had his back to them, and as he turned to look at her, Margo was proven wrong. It felt like being hit in the chest. He was even more stunning than she'd remembered.

"Looks aren't everything," she murmured under her breath as she and Jasmine walked toward their rescuers.

"Where is Alberto?" Jasmine asked Kevin.

The hypnotist frowned. "Why do you want to know?"

"He has my passport, my driver's license, and my credit cards. I bet he brought them with him. Can you use your hypnosis on him to give them back?"

"Of course. Give me a moment." Kevin trotted down the stairs.

"Where is he keeping the men?" Margo asked Negal.

"The grand salon. They won't move from there until he okays it."

"How is he going to do that after we are gone?"

Negal shrugged. "I don't know, and I don't care." He pointed at the boat heading their way. "Our transport is here."

"Awesome." Margo lifted her hand to shield her eyes. "Where is the ship?"

"Beyond the horizon."

"That far away?" Jasmine asked.

"For a ship to be beyond the horizon, it needs to be only about three miles away. That's not so far."

"Oh, I didn't know that." Jasmine smiled in that coquettish way of hers. "I feel so stupid."

"Stop saying that," Margo snapped. "You are not stupid. I didn't know that either."

As the boat came alongside the idling yacht, one of the guys inside stood and pointed at the ladder. "Who wants to go first?"

"I'll go," Edgar volunteered.

He made it down the ladder in seconds and made it look so easy that Margo offered to go next.

As she carefully made her way down, the guy in the lifeboat put his hands on her hips to help her jump the last couple of feet, and she thought that she heard Negal growl, but she must have imagined it.

When he made it to the lifeboat, though, he glared at the guy, and she thought that maybe she'd heard it right.

"Got it!" Kevin waved a passport from the railing. "I have your other stuff, too."

"Thank you," Jasmine called back.

He made his way into the boat with the same agility as his two companions, and when everyone was seated, one of the guys who came with the boat pushed it away from the yacht while the other revved the engine.

As the lifeboat sped away, Margo watched the yacht getting smaller and smaller the farther away from it they got, and a knot of tension that had been hiding deep inside of her loosened.

This part of her so-called adventure was over, and a new chapter was beginning. The question was whether it would be a love story or a drama.

COMING UP NEXT

The Children of the Gods Book 81

Dark Horizon Eclipse of the Heart

To read the first three chapters, JOIN the VIP club at ITLUCAS.COM.

Coming up next in the

PERFECT MATCH SERIES

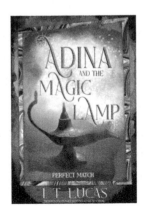

ADINA AND THE MAGIC LAMP

In this post-apocalyptic virtual reimagining of Aladdin, James, the enigmatic prince, and Adina, the fearless thief, navigate the treacherous streets of Londabad, a city that echoes London and Ahmedabad and fuses magic and technology. In the face of danger, the chemistry between them ignites, and the lines between prince and thief, royalty and commoner blur.

JOIN THE VIP CLUB
To find out what's included in your free membership, flip to the last page.

NOTE

Dear reader,

I hope my stories have added a little joy to your day. If you have a moment to add some to mine, you can help spread the word about the Children Of The Gods series by telling your friends and penning a review. Your recommendations are the most powerful way to inspire new readers to explore the series.

Thank you,

Isabell

Also by I. T. Lucas

THE CHILDREN OF THE GODS ORIGINS

1: GODDESS'S CHOICE

2: GODDESS'S HOPE

THE CHILDREN OF THE GODS

DARK STRANGER

1: DARK STRANGER THE DREAM

2: DARK STRANGER REVEALED

3: DARK STRANGER IMMORTAL

DARK ENEMY

4: DARK ENEMY TAKEN

5: DARK ENEMY CAPTIVE

6: DARK ENEMY REDEEMED

KRI & MICHAEL'S STORY

6.5: MY DARK AMAZON

DARK WARRIOR

7: DARK WARRIOR MINE

8: DARK WARRIOR'S PROMISE

9: DARK WARRIOR'S DESTINY

10: DARK WARRIOR'S LEGACY

DARK GUARDIAN

11: DARK GUARDIAN FOUND

12: DARK GUARDIAN CRAVED
13: DARK GUARDIAN'S MATE

DARK ANGEL
14: DARK ANGEL'S OBSESSION
15: DARK ANGEL'S SEDUCTION
16: DARK ANGEL'S SURRENDER

DARK OPERATIVE
17: DARK OPERATIVE: A SHADOW OF DEATH
18: DARK OPERATIVE: A GLIMMER OF HOPE
19: DARK OPERATIVE: THE DAWN OF LOVE

DARK SURVIVOR
20: DARK SURVIVOR AWAKENED
21: DARK SURVIVOR ECHOES OF LOVE
22: DARK SURVIVOR REUNITED

DARK WIDOW
23: DARK WIDOW'S SECRET
24: DARK WIDOW'S CURSE
25: DARK WIDOW'S BLESSING

DARK DREAM
26: DARK DREAM'S TEMPTATION
27: DARK DREAM'S UNRAVELING
28: DARK DREAM'S TRAP

DARK PRINCE

29: DARK PRINCE'S ENIGMA
30: DARK PRINCE'S DILEMMA
31: DARK PRINCE'S AGENDA

DARK QUEEN

32: DARK QUEEN'S QUEST
33: DARK QUEEN'S KNIGHT
34: DARK QUEEN'S ARMY

DARK SPY

35: DARK SPY CONSCRIPTED
36: DARK SPY'S MISSION
37: DARK SPY'S RESOLUTION

DARK OVERLORD

38: DARK OVERLORD NEW HORIZON
39: DARK OVERLORD'S WIFE
40: DARK OVERLORD'S CLAN

DARK CHOICES

41: DARK CHOICES THE QUANDARY
42: DARK CHOICES PARADIGM SHIFT
43: DARK CHOICES THE ACCORD

DARK SECRETS

44: DARK SECRETS RESURGENCE
45: DARK SECRETS UNVEILED
46: DARK SECRETS ABSOLVED

ALSO BY I. T. LUCAS

DARK HAVEN
47: DARK HAVEN ILLUSION
48: DARK HAVEN UNMASKED
49: DARK HAVEN FOUND

DARK POWER
50: DARK POWER UNTAMED
51: DARK POWER UNLEASHED
52: DARK POWER CONVERGENCE

DARK MEMORIES
53: DARK MEMORIES SUBMERGED
54: DARK MEMORIES EMERGE
55: DARK MEMORIES RESTORED

DARK HUNTER
56: DARK HUNTER'S QUERY
57: DARK HUNTER'S PREY
58: DARK HUNTER'S BOON

DARK GOD
59: DARK GOD'S AVATAR
60: DARK GOD'S REVIVISCENCE
61: DARK GOD DESTINIES CONVERGE

DARK WHISPERS
62: DARK WHISPERS FROM THE PAST
63: DARK WHISPERS FROM AFAR
64: DARK WHISPERS FROM BEYOND

Dark Gambit
65: Dark Gambit The Pawn
66: Dark Gambit The Play
67: Dark Gambit Reliance

Dark Alliance
68: Dark Alliance Kindred Souls
69: Dark Alliance Turbulent Waters
70: Dark Alliance Perfect Storm

Dark Healing
71: Dark Healing Blind Justice
72: Dark Healing Blind Trust
73: Dark healing Blind Curve

Dark Encounters
74: Dark Encounters of the Close Kind
75: Dark Encounters of the Unexpected Kind
76: Dark Encounters of the Fated Kind

Dark Voyage
77: Dark Voyage Matters of the Heart
78: Dark Voyage Matters of the Mind
79: Dark Voyage Matters of the Soul

Dark Horizon
80: Dark Horizon New Dawn
81: Dark Horizon Eclipse of the Heart

PERFECT MATCH
Vampire's Consort
King's Chosen
Captain's Conquest
The Thief Who Loved Me
My Merman Prince
The Dragon King
My Werewolf Romeo
The Channeler's Companion
The Valkyrie & The Witch
Adina and the Magic Lamp

The Children of the Gods Series Sets

Books 1-3: Dark Stranger trilogy—Includes a bonus short story: **The Fates Take a Vacation**

Books 4-6: Dark Enemy Trilogy —Includes a bonus short story—**The Fates' Post-Wedding Celebration**

Books 7-10: Dark Warrior Tetralogy

Books 11-13: Dark Guardian Trilogy

Books 14-16: Dark Angel Trilogy

BOOKS 17-19: DARK OPERATIVE TRILOGY

BOOKS 20-22: DARK SURVIVOR TRILOGY

BOOKS 23-25: DARK WIDOW TRILOGY

BOOKS 26-28: DARK DREAM TRILOGY

BOOKS 29-31: DARK PRINCE TRILOGY

BOOKS 32-34: DARK QUEEN TRILOGY

BOOKS 35-37: DARK SPY TRILOGY

BOOKS 38-40: DARK OVERLORD TRILOGY

BOOKS 41-43: DARK CHOICES TRILOGY

BOOKS 44-46: DARK SECRETS TRILOGY

BOOKS 47-49: DARK HAVEN TRILOGY

BOOKS 50-52: DARK POWER TRILOGY

BOOKS 53-55: DARK MEMORIES TRILOGY

BOOKS 56-58: DARK HUNTER TRILOGY

BOOKS 59-61: DARK GOD TRILOGY

BOOKS 62-64: DARK WHISPERS TRILOGY

BOOKS 65-67: DARK GAMBIT TRILOGY

BOOKS 68-70: DARK ALLIANCE TRILOGY

BOOKS 71-73: DARK HEALING TRILOGY

BOOKS 74-76: DARK ENCOUNTERS TRILOGY

MEGA SETS
INCLUDE CHARACTER LISTS
THE CHILDREN OF THE GODS: BOOKS 1-6

THE CHILDREN OF THE GODS: BOOKS 6.5-10

PERFECT MATCH BUNDLE 1

CHECK OUT THE SPECIALS ON
ITLUCAS.COM
(https://itlucas.com/specials)

**FOR EXCLUSIVE PEEKS AT UPCOMING
RELEASES &
A FREE I. T. LUCAS COMPANION BOOK**

FOR EXCLUSIVE PEEKS AT UPCOMING RELEASES &
A FREE I. T. LUCAS COMPANION BOOK

Join my *VIP Club* and gain access to the VIP portal at ITLUCAS.COM

To Join, go to:

http://eepurl.com/blMTpD

INCLUDED IN YOUR FREE MEMBERSHIP:

YOUR VIP PORTAL

- Read preview chapters of upcoming releases.
- Listen to Goddess's Choice narration by Charles Lawrence
- Exclusive content offered only to my VIPs.

FREE I.T. LUCAS COMPANION INCLUDES:

- Goddess's Choice Part 1
- Perfect Match: Vampire's Consort (A standalone Novella)
- Interview Q & A
- Character Charts

If you're already a subscriber, and you are not getting my emails, your provider is sending them to

YOUR JUNK FOLDER, AND YOU ARE MISSING OUT ON **IMPOR-
TANT UPDATES, SIDE CHARACTERS' PORTRAITS, ADDITIONAL
CONTENT, AND OTHER GOODIES.** TO FIX THAT, ADD isabell@
itlucas.com TO YOUR EMAIL CONTACTS OR YOUR EMAIL VIP
LIST.

**Check out the specials at
https://www.itlucas.com/specials**